Jessica Cameron was born in the UK and moved to Spain and Portugal as a young adult to pursue a career in skydiving. After a few years, this career path was put on hold to raise a family, and soon a love for writing and painting was rekindled from childhood. Very quickly thereafter, these passions developed and she is now a full-time parent, artist, writer and skydiver.

Jessica Cameron

IMPLANTED

Hope you enjoy reading this
Milly, love Mum

[signature]

AUSTIN MACAULEY PUBLISHERS™
LONDON • CAMBRIDGE • NEW YORK • SHARJAH

A CIP catalogue record for this title is available from the British Library.

ISBN 9781398411326 (Paperback)
ISBN 9781398414174 (ePub e-book)

www.austinmacauley.com

First Published 2021
Austin Macauley Publishers Ltd®
1 Canada Square
Canary Wharf
London
E14 5AA

The day it all changed.

My day started like any other. It was a typical routine really. A routine I had come to tire of, an endless cycle with no end in sight full of monotonous actions and repeated activities every day. First, each day always started with my alarm bleating in my ears, pulling my sleep dredged mind into the here and now. My numbed sleepy hand fumbled across my nightstand to silence it. 6:30 am. Once again, time to get ready for work. Throwing my legs over the side of my bed, my feet hit the shock of cold on my tiled floors, bringing a little bit more wakefulness into my sodden brain. I shuffled into the bathroom and began the task of trying to remove some evidence of last night's drunken antics. I wish I could say I went out for a good time but it was really out of habit now. Peering into the mirror above my sink, I grimaced. Red rimmed eyes with dark smudges telling their own stories, chapped lips and a patchy stubble spread a shadow across my jaw partially concealing a little scar I had on my cheek from some mishap years ago. I dragged a hand across my face and became aware of a dull throbbing in my knuckles. Flashing back, I can vaguely recall a small run-in with a local over, who was first in line at the urinals. Never mind. Autopilot kicked in and carried me through the motions of my morning routine and before I knew it, I was leaving my sanctuary and heading into the outside world.

****

There are many various noises I have come to associate with office work life. It is a constant low murmuring of people chit-chatting, gossiping and nodding continuously into headsets with the occasional eye roll, like the person on the other end is aware of the action, not dissimilar to a football fan shouting furiously at a TV set as though the players could hear them. The beeping and whirring of the printer never ended, seemingly on a mission to always be printing something or jamming every time someone tried to print anything more than three pages. There is the muted thudding of footsteps as people go to the coffee machines telling anyone who will listen 'You will not believe the day I have had so far'. Yes, Sally, I probably could believe it, we are all doing the very same thing as you. There were many scents too. The musty smell of cheap coffee lingering in the air, too many overpowering perfumes to even distinguish one and the dust and despair is an assault to my nostrils day in day out. as I come to work as a customer services representative of Ianx, an insurance firm for vehicles.

I settled into my cubicle, pulled on my headset and logged in to the system and prepared to count down the minutes until 1:30 pm when I next escape this cell. All the while, I can't help but wonder to myself, is this really what I am meant to do with my life? Why when I see everyone else (mostly) happily doing what they do in here do I feel above that and like I have another purpose or am I destined to be your average office slave for the rest of my working time?

As I mused, I looked around the office and observed all my colleagues with their heads buried in paperwork and keyboards. Many of them had various photos and titbits strewn across their desks in a bid to make it more personal, I guess. Mine was barren in comparison; all I had pinned on my backboard was a couple of numbers of different companies I spoke to frequently and the age-old poster of the cat hanging from the tree branch with 'Hang in There!' written on it. Both of my parents were long gone and aside from a few distant relatives, I was running solo in this world. I thought about how time really could tick by so slowly in here, but when all you would rather is to be anywhere but here, of course, the time was going to drag by. I spent the following hours just typing away slowly and unpassionately fulfilling my rota and picking grime out from underneath my broken fingernails. Finally, locking my screen, seemingly an eternity later, I rose from my desk and headed to the elevator.

Whilst I was waiting for the elevator to reach my level, Jeanie, one of our administration team, a short grey-haired lady with a permanent scowl on her brow, approached me.

"Arnie dear, how are you feeling? You seem to be a touch pale today?" I replied with nothing more than a half shrug and self-deprecating smile. No use in confirming what she was undoubtedly hinting at. Yes, I did go out drinking on a school night. And no, I don't need telling how irresponsible that is in some people's eyes. Her concern (false, I felt) seemed more like a judgement and I didn't have time for it. Thankfully, the elevator dinged open and we both entered, neither speaking further. On the ground floor, I gave my usual cursory nod to the security man, Pete, and made my way out into the afternoon sunshine.

The sun's rays stabbed my retinas like a knife, hangover still not finished toying with me yet. Being locked away for hours, staring at a screen and fluorescent bulbs being the only light source cannot be good for you. I yearned for some magical job where I didn't have to do much and could wander where I wanted, doing what I liked and get paid a handsome sum. A guy can dream, right?

I decided today I would lunch in a small family café on the other side of the train tracks. Good food, friendly unobtrusive service, one of my favourite go-to places on any given day. I made it about halfway across the railway bridge deep in my self-pitying thoughts when I heard a commotion coming up fast behind me. Louts, no doubt. I turned round to see the cause of the noise and sure enough, there was a group of around seven boys, perhaps around the early twenties but not worthy of the title 'men' yet, were storming up the steps screaming obscenities at a young lad. No more than twelve years old I would have thought, he looked petrified and unsure how to get out of his current predicament, he was completely out of his depth. He was trying to run away, but the older boys kept sticking their legs out in front of him and catching his young scrawny ankles.

Having had my fair share of encounters of bullies in my time and not able to stand by and watch it play out any more, I decided to intervene or at least take some of the heat off of the child. I have no idea what I expected to happen, but as is often the case, the events that followed were completely unexpected. Taking a steadying breath, I reached my hand out to the boy for him to come and stand next to or behind me and saw the flash of relief in his eyes. Small motion, it was all I had time to do. The boy made it across the path and fell in place next to me, leaving me with the problem of not knowing what I was going to do to deter these boys. Before I needed to make the decision or had a chance to say anything, one of the older boys, clad in a buff of sorts to conceal his face, had clearly taken a dislike to the interruption of his afternoon fun, reared back and launched his Timberland squarely into my gut. I doubled up trying to work out my next move when a neat uppercut punch pulled me upright again. I stumbled backwards with my hands flailing around fruitlessly trying to find a handhold. This is the last thing I remember before everything flicked neatly into blackness.

****

You see, I like to think of myself as a good person. I, of course, have my times when I allow the darkness to shadow my moves and thoughts, but for the most part, I try to be the best I can be. I do keep myself to myself, I enjoy the company of other people, but there are often times that I need to be with myself. Not to be depressive, I am simply content to have my own time. I love it, in fact. I had some years in my youth where doctors decided I was suffering from manic depression (now known in today's terms as bipolar disorder) and promptly threw me on heavy medication. Whilst it was fair to say I did have moments of haziness and worrisome thoughts, it was just disliked that I didn't blend in seamlessly with the mass of children following the system with nothing more than a nod and acceptance of this is the way it is going to be. Now I have no medication anymore. I weaned myself years back, I had felt like a zombie, what was the use of living without emotions? I would rather deal with a barrage of highs and lows than not feel a thing.

Anyhow, the point I am making, I try to do good things for people, where my patience permits because frankly, no one knows what the next person is going through behind closed doors and it doesn't cost more than a few moments to extend a helping hand or offer a titbit of advice, even if it goes unheeded. We could all try to be more kind and understanding, even when sometimes it doesn't seem possible, I know I am not always of this giving mind-set. But this is why, even though I stood not even a 10% chance against those bullying boy-men, I couldn't stand by and watch a young boy be subjected to their cruel taunts. If only I could have foreseen the repercussions of my actions, I would have maybe done it a little bit differently.

****

A blinding light was searing through my eyelids. A cacophony of noise was raging through my skull. High pitched beeping was sending needle-like shockwaves through my temples. Did I change my alarm sound? Why would I go to bed with the curtains open? Reaching over to silence the alarm, I started to feel uneasy. I didn't want to open my eyes, my arm twitched but didn't respond. Then I suddenly remembered the bridge, the boys. What happened? I slowly started to open my eyes, wincing against the harsh light in the room. A figure came into focus, looming over me. My eyes started to focus and a second light started flashing into my eyes, the glare making me clamp them shut again. I heard the figure shift away from me and I looked again. It was a nurse jotting something down onto a clipboard and nodding her head.

Without looking at me, she spoke, "Glad you are back with us, sir, do you know where you are?"

"A hospital? What happened at the bridge?" I mumbled back, a scratchy throat making itself known.

"You suffered a head trauma. I need to ask you some questions and then you'll need to rest."

I merely nodded my consent back, a few days off work wouldn't be too bad. She went on to ask the cliché questions like in the movies, for good reason. With the exception of the date (to my surprise, I had been out cold for two days apparently), I passed with flying colours. She proceeded to inject something into my IV, ordered me to stay put and rest whilst she 'fetched' the doctor then swept out of the room.

****

I must have fallen asleep again, but waking up this time was much more pleasant. The roaring noise and lights didn't seem so offensive. The doctor was standing checking the machines and turned to introduce himself when he noticed I had awoken.

"Good afternoon, Mr Shack, I am Dr Muggor. How are you feeling?" His voice was unexpectedly high. He must have been a little over six foot tall, built like a rugby player and a rugged face. Funny how we can assume someone's voice from their appearance and why is it so weird for us when it 'doesn't suit them'? Shaking my head, to myself, I told him I was fine if a little queasy and tired. He bopped his head, making approving grunting noises.

"Well, your memory seems to be fine, so this is a good sign post head injury. You may experience some headaches over the next month, easily manageable with Paracetamol, I will give you a prescription for something stronger in the event you need it. Do you have any questions?"

"No, I just want to get home, can I discharge myself?" The knowledge that I had lost two days made me eager to get home. Dr Muggor looked understandingly at me and told me I could go home the next morning as long as everything was OK.

Deciding to look at this head injury myself, I hoisted myself out of the bed and padded over to the bathroom to inspect the damage. It wasn't too bad, but it wasn't pretty either. Some heavy stitching lined what would be a decent scar running across the side of my head. It began just at my temple, went over the top of my ear, coming to a slightly curled end at the bottom of my skull. How badly did I hit my head? This seemed quite large, but if the doctor says it is OK to go home, I won't question it, plus it'll make for an interesting conversation starter – when I feel sociable anyway. Styling wise, no buzz cuts for me then, not that I ever did. I like the unkempt look, my dirty blonde hair doing whatever it may daily. Any other style just never suited me and I was more than content not having to maintain it every day.

The contrast of the shaved section of my head to the non-shaved was pretty terrible though. It almost resembled that punk trend all the teenage girls were doing a few years back. I'll sort that later when I get back home. I turned away from the mirror, ready to head back into the room when something caught my eye. Whatever it was, it made me jump. Looking back in the mirror, I checked for what I had seen. Nothing. A trick of the eyes. I shook my head and remembered hearing somewhere that head injuries could cause all sorts of odd side effects. Climbing back into the bed, I flicked on the TV and settled in for the night.

****

I was walking through my old home town. I couldn't hear a thing and the streets look deserted. The houses seemed to loom up at me, closer together than they ever had been before, as though they were crowding me. Everything had a slightly orangey-red hue. The old bandstand looked to be in bad disrepair with the structure half crumbled and the bricks around it blackened by something. Scorched? The attached steps leading down to where the grass used to be had something all over them, but as I tried to focus, my sight became hazy. I wanted to see what it was, unaware of why my vision was flickering so much. I paced warily towards the steps, towards the bandstand. My ears started to tune in to a crunching noise, I became aware of my footing being unsteady in that same moment. I glanced down to what should have been concrete slabs.

The floor was covered in blackened stubs, all different sizes and shapes. I crouched to look closer and revulsion hit me in the chest like a sledgehammer.

The 'stubs' were body parts. I felt panic tear through me like wildfire. I stood upright and thrashed my head side to side to see where I could run to and shake the images from my vision when I was suddenly standing in the centre of the bandstand. There were fairy lights flashing all around the dome. A radio or something out of my line of sight was blaring out circus music it sounded like. I blinked frantically hoping it would stop but the bizarre sketchy scene continued to play out in front of me, like a scratched DVD skipping and jumping.

A man rose up from seemingly nothing in front of me. His face was covered in grime and red matter. He was wearing an apron of sorts and it was maybe once white, but it was now the canvas for whatever was happening here. The foul stench assaulted me; he was suddenly about two foot taller than me, wide-set eyes barely showing any whites, the blackness of his pupils had no end. His thin slit of a mouth grimaced at me, spreading into a yellow-toothed grin when I cowered involuntarily in response. He wielded a large-toothed blade in his right hand and with a whooshing sound, he brought it towards me faster than I could react, slicing effortlessly through my collarbone. My vision shot to bright red, then flickered between blackness and my attackers leering face as my blood gushed out in a boiling hot stream. My ears echoed with the sound of the blade swishing through solid bone and I could taste the metal. My whole body felt weak and wet, my blood quickly saturated me and I collapsed to the ground, my vision thankfully failed me and turned everything black before I hit the limb strewn pavement below me.

****

I jerked violently, arms thrashing out, amazed that I was still conscious. I dared to open my eyes and to my confusion saw the hospital monitors beeping steadily beside me. Waiting for reality to settle in, I couldn't help the feeling of unease. It had been so many years since I had had a nightmare and although short, it was brutal. Those ruins, the bodies, the eyes especially stuck in my head. Deep haunting pits of malice and madness that looked like they could suck me in and never let me go. I'd never had a nightmare where you were actually caught and injured. Touching a hand to my collar, I shuddered a bit, the sensation of the blade cutting through me like butter fresh.

Pulling myself upright, I glanced at the TV. 7:47 am. Good, I can go home soon, the comfort of my own home would make things better. I had no pain in my head, just a dull ache to let me know it had sustained a recent hit. And as quickly as that, the nightmare faded and the details were rapidly forgotten. Amazing how our minds can make you forget a dream or nightmare within five minutes of waking up, even when you consciously make an effort to remember them. I heard a small movement and saw Dr Muggor watching me in the doorway, I frowned. I wondered how long he had been there and if the guy ever went home. Eyebrow twitching in some sort of amusement, I guess, he answered my unasked questions,

"I picked up a double shift. I wanted to come to see how you were before discharging you."

I managed a half-smile, doctors were renowned for long hours, of course.

"I am fine and will do much better to rest in my own space, in my own house." Nodding his understanding, he approached me. Running through a few routine tests, he didn't say anything further. He told me to take it easy, don't get my head wet and come back in three days for a check-up. With that, I thanked him, gathered my belongings and went to call a cab.

****

A short time later I settled into the back seat of the taxi. The seats were stained and had various stitched patches in all muted colours. None matching the greyish hue of the seat itself though, of course. An overfull ashtray attached to the centre console in front emitted a musty old smell like it hadn't been emptied in a long time. The driver, wearing what looked like a beret, had a haggard world-weary face, pock-marked skin and puffy in places you wouldn't expect. Whilst taking in his appearance, and yes, perhaps judging a little even in my current state, I noticed he was looking at me expectantly. I realised I hadn't told him where we were going. I opened my mouth to tell him but he got there first,

"I said, that's 32 even, can you hear me?" he sounded tired, impatient. 32 even? But we hadn't gone anywhere yet! Confused, I looked out the window and jolted when I saw we were outside my block of flats. How did we get here? I played back, chest restricting as confusion built up. I had climbed into the cab, looked around and that was it. So, how did we end up here, ten minutes' drive away? Was this some karma to pay me back for judging someone a bit on appearances?

I felt a veil coming over my head, it felt physical, so I put my hands up to stop it. There was nothing there. The driver was now frowning at me like I was wasting his time. I blinked slowly, the motion of each blink feeling like a thud. The blackness that came with each closure felt like a trap, heavy. I could feel my breathing accelerate and a flush ran over my body. Trying to hold my composure, I handed over £40 and told him to keep the change. Stumbling out of the cab, I tried to take steadying breaths. What was that? Perhaps just a repercussion of the hit to my head. I'm tired, I will put it down to those factors.

"What!" I practically leapt out of my skin. Looking to the source of the shout, somewhere close behind me on the left. There was nobody there. People minding their own business, heads bowed moving on from one location to the next. All I could think at that moment was I clearly had had a long few days despite being unconscious for two of them and needed to rest. But first I could do with a damn strong coffee to straighten my mind up a little.

****

Back in the confines of my flat, I flicked on my kettle. The familiarity bringing some comfort to my addled brain. Had anyone called to see if I was OK? I realised I hadn't even spoken to Sarah since before the accident. But then again, I couldn't blame her for not having called or checked in. Did she even know what had happened? We have been together for around eight months. On and off. But last Saturday, she told me she wanted to spend the evening with me when I had already arranged a night out with the lads earlier that day. I told her to stop trying to control me and let me live my life. She didn't like that, I didn't like that she didn't like that. So, she had stormed out, muttering about growing up and the lads would always be there so why don't I shack up with them. Right now though, I could have done with her company, her reassurance, her warmth. The funny part was, these lads were not even really my friends, they just occupied the bar space with me. I shook my head as I thought about the ridiculousness of the petty arguments couples can get in to so easily.

Pouring the boiled water into my mug, I contemplated what I would say when I called her in a minute. Picking up the spoon to stir I half-gasped, half-shouted when I saw my coffee was a deep shade of red and bubbling. But the moment I blinked, it went back to dark brown with the little white bubbles swirling in the middle. Unnerved, I just stood and stared at the mug, almost willing it to do it again, to see if I really saw it. I really needed to get my head together. Sarah would have to wait until I was more composed, she would think I had lost my marbles.

Deciding to drink my coffee in bed, comfortably, I peeled off my clothes, slid under the sheets and rested my head against the plush backboard. No point fretting over any of the events, all would be directly related to the head injury, and that was only three days ago. I would feel good as new within a few days, no doubt about it.

****

I was walking through a meadow. Lush and green with splashes of colour in the forms of daisies and buttercups peeking up through the thick emerald green strands of grass. There was some sort of paddock in front of me, on a hill so I couldn't see the end of it. The wooden posts gave me a nostalgic memory of old-style farms. Thick lumps of wood hammered together with the knots and swirls visible, creating river-like lines in the grain. How I could make that out from where I was stood was beyond me, perhaps it was all in my mind's eye. I could see a grey horse over to the far left, grazing happily.

A huge oak tree sat over on the right with a small bench in front of the mammoth trunk. It looked like someone was sitting on it, but nothing was clear. The figure of the person seemed to be there whilst not really. Maybe it is just the haze of heat? Strange considering how well I could see the patterns on the wood a second ago. I turn my attention to my direct left. I was alongside two shacks. Both were wide in a structure. The first one was very homely, terracotta flowerpots laden with roses and earthy green vines climbed and circled the window panes.

There was ivy stretching its pale green fingers over the white-painted door. The gravel pathway led up to it looked inviting, I could almost picture the interior being cabin-like but with soft floral furniture and a large fireplace spitting out warm embers. The building on its right seemed to be in disrepair, like an old workshop. Cracked windows boarded up and slats of wood just hanging off of its frame in places. It was much greyer too, like the building itself had lost all life, even the air surrounding it seemed visibly darker and denser, completely uninviting. What a contrast. I wanted to go and see the bench. I turned away from the decaying building and started to move towards the oak.

14

Suddenly, I felt my feet move away from me, my legs having no choice but to turn too, my upper body followed the movement even though I tried to twist away, but I had no control. I could only liken the feeling to being a puppet and the controller had forgotten for that moment to move my upper half in sync with the lower. I had no sense of fear, only bewilderment. My apprehension grew as the pulling sensation increased and I was, for want of a better word, flying towards the broken building. As the motion took me, everything else started to fade slowly to the colour of the shack. The previously beautiful grass now resembled ash, the flowers were gone. Glancing around, the landscape has become barren, nothing to see but an dark cloud coating the ground, like a fog, for as far as I can see.

Turning my attention back to the direction I was going, I saw the homely cottage/shack was no longer there, all there left was this looming pile of rotting wood and I was suddenly propelled through the door. It took two seconds for my eyes to adjust. Somehow, I was now strapped to some sort of gurney and I could feel my heart rate increasing. I looked around, it resembled some sort of warehouse with a restaurant server's trolley next to me neatly displaying all sorts of tools, including knives and scalpels, metal sheets encrusted with brown and orange rust and makeshift wooden tables lined the far wall.

I tried to look further around the room and only now realised my head was also restrained, I could only see to my left. I could hear a deep heaving sound and a person came into my line of sight. I recognised the eyes but didn't place them immediately. The lower face was covered by a mask, like the ones they use to prevent the spread of diseases or use in operating theatres. A guttural sound was coming from behind the material, slight creases around his intensely dark eyes indicating he was smiling, maybe laughing but I couldn't tell. I was frozen in place, sure that even if whatever was holding me on this gurney released me, my limbs would not respond to my brain's increasingly frantic messages to get the hell out of there.

His chest seemed to expand before me and I saw a glint of something shiny. I was now acutely aware of a metallic scent in the air, unmistakable if you know what it is. How did I know? I felt a tingle creep up my right forearm, a heat followed and something started to pump, I could feel the pulsing. I spotted an aged hand mirror propped up just behind the beast of a man, was it there intentionally? Of course, it is, it reflected off of what looked like multiple shards of mirrors above me because I could see myself from a bird's eye perspective when I looked into it. What is this sick game? Why am I here?

I spotted my arm and started to heave as I saw that it seemed to have been carved open, whites of my bone shining out like a beacon. The dirtiness of the old mirror did nothing to conceal the horrific wound on my forearm. Terrified, I could barely breathe, I wanted to avert my eyes but somehow now I have seen it, I couldn't look away and now I could see the extent of the cut the pain increased tenfold. I watched in horror as the man slowly, calmly, brought a scalpel up towards my neck, the right side fully exposed to him. As the icy coldness swept through my head, a roaring started and I closed my eyes, unable to watch any further.

****

A hot burning pain racing through the side of my skull made me open my eyes. I was sitting almost upright in bed, slumped against the headboard, coffee mug on its side, contents spilt all over my legs. My sweat saturated the bedsheets. Shaking my head, trying to rid the nightmare, I saw it was 6:37 am. Even when I don't have work I am awake, more due to the haunting dream than routine though, I expect. Peeling the wet fabric away from me I heaved myself out of bed. My head throbbing, I reached for the painkillers from the doctors. So, this is the pain I was told may come, not surprising really, but also not welcome. I was starting to get unnerved by all the nightmares and reality glitches. Starting to get unnerved? I laughed silently and darkly at the thought. I had been toting the level of unease I had been feeling like a strait jacket. To say I was unnerved was an understatement, with all these nightmares and glitches. I decided that this was what they will be called to me because that is what it felt like, a glitch.

I blinked and something changed, back and forth. I knew it was all going to be related to the head trauma, but for now, I needed to see if there was anything I could do to lessen the side effects. I truly felt like I was going out of my mind. Picking up my phone, I dialled the number for Dr Muggor. He said he specialises in head injuries and seemed to actually care about my recovery. I listen to the dialling tone and felt disheartened and a little lost when the answering machine picked up. Leaving a short message, summarising quickly that I wanted to make an appointment for a check-up and some more information for post head injury care, I hung up and climbed back into bed to wait for the drugs to work their magic. Sarah's smiling face popped into my mind and I wanted her so badly by my side, a need I didn't normally have so strongly. Clearly, I was feeling the effects of recent events. Picking up my phone again, I typed out a quick text.

'I miss you. It doesn't feel right not seeing you. I had an accident a few days ago, can you come round and talk to me?' My finger hovered over the send button. It would probably be better if I called her, but I couldn't handle the idea of even a bit of noise right now, or the possibility of further arguing. Would she have calmed down yet? If she agreed to come to see me and that was a big if – she may take one look at my sorry state of being and decide to let our stupid argument go and just be here for me. Hitting send, I settled back in and waited for one of them to reply to me.

****

I awoke with a jolt; I could hear a banging from outside my room. I struggled to orientate myself quickly and then tried to locate the source of the sound, I realised it was my front door. Taking a moment to be grateful for the lack of a vivid dream, I paused for a second. Although once again, I had fallen asleep with no recollection of doing so. Flicking back the slide lock on the door, I opened it with a smile on my face expecting to see Sarah. Standing in front of me, waiting patiently with his hands in the front pockets of a pair of stonewash denim jeans was Dr Muggor. The confusion that hit me instantly rattled me. It clearly showed on my face as a trace of a knowing smile flashed across his face and he stepped through my doorway. Stepping back (not having much choice really), I allowed him to pass.

"How do you know where I live?" I asked, accusingly.

"Your address is on file and you told me on the phone. Do you recall our conversation?" That high voice again. Disconcerting. Was he counting the message I left him as a conversation? And even so, I didn't mention my address in the message, having assumed any appointment would be in his medical office. I stated as much, trying to sound reasonable, but self-confident. Paranoia seemed to be rearing its ugly head and I realised I had been a bit short with him. No reason to question a trained doctor, who hadn't recently suffered a blow to the head, I had more than enough odd happenings in the last day or so to question my own sanity.

Even as I thought about my own sanity and strange head injury side-effects, a loud popping erupted next to my ear and then a low growl. I swung my head around, but once again there was nothing there. Now there was just an increased pain in my skull from the sudden movement. Something in my head didn't feel right, my eyesight started to cloud, a misty haze making everything slightly blurry, my tongue felt too big in my mouth and my limbs had gone heavy. I felt a pressure on my right shoulder and someone called my name from a distance, but I didn't care, I was so overwhelmingly tired suddenly that I couldn't even lift my hand.

****

There was someone screaming, screeching so very loud, it made my eardrums throb. Even my eyes ached from the sound, is that even possible? I opened them to seek the source, vaguely annoyed that my sleep was disturbed despite the fact that the cause of my awakening was something clearly in distress. I was faced with a figure and quickly my mind started trying to work out whether it was truly conscious or not, unsuccessfully. The face was no more than a hands width away from my own. Deep black eyes bored into mine, the face hard to make out even though he was so close to me, a wide open mouth, blackened inside, acted as an amplifier for the guttural screaming that erupted forcefully from his throat. Something was glistening on his cheeks, slowly dripping from his eyes, I was frozen, unable to move and make a sound. Fear was holding me in its grip, locking me in place.

I summoned all of my focus, I dragged in a deep breath and the face faded away.

****

Dr Muggor was looming over me, concern etched across his features. He was talking, but I couldn't hear a thing. There was just static noise bouncing around my skull. Blinking rapidly, I realised I had passed out. Sweeping the sweat out my eyes with the back of my hand, I allowed Dr Muggor to help me up and across to my couch. The bizarre thought of wishing I had opted for a nicer material than faux leather flitted across my mind and I shook it away. I assessed myself quickly. No additional pains, nothing to be worried about. My head seemed intact too, Dr Muggor must have somehow stopped me from using it as a landing surface. Reality slowly came trickling back in and I thought this coming and going with all these strange happenings was something I would not like to get used to.

The last few days seemed to be spent repeatedly having to regain a grip on what is real and what is not. I was still reeling from that face I kept seeing over and over again. Most details have gone already, but something, something was strange about it. Not just the pure unadulterated terror that froze me in place, there was something more there and I didn't know what. I glanced across to Dr Muggor, I had lost myself in my thoughts and he was sitting across from me on a dining chair. Arms propped across his knees observing me, like I was an interesting piece of art in a gallery. Sensing my discomfort, he straightened himself and spoke slowly,

"How are you feeling? Can you tell me any events since leaving the hospital that could be described as out of the ordinary?"

A moment passed, where I considered not confiding in him. Funny really as my instinct told me he knew I was not OK anyway – ignoring the fact that I just passed out in front of him. Hell, part of me felt like I could be thrown in a mental hospital with all the recent happenings. But reason has to rule, I couldn't deal with all of this, I felt like I was losing my sanity, not just my memory. So, I described in as much detail as I could the nightmares, the sounds, visual snaps and glitches I had been experiencing. It was with some relief that I noted he didn't react like I was mad or needed to be shipped off to some facility on a distant island. He merely nodded knowingly. After a brief pause, he spoke,

"I understand this is likely all very unsettling for you, frightening even. If you'll allow me, I would like to take on your case personally, one-on-one. It will entail me seeing you on a frequent basis and you checking in with me every time one of these 'instances' occurs. I do understand however that it may not be your first thought nor instinct to pick up the phone and call me, so I may have an alternative option for you to consider." He was staring intently at me, I had no response, so I waited for him to continue.

"I have a treatment if you will be interested in it. Before I explain to you what it is, I need to warn you that all the symptoms you have been experiencing are very rare in head trauma cases. I am specialised in this field, so you can have the utmost faith that I will look after you and endeavour to make this as speedy a recovery as possible. The risk you have at the moment is falling victim to the images and flashes you keep having if unmonitored and untreated they can lead to a complete mental breakdown, often irreversible. So, what I would like to offer you is what can be described as a 'new-age'." (Emphasis made using his fingers, should that have made me accept it more?) "Treatment, a small electronic plate, around the size of a thumbnail, inserted just behind your ear just underneath the skin. What this will achieve is post events, you can insert a small chip into it and review what you saw or heard in your head, as you did the first time round but from an outside perspective so you can try to look at things objectively."

My mind was reeling, was this some kind of joke? A technology that can access, record and replay what happens in my mind? I was sceptical at best. Clearly, this thought process was betrayed by my face because Dr Muggor clasped his hands together and went on, "This will help you establish and ascertain what has actually happened and what hasn't. This is particularly useful now whilst your realities and imagination are skewed. It also gives you the opportunity to analyse your dreams. From what I can understand of your descriptions, they are vivid and traumatising at best. In order to combat these, you need to understand what has been triggered to make these occur. We fully fund the entire treatment and there is no risk of further harm to yourself. Worst case scenario is you will be exactly how you are now."

It felt like a great deal to take in and completely fictional. But then again, medical fields are coming along in leaps and bounds. Who knows what they have developed and not announced? But to become one of the people who use it, something unheard of (to my knowledge, which I suppose isn't surprising with a group of friends I can count on one hand) and sounding like something born from a sci-fi movie, was I prepared for that? What was the worst that could happen? As Dr Muggor said, I would be no worse off, if the plan wasn't successful. Without bothering to give it any more thought, I gave a muted nod of my head, anything was better than this and I knew in myself that I wasn't dealing with it that well. If it all continued this way I could probably safely wager that I would be in the percentage of people who have the breakdown, and if I could avoid this why wouldn't I? I saw a flash of something that can only be described as relief cross the doctor's face as I gave my agreement to go ahead, but just as soon as I had noticed it, it was replaced by a professional expression, ungiving and almost too serious. But this was a pretty serious subject, I suppose. Why did I not feel more concerned about the next steps? I had a feeling of acceptance, allowing whatever would happen next to happen.

****

I arrived in the evening time to a small medical centre just outside of the main town. It was a bland building, only a dull green cross mounted on the wall indicated to me that I was in the right place. The walls were dulled white and the surrounding ground was broken paving slabs jutting up at all angles. They probably looked very neat before, but now they looked a sorry state, uncared for and a trip hazard to anyone who tends to drag their feet a bit, like me. A small nagging sensation in the pit of my stomach made me halt outside the door for just a moment before I shrugged it off as yet another irrational feeling to go with all the rest I have been having.

Rapping neatly on the door, I was surprised when it was opened almost immediately. I was greeted by a woman with a small pin on her lapel identifying her as Steph. She had a big smile spread across a fairly pretty face, hazel eyes that almost glittered at me and a small nose scattered with faint freckles, her sharp cheekbones were framed by mousy blonde, beachy curls and a soft jawline. Very pretty in fact, in a natural way, which I preferred. I still hadn't heard back from Sarah and I missed studying her face, I should probably try a bit harder to get hold of her. Shaking the thought from my head, I took the delicate hand of Steph that she was patiently holding out to me to shake.

"Mr Shack, pleasure to meet you. If you could follow me, I'll let Dr Muggor know you've arrived." With that, she swiftly turned on her heel and led the way. I had entered into a small hallway behind her, it was painted a brilliant white with a lime green border on the floor level. I heard the door click closed behind me, and I ignored the claustrophobic feeling of being shut in a place I didn't know. Following Steph into the main room, I noted the decor choice remained throughout. Just a few waiting room chairs lined the wall to my left and a small antique looking desk was directly in front, with a plain swivel chair behind it. To the right was a heavy-looking wooden door with a plaque reading 'DR. J. F. MUGGOR MD' positioned top centre.

Steph gestured to the seating area on the left, indicating I should sit over there and wait. I obliged and sat in one of the three seats. I'm sure they made these chairs as uncomfortable as possible, maybe to deter people from bothering to come or to tire and leave faster. Steph knocked gently on the doctor's door and slid in opening it just enough to pass through without letting me see in the room yet. My first impression was that although clean, this place seemed a bit backwater. There was no one else here and Dr Muggor had told me to come in the evening, it was now 9 pm. Apparently, it would be the best time to do the implant and prepare me for what I would be able to do following it. When he gave me the address of this clinic, I questioned him on the location and told him I didn't know there was a medical centre here and he explained that it was a new treatment and this clinic was built for it, and as a result of the newness of the treatment pretty much all funding was dedicated to the upkeep of research and treatment itself, the aesthetic aspect of the facilities being less prioritised for the time being. And he did request that I didn't mention the clinic to anyone because until it became a mainstream line of treatment, people wouldn't understand and it would cause more questions than comfort to the public. The public who were not that receptive to such huge leaps in the medical world People didn't like change, and they would definitely find this invasive and try to shut it down before its true value could be shown. I had listened quietly and in all fairness, I could more or less see where he was coming from.

I wasn't sure how comfortable I was with the whole process, so I had zipped a quick text to Sarah before leaving, telling her the address and that I was going for a procedure to help my head injury. Still no reply, I was beginning to think she may have decided against our relationship now, and although it saddened me and I wished that wouldn't be the case I couldn't blame her. Deep in thought, I was pulled back by hearing my name called from the doorway and Steph told me in an overly soft nursing tone, "The doctor will see you now."

I entered the room and was surprised by the size of it. In comparison to the previous room, this was huge. What seemed to be a dental chair centred the room along with the trolley and assortment of tools glinting in neat rows. Kitchen style cabinets lined each wall with overhead cupboards crowded the space above them. A desk overflowing with paperwork and a computer sat in the far right corner and Dr Muggor was perched on a stool in front of it typing away as I came in. There was a second table to my right, just against the wall next to where I entered, the same style that every doctor's office has, lined with the dull green tissue paper. Dr Muggor rose from his seat, strode over and shook my hand,

"I trust everything is OK with you and ready to go ahead?" I nodded my consent back, not knowing what to say really, nor knowing what difference any answers he gave me for my few questions would make. Frankly, although a bit nervous about this process, I was a little excited to see how it would work. It would be cool to be able to replay my dreams and thoughts, like a TV programme or a movie. I made myself comfortable on the plastic lined dentist chair and Dr Muggor pulled up alongside me.

"For sanitary reasons, I am going to need to remove the rest of your hair in this location, the last thing we need is a small infection to occur." He looked to see my response and I told him with no humour to just take the rest off, there was no point leaving the few tufts that would be left over. It seemed silly that they had left the other half of my head the first time round too. "Noted, we will take it all off for you. Your scar seems to be healing well and I don't want to jeopardise that. It will be a small incision in your auricularis superior muscle, just slightly above and behind your ear. I will use the same side as you suffered your injury so as to prevent more scars. The plate I insert has very small, fine feelers that will then extend and implant themselves onto your temporal lobe. I don't know what knowledge you have of the brain, but each 'section' has its own role.

"What this chip is capable of doing is accessing each one and recreating a visual and auditory representation of that is happening inside your mind. As previously said, to be able to view this and differentiate between what is real and what is not will help you in times that reality becomes a bit fuzzy."

Again, a cursory nod from myself. "I will put you under with general anaesthetic and it will be around 15 minutes you will be out. If at any point you become aware of what is happening, do not panic, you will not feel anything and we don't want your cortisol levels to increase, it can have a negative effect on your wellbeing post-procedure."

Whilst he had been speaking to me, I hadn't noticed the needle slip into my right arm. With a small nod of the head from Dr Muggor to Steph, she injected the anaesthetic and within five seconds, I was out.

****

I was sitting in a small alcove, in what looked like a caravan. You know, the seating area shaped like a 'U' and the lower ceiling. A cheap wooden table with the usual garish floral print was in front of me, attached to the wall still. Unlike in a caravan though, this seating section had no window behind it. I rose up and looked around, I had an intense feeling of unease rippling through me. Moving away from the area, I took in my surroundings. There was a hallway directly in front of me lined with gaily coloured drawings by children it looked like. As I

23

look down it, the hallway seemed to extend, growing longer and longer. I felt my state of alarm increasing. I started to move down the hallway because I didn't know what else to do. A section to my left seemed to open up and it quickly turned into what looked like a very old-fashioned kitchen area, from the '60s era maybe. I felt like I recognised it from my childhood somewhere but wasn't sure.

I heard a scuffling behind me and jumped when I felt something on my leg. I looked down and saw a small child, no more than two or three years of age, tugging on my legs. It was a boy, but I couldn't see his face. It wasn't covered, but it was just a blur. I could feel the distress of the child, he wasn't crying, but he was somehow conveying to me a deep fear and need. I sensed another presence and looked further round behind me.

The hallway was now stretching as far as I could see even though I had not walked very far in, and there was a cloaked figure standing a little way off from me and the child. A tearing pain shot through the side of my skull and suddenly the figure launched himself forward into a sprint. A sharp jab of shock ripped through my chest. I didn't know what was happening, but I knew I had to run as fast as I could and I had to take the boy with me. I grabbed him around the waist and he was weightless. I pushed off the balls of my feet and started running, I could almost hear the breath of our pursuer behind me. I glanced back and he was what seemed like less than three feet away. He could easily reach out and grab us. Pushing harder, I ran and my legs were screaming at me. The child was just motionless and soundless under my arm. A sudden corner loomed up and I jump kicked off the wall in front of me and threw myself to the right and could hear myself shouting to my pursuer to get away.

A sudden snip in my mind and I was looking down from the sky at a large complex. A 'U' shaped building, like a newly built school. The roof wasn't there and I could see me running through the halls and the cloaked man right on my tail, it was like watching a video game. I blinked and I was suddenly back on the ground, heaving breaths and using my left arm as a propeller. I saw the end of the hallway. It was almost like a tunnel here, there was a wooden door and somehow, I knew that is where I needed to get to. Having an end destination aided me and I seemed to increase the speed. I couldn't hear the figure anymore. I risked a look back and he had disappeared. The door abruptly flitted away and a corner shot up in front of me, I skidded to a halt and turned quickly. I don't know where this man was and I couldn't let him catch us. Another sharp turn and I resumed sprinting full pace.

Out of the wall, the cloaked figure suddenly appeared, his face shadowed and a long arm shot out to grab me. I slammed myself into the wall on the right and moved harder. The door was a metre away. I yanked the brass handle down and threw us through it. The door crashed closed behind me and I saw we were lying on a grass area. Standing up, I saw a small brick wall and somehow again knew what I needed to do. I had to get over it and to whatever is on the other side. I grabbed the child up from the floor again and ran and neatly jumped over the wall. There was a metal container in front of me and I beelined for it.

Opening the door, I flung myself through it and closed it. There were a handful of locks lining the jamb and I utilised them all. Spinning around to see where I was, I saw my bedroom. Confusion made my head ache, I looked down to the child and he had disappeared. I felt a pull towards my bed and allowed it. I was at home now, I needed to rest. I laid down and closed my eyes. A slow compression started on my chest between my ribs and I opened my eyes again. I found myself filled with an intense, almost indescribable level of fear. My whole body felt like a dead weight. I tried to move my limbs and nothing happened. I fought harder. Nothing. The cloaked figure was standing over me, a shrouded hand placed on the centre of my chest. I couldn't see his face but I could envision it. I could barely breathe. I was paralysed. My head raced with a lot of noise, nothing coherent. I clamped my eyes closed and suddenly, the pressure disappeared and darkness enveloped me.

****

When I blinked my eyes open again, I felt groggy and the throbbing in my skull that had become commonplace seemed to have increased. I half expected to be still in my room, the remnants of the nightmare lingered and I wasn't entirely convinced it was a dream yet. I was in the dentist chair. I could feel some form of restraint on my forehead and when I tried to move them, I realised my arms had been held down too. I could hear Dr Muggor talking to me but it sounded distant like he was calling me from across a street. I heard clipping noises and felt the release of pressure on my head and wrists.

Steph came into view and smiled at me kindly, and if I wasn't mistaken, with a little bit of pity. Looking past her, I could see Dr Muggor taking off some plastic gloves and throwing them into a yellow disposal bin. His mouth was moving, but I couldn't make out the words. Judging from the fact he kept glancing over at me, he was talking to me, I just couldn't hear him yet. I felt something cool flush over me, like a layer of water but underneath my skin rushing through my veins. My hearing came back and the fogginess in my eyesight passed.

"…Success. So, you will feel a little different for the next few days, but this is completely normal. Your brain will need to accept and work with the device, but as of now, it is fully functional. Can you tell me, did you have any out of the ordinary dreams whilst you were under the anaesthetic?" He seemed completely oblivious to the fact that I hadn't heard most of what he said. But I heard the word success, so I was content to leave it.

"I had a nightmare, I was being pursued, I think. There was a child, but I don't know who. There were corridors and a field. But I came back to my flat and a cloaked man followed me. Then I woke up."

I couldn't say truthfully that I would like to rewatch this and come to think of it, any of the other nightmares I had endured recently. Why did I get this? Maybe it would be OK; I didn't have to use it if I didn't want to. I knew that it was just a nightmare, didn't I?

"OK, this is good. We can use this one to review the system and make sure it has no glitches. I will need you to turn your head for me and I will insert the reading chip. I should let you know, because it is rather fiddly you can simply leave this in, like a memory card for a mobile phone." He laughed a little at his own joke and when I didn't respond he continued, "I will leave it up to you in any case."

Not seeing any other way and not willing to tell him I was now having stronger doubts than ever before, I turned my head for him. Bonus is that I didn't even feel it go in, must have some numbness left over from the anaesthetic. Dr Muggor moved swiftly across the room. I could sense his excitement; it was practically oozing out of his pores. Steph was almost jiggling on the spot, staring intently at the computer screen, waiting to see what I had envisioned whilst unconscious.

I followed the line of sight and sat up to see better. Almost instantly, the seating area from the beginning of my dream came up on the screen. It felt strange to see this, like a movie I was in but don't remember filming. It was from my own perspective too. My hands moved around in front of me, it felt alien for me to watch. True to what I had been advised, it played back the entire nightmare with more clarity than I could have described even if I tried to describe it the moment I woke up. There were also points that I didn't recall, but that is, of course, true of any dream or nightmare, some people don't remember anything.

Dr Muggor was humming whilst watching, pausing it here and there and seemingly studying it. Steph was enraptured. I was strangely not, perhaps I would feel differently about it in the comfort of my home, on my computer, without an audience to judge what had been imagined up by my brain. Not that I had any control over it, I just had a dislike for the idea of people thinking I am not of a sound mind. A real sensitive spot for me and a subject that had the ability to rouse a sense of defiance and defensiveness since I was younger.

I gently probed the side of my head looking for the new incision. I couldn't find it although there was a dressing above my ear again but there were no additional sore areas. Then again, Dr Muggor said he would do it near the scar line, perhaps he did it on the scar line. My head felt very exposed with no hair, I was now sporting my first buzz cut in many, many years. Lucky, I had brought the loose-fitting beanie hat that I usually wore every winter, the cold will hit me harder now I'd lost my mane of hair. I looked down, out of morbid curiosity I suppose, to see the surgical tools, to see if they had my blood on them and how many he had used. They looked untouched, exactly as they had before I went under. Efficient, they had cleaned and replaced them already. I wondered briefly how long I had been out for. When they had finally stopped watching the screen, Dr Muggor flicked the monitor off button and turned to face me, clasping his hands in front of him, an action he was clearly fond of.

"This opens up a whole world of possibilities for you and us in the medical field. I know this is a lot to take in, but if you have anything you need me to clarify for you, please let me know. If you would like to be kept under observation for 24 hours whilst you grow accustomed to it, we can provide this. If not, you have my number and I will always be available to assist you if you require."

I declined the offer of observation, the last thing I wanted was someone tailing me continuously and I needed my own space. Everything seemed so curt and efficient, I didn't desire anything additional nor feel like I needed it at this time, at this point I felt like things had been over explained to me and I wanted to shut it all off when I could. We shook hands after Dr Muggor removed the insertion chip from the implant and I made my way out of the building. Patting my pocket as I walked down the path to check I had the little chip in its sealed plastic bag, I headed straight for home. What I didn't see behind me was Dr

Muggor and Steph watching me, talking in hushed tones with a glint of hope in their eyes.

****

Back at home, I emptied my pockets onto the side table next to the door and flopped down on to the sofa. All things seemed dull to me at the moment. I felt listless, wanting to do things but without the real motivation to take any action. I flicked the TV on and was greeted by an orange-skinned middle-aged man reading the news, overacting his lines with false sorrow and concern. A large bush fire tearing its way through Portugal, fed by trees and grass that had been dried out by the harsh summer conditions. No deaths.

I watched for around ten minutes, but my concentration just wouldn't settle. I could feel my eyes bouncing around in their sockets, unwilling to stare at the screen. Strong coffee may help. I rose up and headed to the adjoined kitchen. I had taken around four steps when the ground evaporated from underneath me and I fell, arms outstretched, onto the carpet. Looking around in alarm, the section of floor that I was quite certain a second ago had disappeared as I stepped onto it was once again just the plain beige carpet it always was. I stood again and brushed my hands off on my trousers, and saw the doorframe of the kitchen zoom in and out twice. I blinked rapidly, another one of these trip outs again. It righted itself and I went to make myself a coffee whilst shaking my head in frustration.

Coffee, strong, a good caffeine hit. What I could really do with was an icy cold pint, but I had no inclination to go outside. I could check my fridge but I already knew what was in there, the usual, milk, butter and empty shelves. I was aware of a rumbling and ache in my stomach, when did I last eat? Pulling open the second drawer next to the oven, I hunted for a take-away menu. Perfect, curry it is, only needing the number because I ordered the same thing all the time, I called the restaurant and placed an order for delivery. It felt to me that the only thing I could do right now when my head kept betraying me with unusual sights, giving me the sensation of being on a high hallucinogenic was to push through and wait for it to normalise. It terrified me, but it seemed there was little I could do especially when it was happening.

I made my coffee and went to retake my seat on the sofa. Before I had reached it, I heard a rapping at the door. Sarah? Opening it, I saw a delivery guy standing with a paper bag of food. After handing him the money and not bothering to question how it was here within five minutes because, let's face it, my concept of time was pretty wavy at the moment, I closed the door on him.

Just as I was placing the food on the mahogany coffee table, I heard the door again. Did I not give him enough? I pulled the front door open again and felt the rush of relief and happiness run through me when I saw Sarah, my beautiful stubborn Sarah, standing before me. She took one look at me and a hand shot up to her mouth in an attempt to conceal her reaction to seeing me in this state, not before I heard the gasp though. I shrugged and motioned with my hands like this motion alone was enough of an explanation for the last few days and she threw her arms around me. Burying her face into my neck and I could hear her muffled talking mixed with cries. To my surprise, I felt my own eyes welling up, it isn't like me to be emotional by way of crying, so it was a testament to how I have been feeling that I would cry now.

I pushed her away from me gently and cupped her face in my hands. I rubbed my thumbs across her familiar cheekbones, breathed in her scent, all of her, it made me feel like home, made me feel like it would all be alright. She looked up at me imploringly, waiting for me to talk. But first, I couldn't refrain, I needed her, wanted her to see our petty argument was nothing to me. I needed to feel like me again, it was purely an animal desire for my connection with this woman I love and I pulled her through and onto the sofa with me, she followed so willingly, it spurred me on. Then in a mass of limbs and teary kisses, I felt a respite from all that had been haunting me.

****

Afterwards, we laid in each other's arms and I relished the feeling of her fingertips caressing my chest. I think we laid for around ten minutes before she broke the silence.

"Arnie, what happened to you? You've been leaving me messages at crazy hours, texting me. Every time I have tried to call you back, I just get static noise. Did you block my number?"

I frowned down at her, I had only left one message and sent two or three texts. And why would my phone not allow her to connect when trying to call me? Come to think of it, I hadn't received any calls. I would have a look at it later, plus I hadn't telephoned work to let them know what was happening, even though I'd been signed off by the hospital for three weeks to recover. Ah, they don't need an update, they have been sent the form.

Sarah was watching me expectantly, waiting for me to respond. Do I tell her everything that has been happening to me? Will she understand or run a mile? With a deep sigh, I gently moved her off of me, sat upright and told her everything. From the night terrors to visions whilst awake and memory losses. I even told her about the implant, surely Dr Muggor factored in that if I was in a relationship I would have to tell them at least. Afterwards, she had a distant look on her face, absorbing all the information, I guess. Now was make or break time, she could get up and leave if she decided I was a lost cause. I can't deny the relief that ran through me when she took my hand in hers.

"Arnie, we can work through this. I don't know what to do with all that you have just told me, but I am here for you. I will come and stay with you again for as long as you need, or at least as long as you want me to. We'll do this together, OK?" I felt tears prick the corner of my eyes, I hadn't realised how alone and lost I was feeling, but the comfort I felt in knowing she was by my side was immeasurable to me at this moment. Then a curious thought struck me.

"Do you still have any of the messages that I left you? Can I listen to them?" I am not certain what I was hoping to happen, maybe a memory trigger perhaps. It was worth a shot, surely?

Pulling my phone out of my pocket, I clicked into the call register, nothing. No recent outgoing calls apart from the ones I could remember calling. Odd. Sarah called the voicemail service and put it on the loudspeaker. There were six saved messages. The first one was no sound, just disconnected very quickly. The second was muffled like I was talking into a pillow, I was mumbling about needing to see her and someone was coming to get me. The third message, it sounded like I was crying, telling her I loved her and if something happened to me to understand that. The fourth, a lot of panting as though I was running and then shouting not to let them get us. The last two were along the same lines. All of the messages sounded panicked, not one of them I could recall. The times of the calls were all during sleeping hours too. I knew about sleepwalking but calling people whilst I was unconscious was a new one for me.

I thought again about my phone, it must have something wrong with it, those messages definitely came from my mobile and there was no doubt it was me leaving the voicemails. Just what I needed, a bust phone on top of everything else. I must have sat consumed by my thoughts for too long because Sarah's voice penetrated the flurry of ideas and musings whizzing around my skull,

"How about as you have this insertion device thing, we try to look at one of the things that have happened to you, together? What about the one with the floor disappearing?"

Nodding my assent and understanding she would want to watch a less graphic one at least to start with, I pointed to the table where it was. I didn't really know what to call it for short, so it would just be a chip. Sarah grabbed the chip and went to the door to pick up her bag from where she had discarded it. Pulling out her laptop, she fired it up and settled next to me. As I had a small dressing over the newest section that Dr Muggor had opened yesterday, Sarah had to remove it and finally saw what lay underneath. She gasped when she exposed the full scar and I didn't even want to see it myself right now. She said it was barely noticeable compared to what she had actually expected but there was a really slim skin coloured slit for putting the chip in with scabbed skin around it. It took some time and fiddling with Sarah joking half-heartedly it was like putting in a piercing, but we eventually managed to insert the chip into my still very sore head and I felt something akin to a light electrical shock, zip through me.

Opening up the webpage I had been told about we were greeted by a log in page, we typed in the password to access the portal that pulled the transmissions from the chip and fed via something not too dissimilar to Bluetooth into the database for us to view. Very quickly, the white screen started filling up with video clips, all sorts of sizes. Apparently, the implant would only activate and store what was happening when specific hormones went into a frenzy, either high or low. It seemed that this was a frequent occurrence looking at the volume of footage that had propped up. It felt funny to me that this almost seemed normal to me because I had had slightly longer to come to terms with the strangeness of the concept of this device, but I could sympathise with Sarah, who looked like she didn't really know what was going on but eager to try.

We clicked on the last one, because it was the last 'occurrence' that I was aware of and I assumed it would be the floor disappearing act. It was the right one, it started with me standing up off of the sofa. I watched closely to see exactly what happened, a bid to see if there was a trigger or if what I thought I saw had happened at all or it would show nothing except me falling to the ground. The video answered my unspoken question quickly enough. The floor in front of my right foot crumbled away and I heard Sarah gasp next to me. I could sense she wanted to say something but was holding off. The view starting skittering around as I looked to see what was happening, checking the floor, and you could see me visibly shake my head. Then when I got up, the door started panning in and out like I remembered. It was disconcerting, to say the least, to see this twice, but somehow reassuring that Sarah could witness it now and see what I saw. Does that make me unstable? Either way, it was how I felt about it. The clip abruptly stopped and we sat in silence looking at the screen. Sarah looked at me and I could see the hint of tears in the corner of her eyes.

"That must be so terrifying for you, it looked so real. Do you know if this is a permanent side effect of the bang you had on your head?"

"I don't know, Sarah, I hope not. Frankly, I've been feeling like I am going crazy, like I would be better suited to a mental institution. They have said that it is rare that this happens but it can, and it can be permanent in worst case scenarios. I don't know if my past depressive phases helped it happen, but I want to focus on making it stop. I don't know if I am coming or going when this happens. And the scariest part for me is when it is happening, I don't even question that it is real; it is like watching it happen to someone else and being dragged along for the ride. If I can somehow find a trigger or something that makes these things happen, maybe it won't feel like I am losing the plot."

She nodded back at me, completely at my mercy it seemed. Where did that thought come from? I knew wholeheartedly that she would be here for me regardless of our past arguments. The here and now was far more important than any of that, moving on and past it all, stronger.

"Agh!" I jumped at the sound and clasped my hands to my head. I refused to look around, I knew in reality, there was nothing there, even if my head was twitching to look. I also sadly knew that Sarah didn't hear it because she had no reaction other than concern flashing across her face. Damn, I hated this so very much. Without a word, Sarah looked back at the screen and another clip was already loaded up at the bottom. Clicking onto it, it was just me looking at her face, focusing it seemed just centre of her eyebrows, then a loud distressed shouting noise blasted out through the speaker. This time she jumped.

"You know, if this transmits it so quickly, I wonder if you left the chip in, I could monitor you tonight. If you have anything happening in your sleep I will see what you are dreaming as you dream it. Watch your responses as it happens. I don't know that it will help anything, but it has to be worth a try, right?" It was a pretty sound idea, so I agreed. "I need to go back to mine and collect a few things. Do you want to come with me or stay here? I will be about an hour or so." I didn't want to go out and Sarah knew this already but asked me as a courtesy in case I decided fresh air would be better, but I just wanted to sit and not do anything. I was mentally exhausted, physically too, somehow, despite my idleness. I watched Sarah leave and laid down on the sofa waiting for her return.

****

I don't know how much time had passed. I had been lying on the sofa gazing at the ceiling and simply enjoying the fact that right now my mind seemed at ease. Not even much of a headache, just a dull throbbing that was more background noise than a pressing pain. I was mulling over everything, wondering when it would end. How it would end. The mind is a funny thing, feeble too. I couldn't comprehend how an impact to my skull could result in such drastic changes. I didn't even feel confident that there was much that the medical world didn't know about the brain any more, they have now created a device that can let you see inside of it with realities and otherwise, lord knows what else they can do. It was incredibly daunting to me. However such technologies would almost certainly be interesting if used on people who suffered from hallucinations and/or warped realities all the time. If people could actually see what they saw they could relate better and help more efficiently rather than relying on textbook treatments.

I could hear footsteps to the side of me and didn't bother to turn and look. Sarah must have used my key. She walked round in front of me, but something didn't seem right. She had a faraway look on her face and her very being didn't seem solid, like I could put my hand straight through her and I realised I didn't even hear her come in the door. She leaned forward and extended her right hand as if to stroke my face. Suddenly her face contorted and her eyes went completely black. An unworldly shriek erupted from her; my heart rate shot from 60 beats per minute to a painful 120. I blinked and in an instant, it was the man from my nightmares, the ungodly shrieking started up, coming from the black hole in his face where the mouth should be.

I scrambled up and backwards on the sofa trying to claw my way over the back and away from him, hiding my face. A sudden silence took over the room and I uncovered my head to see if he had gone. He was still there but had stopped screaming. If this was a hallucination, he can't hurt me, right? I tried to reassure myself. I looked back at him, glued in place, utter terror coursing through me, all the while I chanted a mantra in my head, he cannot hurt me and he isn't real. He opened his mouth once again and his face took on a powerfully emotional look, "Help."

It was croaked, full of need. With no warning and nothing more, he disintegrated. I remained on the sofa, not daring to move. I heard the locks mechanism make its tell-tale clicking noise and turned to look full of apprehension. Sarah came through the door lugging a large holdall. She looked at me and gave me a friendly reassuring smile, instantly knowing something had happened and trying to be my calm place. I can only imagine what I looked like at that moment. Pale, wide-eyed and erratic breathing were but a few things I reckon she will have noticed, if she didn't first see the fact that I was huddled over the back of the sofa. I could feel my heart rate stabilising and my short static breaths became easier.

Help? Did I hear that right? I didn't understand, but none of it made sense. I idled and watched as Sarah went through to the kitchen and I heard the kettle start to bubble. Getting up, I followed her and wrapped my arms around her waist as she busied herself making teas. I rested my head on her shoulder and it slowed her in her tracks. I told her what had happened and I could feel her stiffen, unsure how to react.

Self-doubt and paranoia reared their ugly heads again and I wondered if I should tell her about the things I see whilst I am awake. Nightmares are one thing; non-drug induced hallucinations are in a different ballpark. But this was all happening to me and if she couldn't handle it in full effect then she wouldn't be able to help me at all. She gave no answer other than a deep sigh and leaning her head against mine. Time will be the teller on whether she could do this or not, I didn't even know how long I could do this myself, my sanity felt more in question with every event that passed.

We hadn't spoken too much for the rest of that afternoon; Sarah seemed to be wrapped up in her own thoughts. In all honesty, I didn't feel like I was in any way ready to hear them yet. I had too many of my own to contend with and the idea of even one more made me want to run away. It was all overwhelming for me. I wished I could close my eyes and the whole ugly saga would just disappear, like a bad dream. She came and perched on the edge of my bed, softly running her fingertips across my head and scar. It was more soothing than painful, so I let her. I allowed my body to sink into my mattress, the covers giving me a sense of security pulled up to my neck. She was watching me with love and had something like the air of a carer about her, but I could see the concern flitting around inside her eyes. I let mine close with acceptance of the fact I was being mothered, something I hadn't experienced in many years. I ignored the pulsating sensation in my eyelids, my eyes were fighting me to stay open in spite of my dogged tiredness. It felt like a long time that I lay there, but once the darkness enshrouded me, it seemed like no time had truly passed at all.

****

I was blinking my eyes quite a lot, trying to get them to focus on my surroundings. I could see I was in a living room, a very familiar-looking one at that. I took in the garish blue and red walls with embossed flowers on the wallpaper. Two white and orange floral eyesore sofas created an 'L' shape in front of a fireplace about four times the width of me. A small fire was burning and I was standing directly in front of it, I could feel the embers warming my calves. This was my old living room of my parents' house. It even had the same muddy brown carpet that had now been removed many years ago and seeing it made me nostalgic. I heard a chitter-chattering and looked to the source. I now saw my mum, two of my aunts and an old family friend sitting across the sofas, talking idly to each other but not taking their dulled gazes away from me.

There was a small child's toy on the floor at my feet, a plastic baby that crawled when you pressed the button on its back. I remembered it vaguely from when I was small. My attention was drawn towards the mantle above the fireplace lined with various cheap ornaments and picture frames, but I couldn't focus on the photographs they contained as they seem to just be blurred outlines. I was very aware that this was a dream, even though that in itself felt confusing. It was like I had been dropped into a memory and was just stuck in this moment in time.

A low rumbling had started and I could feel the vibrations growing under my feet. I looked back to my family and they seemed unaware of this change. A small child, the same one from before in the hallways had appeared at my side and was facing up at me. Again, I couldn't see his face, but I could feel him imploring to me. But what? The rumbling suddenly rose into a roaring sound. Instinctively, I grabbed the child around the waist and watched, frozen in place as the back wall of the living room crumbled noisily inwards and something that can only be described as a tsunami smashed through.

I watched the others launch up off of the sofas and they ran towards the front door on the right, my mum pausing at the door and looking back at me meeting my eyes. I could see some form of sadness in them. She was ushering everyone out making sure they were safe but didn't even beckon to me to join them. In a blink, she was gone. I tightened my grip on the child and braced myself, knowing there wasn't a chance I could make it anywhere else. The rushing sound of the unforgiving wall of water deafened me and then it hit me. I was crushed into the mantelpiece and I tried to protect the child in my arms. Knowing that above all else, I needed to save him.

We were now underwater and it felt like my whole body had been warped out of shape. My torso was in agony from the impact against the mantle, I was certain I had multiple smashed ribs. I clamped my eyes closed and felt myself being swept with the movement of the tide. I was pulled horizontally backwards and found myself on a surface of sorts and the water drained off of me. I opened my eyes again and looked around, I could still feel the child in my arms but couldn't bring myself to look down at him for fear of seeing the worst. I was in some sort of cabin. Wooden, like the one in the Doris Day movie, 'Calamity Jane' or was it 'Pillow Talk'? Strange that I thought of those movies, my mum loved them and often had them playing when I was a kid. The cabin was homely, anyhow.

I sat upright and realised in that second that the boy was no longer with me again, but I now felt no fear regarding this. I could feel someone in the room with me. Blinking salty water from my eyes, I waited for them to adjust both wishing it to be quick so I could see what was around me properly and also to not be able to see, as if that would protect me. Before I could make out the shadowy figure, I felt him, an oppressive presence. I could feel the level of my fear increase rapidly, I didn't need to see him to know who it was. I couldn't move, he approached me swiftly, seemingly without taking even one step and he suddenly loomed over me. My vision cleared in that instant to give me full visuals of him. He gave me the darkest of stares and I couldn't tear my eyes away. The odour hit me, acrid and burning my nostrils.

I watched paralysed as he unsheathed one of his pale bony hands and presented to me what he had in his palm. It was vicious-looking, it resembled a bull's horn, but sharpened to a deadly point. His mouth sagged open and he screamed a soul dementing scream and it took me what felt like an eternity to realise he was screaming help. I wasn't breathing and my heart was scattering around my ribcage, and gave me a bruising sensation with every thump. His head was suddenly thrown back and the hand brandishing the weapon was brought up with such a force that it pierced my skin and drove under my ribs. I tried to inhale, but my air pipe had sealed shut. I clasped my hands over the area and felt hot sticky dampness oozing out. My vision started to shutter and then I felt an eerie calmness wash over me. As I blinked hazily, the man had gone and I could see my room. Blink, blink, blink. Nothing.

****

I could feel myself being shaken, roughly. Batting the assailant away, I grumbled to stop. My whole body was hurt like I'd undergone intensive one-on-one training with a heavyweight champion. I noticed very quickly that breathing in was a task and my eyes shot open. Sarah was above me, in a state it seemed. She had tears streaking down her face and she was trying to pull me up.

"Sit up and stick your head between your legs, it will help, Arnie, come on." She was speaking rapidly and I didn't really know what was happening, so I followed her orders. In the back of my mind, I registered that I must be having some sort of anxiety attack. The tightness in my chest and lack of breathing abilities couldn't be linked to much else, I'm not asthmatic. She was forcefully rubbing my back and soon I felt my airways loosen up and started to take big gulping breaths to the point I felt myself go almost euphoric with light-headedness.

After a time had passed Sarah helped me scoot over to the side of the bed. I hung my legs over the side without letting my feet touch the floor and had a moment of nostalgia remembering being so little and I couldn't reach the floor. I took one look at Sarah and shook my head.

"They are all this bad before you ask. But I have not woken up like that yet. I think it may be getting worse. I will call Dr Muggor and let him know to see if he has any advice. I can't live like this. It feels like dreams are haunting me. I don't really remember what was happening but just the little glimpses I get now and then are too much, I can't focus on other things. How am I supposed to go back to work? See my friends? Be myself when I feel like I don't know who I am anymore? I don't know when I will have any of my bizarre moments where

I don't know what is going on and that scares me even more than the nightmares."

"I know, but I think Dr Muggor will be able to help you. You said he was a good doctor, right?" I nodded. "I also think that that little child means something, you told me he has appeared in other dreams and in each one you seem to have the desire to protect him. I believe if you find out why you are dreaming of him, you will at least resolve a bit of the confusion and fear. I have a friend who knows someone, a specialist. A psychologist who may be able to work out the meaning of your dreams, if you understand them better it may prevent them or lessen them at least. I didn't know you could have nightmares where the bad guy ever actually got to you, so if you think it is a good idea, we can go over to her place later and speak to her?"

I mulled over what she said, it would make sense to speak to someone about that side of it. Dr Muggor only specialised in the impact and side effects; these dreams were powerful enough to make me believe there could be something else underlying that could be resolved. I agreed, what was the worst that could happen? As long as we didn't divulge any information about the implant and chip device in my head, there would be no repercussions I could imagine. Sarah left the room to go and place a call to her friend whilst I picked up my own phone to call Dr Muggor and let him know the newest development. The line rang out, so I left a message telling him to call me back when he was available. For someone who said he would be around whenever I may need, he wasn't very good at being around when I needed to speak to him.

****

Apparently, the home of the psychologist was only a 15-minute walk away, so we pulled on our jumpers and decided to take a stroll over there rather than a cab. The evening was dewy and pleasant. We barely spoke as we walked hand in hand, just enjoying the normalcy of the activity. Before long, we reached the courtyard where a Dr Smyll lived. As we approached the driveway, the lights lit up on the porch and the door swung inwards. Standing before us was a short middle-aged woman, she looked like a friendly aunt with her wavy auburn hair and glasses perched on her slightly pink-hued nose. She greeted us with a warm smile and beckoned us in. The interior was a perfect match to the woman herself, plush armchairs placed strategically around the room, minimally decorated but effectively so. I felt instantly at ease here, relaxed in such a homely environment. She led us to one of the two-seater sofas and sat in front of us. Her body language was professional but welcoming, unlike many psychiatrists I had encountered in my time, all robotic and just earning a pay-packet without any true interest invested in the 'patient'. She started to speak, she had a soothing voice, not that I expected anything else at this point.

"Good evening, Sarah and Arnold, is it?"

"Yes, but you can call me Arnie, everyone does."

"OK, Arnie it is. Can you explain to me recent events that have led you here to me?"

I took in a deep breath, it felt like in the mere four, was it four or five? Whatever number of days that had passed since I had the accident on the bridge, a lot had happened, more than I could even recount. I felt tired already just considering it. So, we sat for a long period, both Sarah and Dr Smyll listening and me talking, explaining everything but omitting information about the chip reader in my head. Once I was done, I realised I was clasping my hands together on my lap and fidgeting my fingers around. I rubbed my clammy palms on my trouser legs and finally looked up to see the reaction of the Dr Smyll. Would she prove me wrong and now ramble off a bunch of lines that they all learned in their online courses and shimmy me out of her house?

"It would appear to me that the head trauma you sustained has triggered a chemical imbalance. You are not alone with this. This imbalance will have always been present, however, it will not have manifested itself to a noticeable point until the incident. This is not unlike when someone is diagnosed with a mental illness later in life without any noticeable triggers. I have good news for you, however. I will prescribe you a course of medication, Quetiapine. This is an anti-psychotic pill; you will need to take the dosage two times a day for two months. At the end of this period, I will assess you again and hopefully, we will be able to lower the dosage gradually until you no longer need it at all. All of the symptoms you have described to me seem to indicate dissociative identity disorder, which you may have heard of this as multiple personality disorder and schizophrenia."

She paused to see that I was taking in what she was saying. I felt receptive to what she was saying. I didn't like the idea of being drugged up again but it was a means to an end and so I was all for it. I didn't like the diagnosis, however, not questioning her judgement, more just a dislike of being labelled with an illness again.

Sensing this line of thought she continued, "This diagnosis isn't certain yet, we will need to delve more into your mind and the events over the coming weeks. I should also tell you that once the medication has done what it is intended to do, you should be able to live your life as you did before. What is important is we try to get to the roots of your dreams as the stress of these directly impacts your day to day living and will further increase the symptoms of the disorders."

I watched her face as she spoke, she was completely with me in the room. Not just doing her job, she seemed genuinely interested in helping me. "There is a recurring theme of you being pursued or attacked by a male figure and a small boy that you can't see his face. First thing, I would like to speak about is the boy. I would like to suggest that this small boy is, in fact, you. In light of recent events and the strain you have been under, your mind is struggling to digest and process everything. You feel like you are losing grip of yourself and reality and this boy is potentially a manifestation of this. Your mind is telling you to fight and protect yourself and to not forget who you are. Your psyche is aware of the danger it is in, how easily lost it can become in the midst of all the nightmares and day visions."

I sat and absorbed this information. It made sense, even if it sounded a bit out there to my frazzled state of mind. I felt a hand rest on my thigh and looked over to Sarah, she was looking at me encouragingly, clearly in agreement with Dr Smyll. I felt, in that instant, strong fatigue and didn't want to continue this meeting anymore.

"Thank you, for seeing me on such short notice. I think I need a little time to take this all in before analysing anything else if that is alright."

The doctor smiled at me knowingly and wrote out the prescription for me. I took it from her outstretched hand and rose to my feet with Sarah in tow. As we were leaving, Dr Smyll handed me a contact card and told me she would like to see me in three days to see how I was getting on but to call or come by any time if it was needed. I nodded my head, exhaustion making me reluctant to bother saying any more, and left. I didn't want to go to the pharmacy now, but Sarah insisted that it would be best to start as soon as possible, plus it made sense as the dosage was one in the morning and one in the evening before bed. So, I obliged and we made a detour on the route back before heading home.

****

Back at home, Sarah fetched me a glass of water and popped one of the pills from the packet. I still didn't feel comfortable putting myself under the influence of medical drugs, but let's face it, I didn't hesitate when it was any other form, especially alcohol, so what harm could these do? I looked at the clock, 9:48 pm. We had been out for over three hours. I swallowed the pill, all the while hoping and praying that it took the edge off in the very least. With the exception of a couple of mini brain glitches, this night had been fairly uneventful and I was grateful for the respite.

I was out of energy to discuss further the visit with the psychologist, so we agreed to have a relaxing evening and talk more about it tomorrow. We flicked the TV on and allowed ourselves to unwind to the calming voice of David Attenborough telling us about the remarkable lives of bull ants. I allowed my mind to drift to non-worrisome things, avoiding fretting about my mentality, what would happen next, where I would be and what could happen if this was all a permanent situation. Not more than 15 minutes had passed and I started to feel tired beyond anything I could remember experiencing, it was nauseating. My eyes started to flicker and the pressure in my skull increased. I must have managed about four or five blinks before I couldn't hold them open any longer and I fell instantly into a deep sleep.

****

I blinked my eyes open warily, not sure what I would see. All I could hear was a thudding and scratching noise somewhere near me. Was I still asleep? Glancing around, I could see I was sprawled across my sofa, Sarah was fast asleep and curled up next to me. I looked for the source of the sound and saw a scene of gorillas hitting tree trunks with their giant fists and play fighting on the television. I felt a flash of relief at the dreamless sleep. I even felt refreshed, my head barely hurt and my body seemed to have recovered somewhat from the aches and pains of yesterday despite both of us sleeping on the cramped sofa.

The time on the clock told me it was 7 am. I started to stretch out my limbs, long slow movements, enjoying the sensation of the muscles releasing and moving. I reached both of my arms up towards the ceiling and jolted my hands back when I hit something. Looking up, I stifled a shout. Soulless eyes bore into

41

mine and his mouth wrenched open, I braced expecting a scream. Silence, I started to back away and he spurted blackish-red fluid at me from his cavernous mouth. This time I couldn't stop my reaction, I let out a scream and threw myself back and away from the figure dragging himself across the ceiling towards me. I dropped to the floor and covered my head with my hands, not ashamed of the whimpering I could hear coming from me involuntarily. His hands closed on my shoulders and I felt his body come in closer. I had frozen in place again, I let my guard down too early and assumed I was having a period of clarity, how wrong I was.

Then something unexpected, he caressed the back of my neck. Reflexively, I jolted away and looked up. Sarah was kneeling in front of me, hand resting on my shoulder hushing me and telling me I was fine and safe. I broke at this point; nothing was right anymore. I lay across her lap and wept quietly; all the while she stroked my forehead and tried to reassure me. I didn't feel reassured, my only real hope currently was the medication giving me some sort of balance.

Wiping my face, I sat and reached to the coffee table, took that mornings pill, swallowing it without water, I nearly gagged. Pulling myself together, I told her if she wanted to watch what happened, she could. We hadn't removed the chip and I didn't see much point in going through the rigmarole of trying to take it out and put it back in at a later point again, plus Dr Muggor had already said this would be OK if I wanted to do that. I watched her as she rose and collected her laptop, still in the bedroom from the previous night. Coming back in, she didn't bother to sit on the sofa, she sat cross-legged next to me on the floor, knowing without asking that I wanted to see it too. It was somehow easier to watch it afterwards now despite my initial foreboding, I could almost disconnect from the fact that it was happening in my mind. Maybe it was due to having Sarah here with me, it calmed me. We sat in silence and watched what little footage there was, a lot of it was with my eyes closed, so you could only hear my panting.

"He truly is terrifying. It is strange that you can see his face, but he doesn't really have a face." Strange? Understatement of the century, I didn't know what to make of it. But I told her that I didn't have a nightmare, whether that was due to the Quetiapine or a turning point, I didn't know. In light of the hallucination, it didn't feel like a turning point anymore. I wished there was some way I could make it all stop at the click of my fingers. I said as much and Sarah just sat quietly, knowing there wasn't really anything she could say that she hadn't already.

Feeling my levels start to ebb again, I realised I was hungry. I couldn't remember the last time I ate a proper meal. A fry up didn't sound too bad right now, I just wanted to forget the latest episode and get on with my day. In spite of everything going on, I was acutely aware of the fact that Sarah was giving up a lot to be around me right now and taking on more than she signed up for when she entered this relationship with me. Breakfast together would be something like we would normally do and it is something we will continue to do because I will get past this, I was determined. A new force of determination washed over me and I felt quite empowered, this would not leave me crying on my girlfriend's lap, the key to it all is to realise it isn't real.

Nodding to myself, I noticed Sarah watching me, a wariness in her eyes telling me she didn't know if I was present or not. I smiled at her and pulled her up to stand with me, grabbed the keys off the side and strode out the front door, holding her hand and relishing the giggle she was emitting. We may be grubby, wearing slept-in clothes and unwashed, but I didn't care, I was taking this moment and not letting it go. We skipped down the street, ignoring curious looks of passers-by and only stopped when we arrived at the cafe, aptly named 'Breakfast Cafe'. Making a show of presenting her a table and placing a napkin across her lap, I enjoyed feeling a bit of my old self breaking through the miserable haze I had been wading through. Sarah looked joyful, she was loving it and she surely deserved it. The waitress came over fiddling with her pinny and took our order, I told her two number 3s. Full fry ups and coffees. Once she had left our table, I took Sarah's hands in my own.

"I know this isn't easy for you, I know this is all a lot for you to take on. I understand if at any point this becomes too much and you have to go. But I need you to know, I am going to get through this, we will and I will spend the rest of my life trying to show you how grateful I am to have you with me. Whether you are with me or not, you have my word." Completely taken aback by the sudden serious turn and almost maniacal spewing of feelings, Sarah just stared at me for a moment. I already felt in my heart of hearts that she was in this with me for the long haul, but I felt like I needed to tell her that.

"You don't even need to question that. I am here. That is all, no matter what happens you have me right by your side." She had a small tear glistening in the corner of her eye and I reached forward to gently wipe it away. In the motion, a person caught my eye at the edge of my peripheral vision. I don't know what it was about them but instinct told me to look. Just bustling out of the door was someone I recognised but couldn't place. She was holding her hand across her face and moving quickly. Steph, the woman from Dr Muggor's office. I frowned to myself and Sarah followed my gaze.

"What? Who is it?"

"The nurse that worked with Dr Muggor, she was hiding, I think. That was odd."

Maybe she didn't want to speak to me outside of an appointment? Why would she even be on this side of town? *She must live locally to here*, I thought to myself. Or blind date gone wrong and she wanted to escape quickly, and she hadn't actually seen me? Bit out of the way to come across town to this dingy cafe otherwise. I realised then that I hadn't heard back from Dr Muggor after the message I left him yesterday, she could have had the decency to let me know he would call me back or just at least acknowledge me because I was sure she must have spotted me, it was hard to miss me with my shaven head and dressing on one side. The food arrived at the table and putting Steph to the back of my mind, I dove into what turned out to be one of the best fry ups I had ever eaten.

****

Arriving back home, I felt wonderfully at ease. All recent problems a distant memory, I was having a day that finally felt normal. Sarah was relaxed to the point of sleepiness and thinking about it, a nap wouldn't go amiss for me either. Feeling romantic, I picked her up and cradled her in my arms, her wrapping her own around my neck and nuzzling into my chest. Taking her through to the bedroom, I laid her down and joined her on the bed. Gently running my fingers across the familiar bumps and curves of her stomach I felt myself drifting off, sleepiness wrapping its seductive hands around me and pulling me in. I let my eyelids droop and saw Sarah sat upright quickly and lean over me. She started to shout something but I couldn't pull myself back to present, I was drifting off to another dimension and there was no way to stop it. I was falling, endlessly, with no bottom in sight.

****

I finally landed on something after what seemed like forever. In that usual dream way, there was no unusualness to me having landed softly after an extended fall, it just felt normal. I got to my feet and looked around and the brightness seemed to ramp up like someone was fiddling with the graphics in my vision. I was standing on a pier, it seemed I was far out to sea because I couldn't see a shoreline anywhere I looked. The pier was vast, walkways were going in all directions, there were shops and arcades dotted here and there, with toilets that reminded me of a cowboy era, each with their own walkway leading up to the doors. The sea was lapping up against the posts and I looked at how feeble the rails looked, you could probably give a good blow and they would disperse.

I took one step forward and felt myself lurch, looking down to see why, I saw to my horror the slat of wood was crumbling away from under where I just had my foot, it was of a sand-like consistency. Panic welled up and I moved my other foot forward and the same thing happened. Behind me, there was a commotion and as I turned to see, I saw huge amounts of piers and buildings dropping into the ocean and being swallowed into the icy depths. I knew there was no time and started to run, progress hindered by the wood falling away underneath me.

Then ahead of me I saw my family, my mum came out of one of the cowboy bathrooms, other family members scattered around not knowing which way to run. I watched as the toilet tilted with a cartoonish effect and my mum leapt across to the main walkway. She grabbed one of my cousin's hands and started to run ahead of me and then I saw the little boy. He wasn't far in front of me and I was gaining on him. As I caught up, he threw out an arm and I grabbed him, yanking him along with me not slowing my pace. I launched myself over a gaping hole in the floor and stumbled on the other side. I tried to regain my footing but couldn't and I fell in slow motion into the now raging sea.

The boy was now standing on a lone square of wood just floating in front of me and the water was suddenly very still. He was looking down to me, reaching out but not far enough. I then saw my mum similarly standing on a bit of wood disconnected from everything else, watching me, helplessness written across her face. The water encased me, stabbing me like knives with its coldness. My breath caught and I struggled to stay on the surface when I felt something grip my ankle. I watched as both my mum and the boy faded from view and the grip on my ankle climbed up my leg. Pain was tearing through my limb and yet I couldn't resist looking down. I was now fully submerged, but what faced me was clear as day. Those eyes again, his fingers were now gripping into my thighs and blood seeped from the wounds he inflicted. His nails tore into me like a fillet knife. I tried to shout out, inhale, anything and was rewarded with a choking sensation. My throat expanded and stretched beyond its capability and my lungs filled with salty seawater. I could picture in my mind them filling up like a jug in a sink. I watched in horror, wondering when it would end as the cloaked man turned my legs into shreds gargling at me. His eyes portrayed nothing, no glee at his actions, nor sadness or anger. Unreadable. His hand suddenly retracted from me and unable to react, I could only watch as those razor-sharp nails swept up through the water and hooked into my face. I felt something pop and couldn't see anymore. The pain was beyond anything I could endure and as that thought entered my mind, it all disappeared.

****

Something was vibrating, disturbing my whole being. I could even feel it in my teeth. I felt my eyelids being pulled apart and opened them myself. I was drenched, coated in a layer of my sweat. I pawed at my face and my legs and needed to assert to myself that I was in one piece. Hands restrained me and I saw Sarah standing to one side of the bed, hand covering her mouth. Standing over me and holding my arms and legs were Dr Muggor and Steph. I had no idea what was going on, I felt completely disorientated and fearful.

"Mr Shack, I need you to take deep breaths. In for five seconds, out for five seconds. You have just experienced a seizure. You need to remain where you are until I tell you otherwise, understood?" I nodded. A seizure? I didn't even want to imagine what this entailed now. I lay there, saturated in my sweat whilst they carried out a few routine tests to make sure I was OK. When they finished, Dr Muggor extended a hand to me and helped me up, slowly.

"What are you doing here? Not that I'm not grateful, but why are you here?"

"You left me a message and I tried to return your call today, but you didn't answer, so I decided to make a home visit to ensure you were doing well, your message gave me cause for concern."

"What caused the seizure?" Dr Muggor picked up his briefcase and pulled out a clipboard before answering me.

"The seizure was induced by some pressure on your brain. The internal swelling caused by the impact seems to have localised, luckily. There is nothing we can do to assist this right now, but it should be a one-off event. You need plenty of fluids and plenty of rest. You have been having a series of hallucinations and nightmares that will also be creating a strain, so you need to take it more easy. No more adventures running around like an adolescent, understood?" I frowned, so he did know I had been out, which means Steph definitely knew I was in the cafe. How did he know about the frequency of the episodes though? Seemingly reading my mind, Dr Muggor spoke over my train of thought.

"You need to remember I have access to the chip reader on my computer. When a new incident occurs, it flags up with a notification. You have my complete confidence and none of what I see or hear ever gets relayed anywhere else. Also, I only see when you have a flux of hormones, I do not see your day-to-day business, remember." I'm not sure if that was supposed to give me any comfort, but I nodded back at him, I suppose I gave him consent when I agreed to the implant. "Can you tell me, has this access been of any use to you? Has it helped you to understand better between reality and dream?" A nod again whilst I thought about my reply.

"It has helped somewhat, if only to reassure myself that it isn't real. The intensity doesn't seem to have subsided but I assume with time, it will?"

"For now, this is the purpose of the implant. For you to ascertain what is real in your life and what is fictional. I have another appointment to get to, so I suggest you get some rest and don't leave until you feel 100%. All of these occurrences will stop eventually, you will just have to ride it out until then."

I wondered briefly why he hadn't offered some kind of insight to the nightmares or a method for coping with them, but I guess that wasn't something he would have any knowledge about. Nagging in the back of my brain told me not to mention the visit to the psychiatrist, I don't know why, but somehow I felt he wouldn't take the news lightly. Like he would feel someone was interfering perhaps. I said goodbye to them both and Sarah climbed on to the bed next to me and asked if I was alright. I just nodded whilst trying to make sense of the jumble of thoughts in my mind. Paranoia really wasn't something to be taken with a pinch of salt. I heard the front door click closed and once again wondered about the timing of his visit. I was starting to get a bad feeling, but self-doubt meant I couldn't be sure that the feeling was justified or not.

****

The afternoon passed by fairly uneventfully and we decided to watch the video from during my seizure. It was graphic and Sarah was distraught by it. It was terrifyingly realistic, but then, of course, in comparison no horror movie can re-enact 100% convincingly the intensity of a real-life gruesome event or for that matter, what your mind can conjure up. Watching this to Sarah must be almost as distressing as being there first-hand was for me, so to speak. She pushed her head into my cheekbone trying to give as well as take comfort from me. I allowed the weight of my head to rest on her and I paused the clip on the moment I looked down at the man. His face was unclear, but the eyes were a glittery black. I hadn't noticed it before really, but his skin had a greyish hue to it and leathery texture. The nose was slightly hooked but nothing out of the ordinary. In spite of the monstrous aura he had, with the exception of the skin tone and lack of whites in his eyes, he looked remarkably human.

I sat looking at his face for a while and felt a small tugging in my mind. My heart was racing just looking at him, remembering segments of nightmares that he was the sole cause of. His face was drawing me in and I didn't know why. I took a screenshot and sent it to my phone. I had a desire to study it with no real idea of why I was inclined to do so. Sarah just watched me and didn't say anything. I could see her brain ticking behind her pretty eyes and knew better than to ask whilst she was assessing it all. The drowsiness post-seizure was still affecting me and I wanted so much to go and rest, but fear stopped me. I just sat on the sofa, praying – without effect really, I am not religious – that I didn't have to deal with any more crazy turns any time soon or ever if possible. I'm not sure how long I sat there staring into space but was drawn back to the present by Sarah placing a mug of coffee in my hand. I noticed the lights had been turned on and it was now dark outside, confused I looked at the clock. I had been sitting there for more than two hours? It felt like five minutes!

"I'm just going to serve up, do you want to help?"

Was this another glitch in my memory? Serve up what, dinner? I asked and watched as a look of confusion passed over her face, "Well yes, dinner. You told me you wanted spaghetti Bolognese, so I went to the shop and came back and cooked it for you. Do you not remember?"

I shook my head and wearily decided there was nothing to be achieved by panicking about it or worrying, I just had to try and roll with it as best I could. With a small, almost unnoticeable sigh, she wandered back out of the room into the kitchen. The smell wafted out behind her and my stomach grumbled in anticipation, I had to give her credit, the girl could cook a damn good meal.

She came back through balancing plates and set them down on the coffee table. I picked mine up gratefully and started to turn my fork into my pasta when a shooting pain lurched through my head. Blinking it away and trying to focus, I held back a gag at what I now saw before me. On my plate, there was a mass of coagulated blood oozing around and dripping onto my legs. It soaked into strands of what looked like hair, dying it an intense red colour. I blinked rapidly at it and it faded back into a plate of spaghetti topped with the meat and sauce. I tried to slow my breathing and not make a scene. A small noise escaped me, a titter, I think. Then with no control whatsoever, a laugh erupted from me, high pitched and unbalanced. I wasn't happy right now, why was I laughing? A manic wave hit me and I couldn't stop it. I could picture launching the plate of food across the room, hearing it smash against the wall, imagine the tomato sauce dripping down. I could see myself doing a cartwheel into the TV and thrusting my leg through the screen, simulate the pain and blood as the glass embedded into my skin.

I was almost panicking now; my head was running away from me and I was being dragged along behind it putting up a poor fight. I looked at Sarah and imagined her falling backwards off the sofa and hitting the floor with a thud, shaving her head and plaiting the hair to make place settings on the table. I laughed harder, the more I tried to stop it the more uncontrollable it became and I wondered if this was what a full breakdown felt like, if it was now finally happening to me. The pictures were running through my head and I didn't know what to do. I suddenly saw myself running towards the window, opening it and flying through the air, could see the aftermath with my crushed body and crowds gathering to ask what happened. Then a sudden ringing silence filled my ears. The maniacal laughing ceased and I sank back into the sofa, drained. I closed my eyes and wanted to curl up in a ball.

At this moment, I wanted my mum. My dear mum, with whom I had always shared a strained relationship, who passed away a few years ago, who may not have ever known what to say, had always, without a doubt, been there to tell me not to worry. I craved that detached comfort right now. Running my hands down my face, I felt hard stubble. Then over my skull, the hard sensitive ridge of the scar, the prickly grow back of hair on my head. It all felt so foreign to me, my head was swaying, full of cotton wool. I opened my eyes again to get my bearings and Sarah was observing my movements, no fear on her face just a strong concern. I don't know why but it seemed to ignite anger inside me, powerful and overwhelming.

"I am not a child, don't look at me like that! You're making me feel worse, is that why you are really here? To rub it in my face? To see what happens next like in a freak show?" my voice was raised, but I couldn't lower it, the words pouring from me like acid, I didn't even mean them but couldn't make them stop. "Get out. I can't stand to look at you whilst you have that pitying look on your face. I don't know why you came back; do you want brownie points for looking after the head case? Think it will make you seem like a better person. That is so low. Leave. Now."

Internally, I could hear my head shouting at me that I didn't want her to go, but I could feel my body language and spoken words telling her otherwise. This wasn't me, but I felt helpless to the actions I was undertaking right now. I pulled her up off the sofa and practically pushed her out of the front door, slamming it behind her. I could hear her crying, feel her hurt and my heart was aching. I trudged back to the sofa and slumped down. I felt a complete lack of hope at that moment and so very alone.

****

Downing that evenings pill, I set up my computer. Pinging the screenshot I had taken earlier over to my email to see it on the bigger screen, I zoomed in closer to my personal demon's face. I have always been fairly adept at all things computer-related and now I tried to put it to good use. Opening up an application that allowed me to edit pictures, I set to work. I started by changing the skin tone to something more human, spending more than an hour altering the shades until it looked right. Then I focused on the eyes, this was quicker; I just shaded in each corner with a bit of white to make them look more like the average persons, the iris colour wasn't significant to me. I was looking for an overall effect and didn't need specifics. Last was the mouth, I needed to change it from the harsh slit and add some lips. As I was working, I felt my heart rate accelerate. I already knew what I was going to see at this point when I zoomed out, but I didn't want to acknowledge it or face it.

Before doing anything more I pulled a backup packet of Mayfair cigarettes from my desk and lit one with unsteady hands. I am not really a smoker, just your average run of the mill social smoker with the occasional treat smoke every now and then. This one was more for a calming effect. Hoping I was wrong, I placed the mouse cursor over the zoom out button and clicked. The full image filled the screen in all its glory. I couldn't fathom what it meant, but I was sure it wasn't good news. The image now resembled me. Sure, rough around the edges, but there was no denying that this was a picture of me. Why would a monster version of myself be haunting me?

It was freakish enough to me that the child was allegedly a form of myself and now it seemed that the man, the one causing me so much pain and fear was also me. I truly am my own worst nightmare. So, if he is attacking me, but sometimes asking me for help, what does it mean? Thoughts raced around with no definitive answers. Maybe much like the child, he is a manifestation of something much deeper and it is part of the split personality. A damaged part of me that needs to heal, but then why is he hurting me? To make me feel his pain? But if he is me, I should surely feel it anyway? I didn't know, but I knew who might be able to shed some light on it. It was too late to call her now, so it would have to wait until morning, but Dr Smyll may have some insights that could help me.

I opened the viewing portal for my chip and tried to find the most recent one where the non-me me screamed at me for help. So many videos, varying from ten seconds long up to thirty minutes. I finally came across it and watched the clip through new eyes trying to fathom the meaning of it all. Thoughts of Sarah kept flicking in and I ignored them for the minute, there was nothing I could do at this moment to resolve that. Well, there probably was, but my grip on myself felt so loose, I didn't trust myself around her right now.

Something in the corner of the screen caught my eye, a small translucent box, so small, I would have missed it if it wasn't for that side of the screen being dark at that very moment. Curious, I tried to click on it to see what happened. A pop-up box arrived on the screen, not dissimilar to what you would see when creating macros on a document. It was just a bunch of numbers and letters reading:

1645-DPMN/LWR-S1
1915-DPMN/LWR-SRTNN-S2
1930-DPMN/LWR-NRDRNLN-SRTNN-S2
1200-SRTNN-S1
1445-NRDRNLN-SRTNN-S5

Must be something to do with the system, the list went on for a while and I didn't bother trying to decipher it. Saving that thought for later, I returned my attention to the video. I replayed the section where he shouted help to me a handful of times. Each time I played it, I felt myself feel less intimidated by him, in a bizarre way. I was trying to acclimatise myself to him, make it so that when he next made an appearance, my first reaction wasn't to run or cower regardless of what he was doing to me. Then another thought struck me, if he was a manifestation of my own self, then maybe, just maybe I could ask him what he wanted from me.

With a renewed vigour, I had made my decision; I would go to bed tonight and try to see him, on all bar two occasions since my head injury he was there, so it shouldn't be too hard a task. Taking one more cigarette from the packet, I lit it and took multiple deep drags. I needed it, I told myself, readying myself for what I was going to try and do. Stubbing out the butt, I rose and moved over to my bed and closed my eyes, waiting for sleep to come.

****

Something hot brought me to full consciousness; it was prickling all along my back and legs. The stinging brought me up to a standing position. I looked around, even in my sleep state, I was aware this was a dream. I was grateful for this knowledge because what faced me wasn't something I would want to encounter in the real world. Buildings surrounded me, all in varying states of decay, some just heaps of rubble. The entire ground was covered in glowing embers with ash lazily floating in the air above it. My feet didn't seem to be affected by this heat, they were clad in heavy-duty army boots. In the buildings that were barely standing, I could make out shadowy figures, whether it was people or plumes of smoke, it was hard to say.

I started to trudge along, no real direction, just allowing myself to be led where I may. I passed what must have once been a beautiful fountain, now full of debris and a dark fluid. Despite my best effort, I felt myself starting to lose my nerve. Rallying myself up again, I push on, repeating to myself that it wasn't real. My mantra of late. A howl in the distance caught my attention and I looked for the source. I could see the silhouette of a wolf upon a hill between some buildings. The sky is bright orange, the moon a rich burgundy shade, if it wasn't for the location, I would appreciate the beauty of such a sight.

A low growling closer to me spun my head around so fast that it jarred. Flinching and searching for the danger, I spotted him. A mangy wolf, malnourished and hungry for any food it came across. Me, in this case. His eyes were murderous, glinting red in the light from the moon, saliva dripped down around his jaw, teeth bared and crouched low ready to attack. My heart stopped in my chest and I could do nothing but turn on my heel and run. Crunching underfoot, the embers created a firework-like spray behind me as I pounded along. I looked back and could see that it wasn't just one wolf anymore, there were four and they all looked fit to tear me into shreds should they catch me.

I came up to a narrow alley between two standing buildings and raced along, propelling myself off the walls with my hands to get more speed. At the end, I realised there was a gate and a choice of left or right. Using my foot, I booted off of the gate and pushed my weight to the right, losing as little speed as possible, shouldering into the wall to regain my balance. A small heap was lying on the floor in front of me and I knew instinctively that it was the boy and I couldn't leave him, real or not. Scooping down I pull him up by his ragged top and into my arms. I could almost hear the snapping of teeth at my heels and I saw one building, half-collapsed, just a hundred metres in front of me.

On the ground level, there were windows, they were quite wide and one was pushed open, the mechanism making it open by being swung upwards rather than sideways. I narrowly avoided tripping over different obstacles and prepared myself for my next move. Bracing the boy against me, I threw myself into a skid, feet first facing the window and the opening was just tall enough for us to make it. Clattering into the room, I smashed my back and head on something hard.

Taking no time to recover, I launched upward and grabbed the handle of the window, yanking it closed just as one of the wolves reached it. His head had made it through the opening and I used all my weight pressing my feet against the wall to try and close it. The wolf let out a keening sound and with one final hard pull, his head cracked and he became motionless. Using my hand to push his crushed skull out of the way, I cried out, his skull had turned into a gristly paste and my fingers squished straight through it. Withdrawing my hand in disgust for just a moment, I remembered it wasn't over yet and shut the window and locked it. The other wolves stood back, not moving, just observing us from outside. I realised we were standing in a bathtub, grimy and half full with murky water. The boy was crouched next to me cradling his head in his hands and rocking himself back and forth. I put my hand out and touched the top of his head and he abruptly stopped moving and looked up at me. At that moment, I could finally see his face. He was so very young and innocent looking. Dr Smyll was right, he was me as a child. I felt a hard jolt in my chest at this confirmation.

"I will protect you," I told him and I recognised the look on his face, relief and determination. Taking in the rest of our surroundings, I notice we were in what must have once been a fairly upscale bathroom. A large gilded watermarked mirror hung above a cracked marble sink. The floor looked like it had before shone a brilliant white, now a greyish layer of muck covered it. The ceiling depicted something that wouldn't be out of place in a museum, a knock off of the Sistine Chapel.

One corner of the room was really dark and I couldn't make anything out, but I could feel his presence, I knew he was there somewhere, lurking. I took a deep steadying breath, trying not to submit to the growing terror inside of me. My first attempt to speak came out as a mere croak and he moved a little in the shadows, feeding off of my fear. I opened my mouth once more and a rapid scratching noise and growls from what sounded like no more than an arm's reach away behind me yanked my head round in shock. One of the wolves, who could easily be the leader of the pack, was taking action. He was substantially larger than the others and clearly got a larger share when it came to feeding hour. His coat was matted with patches of dried blood and I felt confident in assuming the bloodstains were not from him. He was gnawing at the hinges, teeth grinding against the metal and I could hear it moving under the pressure. It already felt like I had lost this battle, if there had ever really been a chance of me winning, it was long gone. Looking back to the more immediate threat, I jumped hard enough that I smashed the back of my skull on the window behind me. The cloaked man, or maybe I should start to refer to him as the evil me, was less than a foot away reaching out one of his hands. The time was now.

"What do you want from me?" the hand-kept coming in slow motion, "What do you want from me?" I said with more force. I could hear the boy next to me mewling and renewed my strength again, with all the power I could muster, I shouted as loud as I could and with all the force I could muster, "What do you want from me?" It came out like a roar and the room span rapidly. I lost my footing and slipped in the bath and as I descended, so did darkness.

****

I woke with a start, hands clenching the blankets around me as though for support. I put myself straight into the action, this felt like the right way to work this all out, so I was going to put my all into it. Sitting at my computer once more, I fired it up. Tapping the desk impatiently, nervous energy was pulsing through me. Finally, it was up. Going straight into the folder with the footage, I pressed play. My nervous energy increased; I was jiggling in my spot unable to stay still. Skipping to the last part, all I needed to see was the reaction of the cloaked man, see the result of what felt like an immense effort. I could now feel my heartbeat in my throat and my head was throbbing and there was a pulsating in my fingertips. Shaking my head in a vain effort to ward off what I could sense was coming, I almost fell off of my chair.

As I attempted to focus on the screen and ignore the increasing haziness, I saw the little box in the upper right corner was flashing a brighter white than before, and I spotted it very easily, perhaps because I had seen it before and knew it may be there. Moving the cursor over to click on it, I felt a pain shoot up my right arm. Pulling my hand back, I saw that my mouse had pins projecting from it and bizarrely, I thought of a porcupine. Blood was dripping from the pinprick wounds in my palm at a fast rate and it created a river flowing across my desk and ended with a waterfall of my blood cascading onto my lap. I leapt up and stepped back and subsequently tripped. Landing with a thud on my back and clasping my injured hand with the other, I looked to see what caused my fall. I watched in abject horror as a gravestone slowly rose from my floorboards, grinding upwards until it was sitting neatly in a pile of splintered wood and mud. I looked at the engraving:

0815-DPMN/LWR-SRTNN-S5MAX

I rolled myself on to my front and pushed myself upright. When I looked back everything was normal. No bloody river, no gravestone and an ordinary mouse. I looked at my palm, a tingling remained but no injury. What was that one about? I was beginning to feel like all of these things were signs, I just needed to know how to interpret them. I had a strong sensation of determination pulsing through me, I just knew that once I worked it all out, everything else would start to go in the right direction.

Still swaying slightly on my feet and repressing the fogginess that swamped my brain, I sat back at my desk. Looking at the time on the screen, I noted it was 8:19 am. I never used to be an early riser, even when I started working for Ianx, it felt like more effort than it was worth to get out of bed in the mornings. Now I was waking up early, admittedly not through choice, but I wasn't feeling inclined to lounge in bed and go back to sleep. I looked at the time again, 8:21 am. Something was ticking in the back of my brain. Deciding to let it come to me in its own time, I focused on the clip on the screen, I must have managed to click on the little corner box before my episode because it was gleaming brightly at me with all the letters and numbers jumbled about. The gravestone! Excited, I pulled up the shot from the gravestone to see what was written on it and jotted it down on a scrap piece of paper. Reopening the window with the codes, I looked at the last entry:

0815-DPMN/LWR-SRTNN-S5MAX

It matched. I didn't know what it meant, but I was willing to wager that there was some significance to it. If my subconscious focused on it enough to make me hallucinate it, then surely it had some weight. Then I had a rush of excitement as an idea struck me. The four numbers at the beginning of each row, although the first two were seemingly completely variable, they were all ending with either 00, 15, 30 or 45. There was a pattern. Right-clicking on the last video, I checked for the entry time and felt a jolt of glee when I saw it said 08:15. So, the numbers were the time, maybe to when each episode occurred. The first two numbers of the four were not completely variable, it was the hour. Jotting them all down excitedly as I went, each video, sure enough, matched each row. All accounted for. So, this wasn't database macro type stuff, it was a log of every time my brain skirted away from my mental grip and had a little fun at my expense.

Opening the internet browser, I typed in each of the combinations of letters to no avail. Nothing. Zilch. Feeling stumped, I sat staring at them for a while hoping something would jump out at me. Pulling up a blank, I gave up. Feeling like I had been staring at the screen so long doing nothing, I could have been in the office, I decided on a coffee break. As I absentmindedly stirred my coffee, I pondered once again what the rest of the codes could mean. On one hand, I could sit and try and work it out whilst not being 100% certain that I was right, on the other, I could call the expert and ask. After all, it was to do with my brain, there couldn't be any reason he wouldn't explain it to me. Pulling my phone from my pocket and dialling his number, I slowly wandered back into the front room without much hope that Dr Muggor would even pick up, his track record didn't say much for him. To my surprise, he answered after just two rings.

"Dr Muggor here, how can I help you, Arnie?"

"Ah, hello. I just had a quick question really, about the implant? Just wanted to have something explained to me that I don't understand." Why was I feeling so hesitant? I felt like a schoolboy asking out his first crush.

"Of course, anything. Would you like to pop in? Or I can come by your place if you don't feel up to it?" He sounded fine. I was clearly letting my fragile state of mind get the better of me. I decided to get out of the flat and get some fresh air.

"I can be with you in 30 minutes or so if you are available?" I said. He confirmed he was and terminated the call. Idly chewing my thumbnail, I allowed myself to feel that hope grow again. As long as I had a purpose, I had a direction. As long as I have a direction, I have a destination/goal. And that destination/goal for me felt like two options right now, a mental home or regaining my full sanity, I knew which one I preferred, although I wouldn't knock the idea of someone cooking me meals all the time and cleaning my room.

****

I got to the medical office quicker than anticipated and had to wait a few minutes outside for someone to open the door for me. Steph opened it and ushered me in, not before scanning the surroundings quickly though, then shut the door behind me. The more I saw of her, the more she struck me as an odd character, but then we all have our quirks. Considering the amount of quirks I currently had, who was I to judge? I followed on her heel through the hallway and into the reception area.

Not paying any mind, I tailed her straight to the office door and stood behind her as she knocked. I heard a scuffling and what sounded like papers being moved around as Steph opened the door to speak to Dr Muggor. I saw him shoot a scathing look in Steph's direction and hurriedly stuffing some papers in a drawer and slamming it shut. He turned his full body to face us and smiled in greeting, just a slight hint of the annoyance he just expressed to Steph was left in his expression. I noticed he had slammed the drawer in hard enough that it had come open halfway again having rebounded off the back. He gestured for me to come and sit in the central chair like before, the dentist chair. I obliged feeling like I was a bit of an inconvenience to him at this moment. He started straight away to examine my head and was mumbling to himself about sealing and scar tissue when he directed his next words at me.

"You caught me at a busy moment. Mr Shack, apologies. First and foremost, can you tell me how the site of the injury is feeling? Any numbness, pain, tightness? I can see there is no sign of infection, so that is good." He was prodding and poking my head, for medical reasons I know, but it was irritating me and still sore. I tried to keep my irritation out of my voice as I replied.

"In all honesty what with everything that has been happening, aside from some dull headaches, I haven't noticed it too much." He was bopping his head up and down as though nodding in agreement with me.

"Good, good. So, what were these queries you had? Are you having trouble with the chip or accessing them on the computer?"

"No, not at all. I was wondering what DPMN/LWR meant?" Strange, I'm sure that as I said it, some colour drained from his face. His eyes skittered slightly and he regained himself quickly enough that if I wasn't on edge and watching everything intently, I would have missed it. Or did I imagine it?

"Where did you come across it, if you don't mind me asking?" There was an edge to his tone but his expression now belied little emotion.

"The box on the videos that highlights sometimes, I clicked onto it and there was just a list, I assumed it was just a log of each entry. I am just curious what the letters meant." I could feel the edge coming into my voice too, did I pry where I wasn't meant to? If so, I shouldn't have been able to access it. I watched Dr Muggor's facial muscles twitch, whether it was a smile or frustration, I couldn't work it out.

"You are right, it is an entry log of each event. Well spotted. I'm happy to see that your skills of deduction still intact after all that you have incurred." Now I was sure, it wasn't my paranoia or sensitivity, there was a bit of sting to that.

"But it is not anything for you to worry about, it merely tracks the frequency for you, and us. The other letters associated with them, do you remember them all?" I shook my head, deciding to omit the fact that I had them all written down on my desk at home. "Well, not that it matters, of course." Of course. "They are just codes for each video without any real significance, much like when you make a recording on your phone and it automatically gives it a name with varying digits." He was nodding along whilst he spoke, really getting into his explanation, but I wasn't buying it. It felt like there was something he wasn't telling me.

I spoke up, "So, that explains that for me, thank you. On to the next thing that I wanted to speak with you about. You told me to keep you updated on the events and happenings if they got a bit too much. My nightmares and hallucinations are vivid, but there seems to be a recurring pattern in each one of them. I think there is a reason for it and wanted your input as to whether I should visit a specialist to analyse them?" I was testing the waters. If they were keeping a close eye on my progress, which I was certain they were, they will have likely noticed the repeated appearances of the boy and man in each scenario. I saw Dr Muggor's hand clench ever so slightly and relax again. I could hear fidgeting and saw Steph in my peripheral vision, looking uncomfortable and shifting around playing with her hands.

"That won't be necessary. We can provide all the assistance you need here; all you need to do is discuss it with us. Steph here can help give you an insight into these patterns if it will give you peace of mind, she has an extensive knowledge of most things pertaining to the subconscious mind. From what I can ascertain, your case is more severe than we initially thought. You are now suffering from post-traumatic stress disorder and this can lead to you questioning things that are, in fact, ordinary and a heightened sense of paranoia. Even bouts of uncontrollable anger and blackouts, even moments of visions of doing things completely out of character. Have you had any of these?"

Now I felt like I had lost my footing, was that what this all was? I had heard of post-traumatic stress disorder but didn't consider it to be something I was suffering from, but then I guess it wasn't something I would have considered. Dr Muggor sensed me questioning myself and pushed on, "I can see from your reaction that you have, in fact, experienced these symptoms. This is entirely expected and with time and patience, you can overcome them. You must remember you were the victim of an attack and sustained a substantial injury, it is a lot to process. I will arrange for Steph to attend your home at some point soon to talk it through more with you as it is more her area than mine." I nodded mutely.

A sudden commotion outside made us all turn. It seemed to be coming from outside the room. Shouting and clattering echoed through the building. Both

Steph and Dr Muggor reacted simultaneously with a quick exchanged look of surprise and forgot about me for the moment. They rushed out of the room, the door swinging to a close behind them. I don't know what possessed me at that moment but I couldn't resist, maybe it really was post-traumatic stress disorder, but I couldn't ignore my instinct. Jumping up from the chair, I ran to the desk in the corner with the drawer open. I didn't know how much time I had and my heart was beating a hard rhythm in my ears. I could still hear the noises outside and moved as quickly as I could. The papers that he had dashed away in here so quickly had made me suspicious, I didn't even for a second consider they may not even relate to me. Pulling the top sheet out, I saw a bunch of charts that meant nothing to me, the one underneath much the same. The third one was a sheet with boxes filled in with all my details.

The next one proved more interesting. Flicking my eyes back to the door, I scoured the page. It was titled 'Administration of Chemicals', didn't need any explanation for that. Handwritten with bullet points was a list much like the one on the computer. Without dates, I didn't know if these were past ones or ones to come, if that was possible. The title of the sheet alone unnerved me, what was this? I realised the commotion outside had stopped and with mounting fear realised I didn't know when it had stopped and no idea when they would come back in.

Putting it all back hastily, I ran for the chair, I had just reached it when a sweaty dishevelled looking Dr Muggor re-entered the room. I stood alert, trying to act normal like I hadn't just invaded his paperwork and tried to conceal the fact that I was now wary of him. He didn't seem to notice. Running a hand across his head in a gesture of tired frustration, he told me that the appointment was over and Steph would be in touch to arrange a meeting. Thankful for the dismissal, I scooted past him and out of the door. I didn't bother to say goodbye to Steph, who was sitting at the desk in the reception area with her head turned away from me. Wanting to be out of there and in the fresh air, I clicked the door behind me and sped away from the building, only stopping when it was out of sight and sat myself down on a random street bench. I didn't know what to make of it all yet, but I did know that I needed time to figure out my next steps.

One thing that concerned me was his reaction to my suggestion of seeing someone else about the dreams and visions; he didn't like that idea at all, in fact. Thinking about it, I began to feel like he actively tried to deter me from it. Not knowing what else to do, I called a cab to take me to a place where I felt some insight could be shed from an outside perspective.

****

Pulling up outside, I handed cash to the driver and stepped out, greeted by a warm breeze. I looked up at the house for a moment, taking it in. Was I making a mistake in returning here after what Dr Muggor said? I decided, quite rashly and unfairly maybe, that if it came down to it, I would tell them I didn't know what I was doing, having one of my episodes. For now, I didn't know who to trust and I was turning to the person who I thought would maybe be my best bet based on gut feeling alone. I know I had only met her once, but sometimes you just know when you meet someone what kind of person they are and Dr Smyll had a good aura.

I buzzed her door and waited for her to answer, there was some shuffling on the other side and clicking, which I assumed was her looking through the eyehole and the door pulled inwards. She looked surprised to see me, but not unpleasantly so. Without a word, she stood back for me to pass. I went straight into the room that we had been in before with the comfy sofas and sat, waiting for her to come in. She didn't come in for five minutes, but when she did, she bore a tray laden with coffees and biscuits.

"There is nothing that a warm drink and sweet treat can't take the edge off of, in my opinion." She said this with a smile and I became aware of my appearance once more. I must look a state, I didn't really care and luckily, it seemed she didn't either. She perched opposite me again and we were in the same positions as my last visit. She waited patiently and I tried to gather my thoughts, decide what to say and how to say it. In the end, I figured that without her knowing the full picture, there was nothing she could really do to help me or see why I was feeling the way I was. Plus, she was bound by patient confidentiality, right? Only allowed to be broken if I myself was a threat to myself or those around me.

That was it then, a decision made. I clasped the mug of steaming hot coffee between my hands and started to speak. This time leaving nothing out. All from the moment my day started nearly a week ago, down to my last encounter in the medical office. Not once did she interrupt me and on a couple of occasions, I looked up to see she was following me, she was listening intently, taking it all in. Her brows furrowed when I mentioned the implant and deeper so when I told her about the medical office. But she waited until I had finished, knowing that if I stopped now I would lose my roll. Once I was content I hadn't left anything out, I allowed myself to relax back into the chair and sip my now cooled coffee, I noted with silent approval that it was good coffee. I felt mentally drained and was grateful for the respite when Dr Smyll excused herself to go to the bathroom. Now regardless of what happened to me, two people knew what was happening to me that I trusted and I felt safer having more than one place to turn to. When Dr Smyll came back from the bathroom, I saw she was holding a laptop. She sat back in her seat and took a breath.

"What I want to address first and offer some praise for is your discovery of who the cloaked man is. And the courage it must have taken from you to try and face him. I thought this on your last visit and I am impressed you worked it out for yourself. This man you keep seeing is yourself, it is the darker side of you trying to break out. He is asking for your help because as a part of your subconscious, he is aware of some things that are happening and ideas you have before you consciously are. The pursuing and capturing of you and the boy is a different part to think about though, it is a far more concerning part of it. These two characters are two very conflicting parts of your personality trying to gain power in your mind and become the controlling force. You, as you are now, placid and yourself, are the only thing preventing this right now. Your mental strength is what stops the other personalities from having permanent control over your day to day living. Your medication will also help with this, but it requires you to fight with it too." She hadn't said anything I disagreed with, so I sat listening and she carried on.

"Something you have said has concerned me deeply. This implant that you referred to. Right now, I need to know if this is the truth, that you are certain this is what has happened?" I was taken aback by this, I knew it was an out-there concept when it was offered to me, that people would find it hard to understand but, I didn't appreciate being asked if it was real or if I was making it up. She held her hands up in apology having seen my reaction.

"Then I have much deeper concerns than the ones relating to your dreams and hallucinations. Something that I must tell you and I hope it is just coincidental that they share the same name, I attended medical school with a Dr Joseph Muggor. He was expelled for reasons that I don't need to relay to you. To my knowledge, he never completed his degrees and I haven't heard his name in many years. If it is the same man, I think I should have heard his name in one circle or another if he was working on such a complex device. Plus of course, the chances of it being a different person strikes me as slim, given his name isn't exactly common."

She paused and allowed what she said to sink in. If it wasn't a coincidence and this was the same man, was he allowed to practice medicine? He must be, he was in the hospital with me, that was where I had met him. I shook my head at her and told her this again and she nodded her understanding at me. Turning her attention back to her laptop, she opened up a vast spreadsheet. Typing away, she concentrated on what she was doing. As yet, I had no bad feelings about Dr Smyll, but I could see something akin to worry etching lines into the sides of her mouth as she worked. After a few seconds, she sighed and rubbed her thumb against her chin in thought.

"Dr Joseph Muggor is neither a registered nor qualified doctor, in this country at least. I am not happy about this situation, Arnie, I need to know absolutely everything. Down to the finest details. I am worried you have fallen victim to some sort of foul play and I want to help you. I just can't see what it is all about yet."

With that, I rehashed everything to do with Dr Muggor and Steph again and pushed her attention towards the codes. If we knew what they meant, we could potentially fathom part of what was happening. I felt a deep-seated fear curdling in my gut. If Dr Muggor wasn't a real doctor, where did that leave me? How did he get into the hospital room I was in? Why did he have a clinic? Who was Steph? What were they doing to me? What was this implant I had let them put in my head? Considering it did exactly what I was advised it would do, I couldn't see why he would go to such lengths to administer it. How did I get it out? If it had little connectors linked into my brain I couldn't just cut it out, surely it would do some serious damage? I felt used, alone and scared. I thought of Sarah and thought back to what she had said at one point when we were talking about it all, about not being sure about Dr Muggor and Steph, oh, how right she was. But maybe, on the other side of things, he could be doing this experiment to make waves in the medical world and had no ill intention, with the way I was feeling that seemed too far-fetched to be plausible.

My head was whirring with too many unanswered questions. I jolted when Dr Smyll reached across and touched my hand, bringing me back to the present.

I looked up at her, realising she was saying something, but there was a roaring in my ears. Shaking my head a little, it mostly cleared.

"I know you are going to have a lot of questions; I have many of my own. But until we know what this is all about and the risks involved with the implant in your brain, we cannot make any rash decisions. We need to decide step by step what we are going to do and how to go about it without causing an uproar in the medical community, or anywhere else for that matter. As you are a friend of Sarah's, I will take personal interest and care in solving this with you, but I need to know you are on board and won't confront Dr Muggor yet. If the medical community finds out about this, you will become the subject of many people's interests, both good and bad. I don't want to see this happen to you. For now, we must keep it under wraps, understood?"

I tilted my head back and forwards in a weak effort at nodding. "I need you to stay with me Arnie and I want you to get back in contact with Sarah, you will need someone by your side. I can speak to her and explain for you, but you can also do the same. She will understand that everything you said was not really you. The Quetiapine should be taking full effect in the next couple of days, providing you don't miss any of your doses. What we need to do next is work out the meaning of the letters you said you saw. Do you have them with you?" I shook my head and she chewed her bottom lip, obviously eager to get the ball rolling.

Finally, I spoke, "I don't have the paper with me, but you can access them from your laptop if you log into the viewing portal, I can show you where." Dr Smyll smiled reassuringly at me again and pulled her laptop back round. I showed her how to access it and log in. Within a few minutes, we were in. I didn't know how to access the codes any other way than watching the footage again, so she clicked into the last sizeable file with my permission. We both stared at the screen as it replayed the vision with the gravestone. Dr Smyll clasped her hand across her mouth as she watched, disbelief written all over her face, which had significantly paled. If she thought this one was bad, I didn't want to see her reaction to the nightmares or other conscious visions, this one was pretty tame despite the graphicness of the blood river, in my opinion.

I looked for the white box but it never came up. Luckily, I guess, the gravestone had the letters written across it and we paused it whilst she wrote it down in her pad, circling it multiple times and scribbling a question mark next to it. Wondering about the absence of the box, I remembered Dr Muggor's reaction to my being aware of it. Perhaps I wasn't meant to have been able to see it previously and they had now altered the programming somehow. Seemed entirely possible, if what I had just discovered was true. If it could lead me to information he didn't want me to have, of course, he was going to remove it. Again, I was thankful that I opted to go to his office rather than him come to my home, he would have seen the notes I had made and probably gotten rid of them somehow.

"For the meantime, Arnie, I need you to continue with your medication, this will take the edge off for you. You don't appear to have had any noticeable episodes in the time that you've been here and whether that is due to the Quetiapine taking effect or you are having a docile period I cannot say, but you should not have any negative reactions to remaining on the medication, apart from some fatigue. I need to think about all that we have discussed and I will be in contact with you soon, or you can call or visit me. I shall make sure that I am available to you to the best of my abilities, without cancelling any of my current patients. Will you be OK?"

"I'm sure I will be. It is just a whole lot to process for me right now. I will call Sarah on my way back and see if she will come and talk with me. Thank you for today, I don't mean to be a burden, but I didn't know who else to turn to." Dr Smyll waved her hands in dismissal at me and assured me I was no burden, she was glad I had come to her in spite of the weight of the situation. We said our goodbyes and I wandered down the pathway, pulling my phone out of my pocket as I went. I called Sarah and left a message; at this time of day, she was probably still at work. Placing the phone back in my jeans, I took the walk home slowly, mulling all that I had discovered over in my mind.

****

I was about halfway home and thinking about all that Dr Smyll had said in our meeting when a thought struck me, I didn't know what to make of it all, but I could check one thing. Pulling my phone back out and dodging a pedestrian at the same time – why do some people insist on beelining for you on the street sometimes, was it a power play to see if you would move out of their way before crashing into each other? – and I looked up the number of the hospital I had been in and called the main reception. A polite yet harried sounding woman picked up the line and confirmed I was speaking with the hospital.

"Hello, I was a patient there recently and was wondering if you could maybe put me in contact with my doctor, Dr Muggor? He did give me his number but due to my head injury, I seem to have forgotten where I put the card down."

"Hmm, give me one moment and I'll find his pager number for you, sir." I could hear her rummaging around on the other end of the line, then there was a muffled sound where someone had covered the mouthpiece. "I'm sorry, sir, did you say Dr Muggor?"

"Yes, he treated me there a few days ago."

A tut, then muffled sounds again, then she came back, "Are you sure it was here you came? We don't have any doctors here with that name." Rather than insist I was, I hung up the phone. That was all I needed to know. Thinking back, as patchy as my memory was, I couldn't think of any point that Dr Muggor was in the hospital room with me at the same time as anyone else. This information solidified what Dr Smyll had said to me and left me with a stronger feeling of being lost and in the dark.

****

Back at home, I realised, with a hint of sadness, that I didn't feel as at ease here as I had at Dr Smyll's. I imagined it was something to do with the fact that I had had so many visions and nightmares here, now it just wasn't a positive environment to me right now. I knew what could aid in changing that, I just needed to get Sarah to come over here. If she could forgive me for what I had said and the way I behaved that is. The worry I had niggling at me was what would happen if my mood struck like that again. I would be lucky if she forgave me this one time let alone more.

I had made it around two metres into my apartment when my legs gave out underneath me. I was helpless to stop myself as my arms didn't respond, I could only watch in horror as the corner of the wall rose up to meet me in slow motion as my adrenaline levels increased rapidly, I managed to turn my head in the nick of time to avoid it being a full facial impact. I felt the thud as my collarbone took most of the hit and my head bounced off the floor. My arms started to function again and I rubbed my collar and head as I lay there slightly disorientated, I felt the haziness start to come over me, the veil of confusion and distress. I batted my head trying to stop it but I couldn't, it was drawing in too strongly. My blinks became heavy like mini weights had been attached to my eyelids. Everything in the room became wavy and echoed talking that sounded like it was a mile away reverberated in my head.

I tried to get into kneeling position but it was like I was heavily intoxicated. I could feel the coherent side of my brain fighting with the side that was malfunctioning. Clear thoughts interspersed with bizarre nonsensical ones only heightened my feeling of fear. With an effort, I hauled myself upright and leaned against the wall, steadying myself with one hand whilst the other rubbed my collarbone. My hand felt detached from me, I could feel myself touching my collar but it was a foreign sensation. I looked to make sure it was my hand because it felt so strange, it was, but it only served to feed my confusion. In a trance-like state, I moved further into the living room, not sure if it was a conscious move on my part when the couch folded in on itself and a gurgling sound came from within the folded of fabric.

Moving forward again, I looked at the contorted piece of furniture and was horrified to see a distorted face being pulled into the centre. Multiple hands were clasping at the edges like there were people trapped in the folds trying to escape and they were making crying noises but not like an adult, it was a baby's shrill cry. Not sure what else to do, I reached forward and grabbed one of the hands and tried to pull it free, not wanting to look at the face of the person in the middle being suffocated but unable to help myself. They didn't seem to be male, nor female, just a generic face with no distinguishing features.

Yanking harder on the hand, I was suddenly pulled forward, off-balance. My arms plunged into the sofa and my face was inches away from the crying persons. In a blink, it transformed into an ugly nightmarish mess, the skin bubbled and turned black, the eyes sank into the skull and I tried with all my might to get backward, but I was held fast in the grip now. As I watched, my breath caught painfully in my throat, the face became that of the cloaked man. His mouth was open beyond any human capacity and the crying noise changed to a guttural shouting that I felt through to my bones. I had no courage at this moment, I was completely at his mercy. In his eyes, I could see a fire raging over a roaring sea surrounded by inky blackness. I renewed my effort to get away when I felt him pull me even closer. With a big heave, I launched backwards. For a moment, it felt like I was flying, my return to solid ground delayed. With a crash, I landed slumped against the TV stand and everything faded into darkness.

****

A gentle tapping on my cheek brought me back to consciousness I looked to see who it was and relief bombarded me when I saw Sarah kneeling in front of me, one hand on my chest and the other on her knee. She had looked better, bags under her eyes and gaunt cheeks, I had no doubt that I played some if not all the part in causing this. Guilt edged its way in and I grabbed her wrists and pulled her to me, seeking to share comfort. She didn't resist and sank against my chest drawing in a deep breath. The pain exploded in my collar and I pushed her away from me, crying out. She rolled back in front of me and looked at me quizzically. It must have been fairly obvious that something had happened considering I was laying on the floor pushed up against the TV stand. Looking past her, I could see the sofa cushions were scattered across the room, did I do that? She reached forward and pulled my top down a little, wincing at what she saw. I looked down too but couldn't quite see.

"What happened? Did you have another seizure?"

"I don't really know, I fell over there by the door and then the sofa was trying to take me, the man was pulling me in and I fell backwards to here. Then you came. You came back, Sarah, I didn't know you would after what I said and how I treated you. I'm so sorry." Her eyes glistened and she stroked my head, shaking her own like my words weren't necessary.

"I know you didn't mean it, I shouldn't have been so angry and not come back. I have been trying to call you but you didn't answer, so I figured you needed space. But I came as soon as I heard your message."

Again, with the calling thing, this had happened before. I had no missed calls from her, what was wrong with my phone? In fact, thinking back on it again, I still hadn't received any calls. I knew my circle was small, but not that small. Unless it had been ringing and I somehow was blanking it out, but my episodes were varying, no one thing seemed to trigger them and it would be too much of a coincidence if it happened every time my phone went off. I pulled my phone from my pocket and checked, no missed calls or messages. I looked at her log, nine outgoing calls to me within the last day. I really should get that seen to, but it was the last of my concerns at the moment.

I gave her a quick kiss on the forehead as I got up, I wanted to see my collarbone in the mirror. Padding through on aching legs to the bathroom, I still felt a bit wobbly. Looking in the mirror, I examined the area, thin red lines streaked out from the impact site and a neat thick purple line highlighted the bone. No split and seemingly no breakage, I checked by rolling my shoulders around. Aside from the expected pain, there was no jutting out bits to worry about. Sarah came in behind me and handed me a tea towel, I gave her a questioning look and she told me it had ice in it to help the swelling. Taking it gratefully, we went back through to the bedroom.

"If you want, I can call the phone company. I think that now of all times, it would be ideal for you to have a working phone."

"Yeah, if you want. But I need to talk to you, there have been some crazy things going on since I last saw you." She crossed her hands over her legs, which I noticed at this moment were bare, she was wearing a pair of floral shorts and a vest top. It must be warm outside, but seeing her like this combined with missing her made my internal temperature peak. She was looking at me expectantly and I pushed my wayward thought to the back of my mind and told her about my meeting with Dr Smyll and the events in the medical office with Dr Muggor. Once I finished recounting everything to her, she rose up and started pacing the room.

"Then what does all this mean? He isn't a doctor, but he has an office? An assistant? He has access to medical supplies and he was in the hospital with you, so maybe the database that Dr Smyll checked was wrong? If it isn't, what does this mean for you, can the implant actually hurt you? You said you called the hospital too? You said the woman you spoke to didn't sound certain so maybe she just missed something or misheard you? What, just what is any of this?" The last part her voice hitched up an octave and I had to pull her back down to sit next to me. The last thing we both needed was her becoming hysterical when I was barely holding on, we wouldn't achieve anything.

I spoke to her in a calm measured voice, "What I am going to do is not let Dr Muggor know anything that I know now. Since I asked him about the codes, he has removed access to them or at least I cannot find them. The papers that I saw in his office seemed to be some kind of schedule if I was reading it right. Maybe if I can see the rest of them or something, I can work it out more. But I don't know how. For now, I play it normal, as normal as can be anyway," I gave a self-deprecating smile and gesture of my hands to show I was aware nothing could possibly be classed as normal right now, "and wait for Steph to call me and make a meeting with me. Dr Muggor said rather than seek someone else, he would like to offer her as someone to analyse my visions and dreams, so that is what is going to happen for now. Apparently she knows what she is doing so another

69

perspective doesn't hurt. Dr Smyll has one of the codes and she is trying to work it out at the moment for me."

Speaking of the codes, I remembered I said I would text them through to her, so she had the rest. I thought it would be best to send it with Sarah's phone as mine wasn't working at the moment, so I took it from her and went through to the desk, I snapped a picture of the notepaper and pinged it across. One less thing to do for now. Sarah had joined me again and I got the impression she didn't want to be too far from my side considering the state I was in when she found me. Taking my hand, she pulled me over to the sofa and indicated I should lay down. She perched next to me and started running her hands all over me, stroking away the pains and aches, filling me with a feeling of warmness. I simply sank in deeper and allowed her to trail soft lines all over me, letting everything fade to the back of mind.

****

I woke slowly and dozily. It was dark in the room and a small green flashing light somewhere across the room caught my eye. I could hear Sarah's deep breathing and moved gently so as to not wake her. Prying her away from my chest and suppressing a wince at the pain in my collar, I slid off the sofa and trudged across to my phone. The time flashing on the screen told me it was 5:32 am, early enough to make me cringe inwardly. I must have slept a solid nine or ten hours though, with was good. Gingerly touching my fingers to my collarbone, I checked how it was feeling. Not too bad but not particularly good either. Opening my phone, I saw a message that I had received whilst I was sleeping:

'Arnie, I think I have worked it out.
When you can, call me and we will meet.
Important.
D.S.'

D.S.? It took second for me to realise it was short for Dr Smyll. I felt a surge of excitement and anticipation at this news, like when you finally finish the nigh on impossible to complete the daily newspaper crossword puzzle. All my sleepiness was instantly forgotten, I could barely wait to see what she had found out and rushed across to Sarah.

"Sarah? Wake up!" Sarah stirred groggily, not pleased to have been rudely pulled from her peaceful slumber. She grumbled at me and sat up rubbing her sleep-filled eyes. Despite the early hour, I was pumped, energised, having a positive turn. I told her I was making coffee and all but skipped into the kitchen. A few minutes later, I re-emerged and as I stepped over to Sarah, I felt my mood plummet like someone had just poured lukewarm water over me. Momentarily caught off guard, I paused in my tracks and felt wave after wave bashing into me and was left feeling devoid of anything happy. Gloom swamped me and I sank into the sofa, perplexed as to the sudden mood shift.

"Are you OK?" Sarah looked just as confused as I felt. "What happened?" I shrugged my shoulders, energy zapped and feeling like even speaking was too much.

"You're losing." It was growled at me, low and menacing. Startled I looked at Sarah.

"What? Losing what?" I saw her eyes shutter, thinking.

"What?" I realised that it wasn't her who said it, it was in my head again. Gritting my teeth, I massaged my forehead in frustration. As I lifted my head back up after a few minutes, I felt something move and the tension in my shoulders and neck released. Everything shone a bit brighter and as quickly as that, the dark mood that had enveloped me released its grip. Moving past it and refusing to dwell on it as I didn't know how much time I had, I told Sarah about the text from Dr Smyll and saw her share in my excitement.

"So, what happens when we find out what the codes mean?" she asked.

"I don't really know, I guess the answer to that depends on what they are. But it could help us, it is something to aim for." We agreed it was too early to try and get hold of Dr Smyll and decided to wander down to the cafe again for breakfast and fresh air. I sent a quick text from my phone to Dr Smyll anyway, it shouldn't wake her like a phone call would. I mentioned where we were going and if she wanted to join us, she was welcome, if not I would call her when we got back. Clicking off we left and faced the brisk morning air, the cool breeze whipping around our faces removing any remaining remnants of sleepiness. We walked hand in hand, talking about idle things such as the weather and how her work as a sous chef was going, the local road works down by the secondary school.

****

Before I knew it, we were outside the cafe and there was no-one in there except the waitress and chef, this was how I preferred pretty much any place I went to. We took our usual booth and waited for our orders to be taken, she didn't even bother coming over and just called out that she would make the usual and we nodded in appreciation. Maybe we came here too much, but to be served without having to socialise was sometimes all I wanted. The food was brought to us quickly and two steaming mugs of coffee placed in front of us. I smiled gratefully at the waitress and she took her leave, going to perch on a stool behind the counter, the illumination on her face giving away the fact she was playing on her phone. A small giggle came from Sarah and she quickly put her hand across her mouth looking apologetic. I looked at her waiting for an explanation and could feel a little smile twitching at my lips as I looked upon her clearly amused face. I felt deep happiness emanate from my core when I looked her like this, her smile tugging at the corner of her mouth making her eyes crease and twinkle.

"I'm sorry to laugh. I shouldn't really, it isn't right." Guilt came across her face at that moment and I wondered what she was talking about and asked her as much.

"Well, I was just thinking about how awful everything has been the last week or so," so far I failed to see where this could go that could be even remotely funny, "and how very surreal it has all felt. I can't even begin to imagine how it must be for you as you are the one going through it personally."

"Right…" I paused and waited for her to continue, feeling a bit annoyed and hurt now considering she had started the conversation with a giggle.

"Do you not find it almost funny, how it is like we are in a movie? Like a thriller or something? Any moment now, I am half expecting someone to leap up from somewhere or out from behind a wall and shout 'Cut!' And someone will come out and start to do our makeup and costumes? It's so surreal, don't you think?"

I couldn't help it, I had to smile, even a little laugh came out of me. Maybe it was a release of our stresses, but it felt good. We both sat and laughed together from the pits of our stomachs about the bizarreness of it all and the prospect of it all being a big hoax. It really was absurd and the stuff of movies, the crazy doctor, the sweet psychiatrist, the troubled lead and his dedicated girlfriend all mixed in with the horror story monsters. We sat for some time, just thinking about everything, taking occasional mouthfuls of our food, letting the time pass us by. In this booth right now, it felt like it was just me and Sarah in the world and honestly, that suited me just fine.

As if to taunt to remind me that this wasn't the case, a beeping noise started up from inside Sarah's pocket. Pulling her phone out she frowned and stepped away from the table as she answered. I patiently waited for her to come back and checked my phone to see if there was any response from Dr Smyll. Opening up my messages and clicking on her name, I saw that there were no received messages. This would have been OK if it weren't for the fact there was literally no messages from her at all in my inbox, including the one I had read this morning. Did I imagine it? My reply was there, but it looked like I had just sent a random message to her. Scratching my head, I didn't notice Sarah come back to the table. She looked a bit disgruntled and didn't wait for me to ask.

"It's my work, they've revoked my holiday for today and told me I have to go in for a couple of hours, the other chef has called in sick. Will you be OK?" A bit bummed, to say the least, but I nodded and she stood up, taking a moment to kiss me softly, then swept out of the door in a hurry. Stirring the remainder of my food around my plate feeling bereft, I wondered about the missing texts. Was it my phone playing up or something else, had I been deleting things from my phone when in a memory glitch? Was that even possible? At this point I didn't question it, none of it was a surprise to me.

Throwing a £20 down, I stood up ready to leave the table. By now, I was starting to learn the signs of something being amiss and quickly grabbed onto the side of the table as a huge head rush threatened to unbalance me. It passed after a few seconds and I knew I wanted to be at home if anything happened. Something in my brain snapped and my feet didn't respond to the signal to move. Darkness fringed my vision and I fell unconscious before I had even hit the ground.

****

I seem to be in some sort of marina. Once again, I was acutely aware that this wasn't real but somehow not fully registering that fact. I wondered as to why a large portion of my dreams involved the sea, perhaps an underlying fear I didn't know I had. I was standing next to an old school friend, one I hadn't seen in years. He wasn't talking to me, just looking over the balcony to a large ship on the right. Its hull was painted a vivid red and had a black band atop it. The handrails glistened in the sun and I could see people roaming around, holidaymakers I assumed. The boat had a huge built-up section in the middle and I could see the staircases and huge richly decorated rooms through the floor to ceiling windows. People were jovially dancing and swinging around to music I couldn't hear but easily imagined. I was drawn to it, watching with fascination, it looked like it was from another era.

My attention shifted to the left for no real reason other than knowing I had to turn and look and I felt bubbles of shock and panic loom up in my stomach. In slow motion, I watched as a second ship, absolutely mammoth in size, so big that it dwarfed the red-hulled one, came sweeping in sideways, riding on the crest of huge wave. I was motionless and couldn't react as the underside of the boat became exposed, listing beyond its capacity to roll and the razor-sharp jutted section tore into the first boat with a horrific noise that I couldn't even describe, I felt it more than heard it despite its loudness. Glass flew everywhere and with the shattering of the windows, I could now hear the screams and terror of the people inside. Splashes of red-coated the two boats and crushed figures sprawled everywhere, some of them were not even whole anymore, they lay scattered across the destroyed deck. The ship that caused the impact had fallen away and was starting to sink in the now frothing blood-stained waters. I felt my legs move of their own accord and turned to enter a building behind me, blindly pushing people out of my way and shouting that they all needed to be helped. A tan man suddenly grabbed my arm as I ran past and pulled me into a little room. He looked at me with a glint in his eye and handed me a cap. I held it lamely, not sure what was going on.

"Do you want it laminated? To commemorate the occasion?" He asked me in a bizarrely calm voice as though the world wasn't ending just outside, and what on earth did he mean about laminating a hat that didn't even make sense. I shook my head violently and handed the hat back to him. He pushed it back at me and told me it was a gift. I tried to refuse again and he lifted it above my head and brought it down onto me quicker than I could react. Pain shot through my skull and I ducked. I blinked and the man was suddenly gone, as was the room we had been in.

Spinning on the spot, I realised I was now on the boat that had been smashed into. Something wet was dripping down my face and I reached up and felt it with my fingertips, pulling the cap off that had been forced on to me. As I took it off, I felt sharp stinging all across my scalp and then more wetness, it was hot and felt like it was pouring from me now. Looking at the cap, there were hundreds of shards of glass embedded into it. Numbly, I reached to touch my scalp and found countless bits of glass there too. I needed to get out of here. Looking for an exit amongst the masses of bodies, broken furniture and jutted decking, I heard the sound of the melody. Very old style. As I listened it scratched and jumped then stopped altogether. Then louder than the music had been, a laughing sound filled the air, not a pleasant laugh, it was malicious.

Completely on edge and lost, I realised I was holding something. It was the boy. He had his head buried into my chest and legs wrapped around my waist. The now-familiar paternal like instinct kicked in and I ran to the bow, looking for a way off when one of the mangled bodies on the floor started to twitch. I heard myself murmuring no, no, no and the broken body brought itself upright. Its hand came up and wiped the blood from its face and I recognised him although I knew who it was in my stomach before the reveal. Turning and running the other direction, I leapt over more bodies that had all been crushed and broken beyond recognition by the other boat and falling debris. A creaking roaring sound was coming from the boat itself and I knew it was a matter of time before we went down with it.

Something caught my ankle and I tore it free. Sparing a glance back, the cloaked man was laying with an outstretched hand. Not looking where I was going, I crashed full bore into something solid. Falling back and groaning, I instinctively shrank away. He was now in front of me, larger than ever and more menacing. He lunged forward, bloodied hands outstretched aiming for somewhere around my throat and I threw my arms up protectively, the young boy had disappeared and I didn't know where he was. I felt the heavy thud of his full body weight bear down on me and my vision started to turn red. I felt his fingers prising my arms away from my head and neck and one of his hands slithered around my windpipe. He pressed down hard and the redness increased. I felt his nails puncture my skin and gasped for breath, hopelessly now grasping at his bony forearms, trying to lessen the pressure. The red mist got worse and the next thing I knew was that I could see nothing.

****

The haze cleared and I restarted my efforts to prise the arms off of me and I was confused to see a bright light above me. My head throbbed and there was no pressure on my throat anymore. There were the sounds of people speaking in hushed tones and I let my arms drop down to my sides. I could feel a blanket of disorientation clouding my mind and it took a while for me to register. I was in the Breakfast Cafe, laying on my side on the linoleum floor. Someone was leaning over me, holding one hand on my shoulder and declaring that the fitting had stopped and the show was over. It was Dr Smyll, concern etched lines into the corner of her mouth and she shouted at someone behind me to fetch a glass of water and ice pack. Rubbing my head, I groaned. It all came crashing back to me; I had a seizure in the middle of the cafe. How long had I been out?

"Lucky timing really, I was just walking through the door as you landed. I don't think any of the people in here know basic first aid; they just jumped around like they had a bee in their underwear." I chuckled lightly, what an odd description. "Can you sit up?" I wasn't really sure, but I grunted yes anyway and she helped me back into the booth.

The waitress came over with the water and ice pack and Dr Smyll put the ice pack straight onto the back of my head and made me lean with it trapped between my head and the wall so as to not have to hold it. The relief was almost instant. She asked where Sarah was and I told her she had been called into work. A slight pout of the lips was the only response to this, but imagine she knew full well how much time Sarah had devoted to me recently, I couldn't expect her to be around 24/7.

"I need to know you are fully aware and listening to what I am saying. Are you ready or do you want to go home and rest first, get your bearings and we meet later?" I thought about it for a second and tried to probe inside my mind to see how alert I was. Slightly sensitive, but I didn't feel like I was about to lose it anytime soon, not that I ever did. I told her I was ready and she leaned forwards, elbows propped on the table and started to tell me about Dr Muggor.

"So, as I told you the last time I saw you, Muggor left his medical studies early." It didn't escape my notice that she chose not to refer to him as Dr Muggor. "I don't know if this information will be of any use but it won't hurt you to know what happened in case it helps us down the line somehow. Please remember the majority of my knowledge on the matter is hearsay, so it may not necessarily be as bad as it sounds, you know how people can blow things out of proportion." Yep, I truly did.

"But as I know it, it is more or less along the lines of what happened back then. He was made to leave quietly and without warning. None of us knew what he had been doing in his dormitory room. Those of us who shared a classroom with him knew he was something else, the level of his intelligence was beyond what many of us had ever encountered, that stands true for the professors too. He was quicker to learn than us all and was always shooting out new found ideas, most of which sounded completely foreign to us normal students who just wanted to help people the traditional ways. The ways we knew for a fact worked. His interest lay mostly in psychology and the alteration of the chemicals in the brain in people who suffered from any form of mental illness. He always had his nose buried in a book, he wasn't well-liked, you see, his character was too much for the general populace. So, he kept himself to himself."

She paused a moment, catching her breath and thinking before continuing, I was enraptured. Dr Muggor didn't strike me as the type who didn't fit in, but as we all know too well, we change a lot when we come to adulthood and the school years and the people we were can often fade away as we develop for better or worse.

"To get to the point, he had started hanging around with a newcomer, who only too eagerly latched onto this person who could teach them so much. I imagine she thought it would aid the progression of her studies at a faster rate. Who knows? Anyway, we all noticed that this new girl, I forget her name," she mulled for a second and her eyes lit up in remembrance, "Jane was her name. Jane became more and more subdued and didn't speak to anyone much. Soon she started having seizures and acting out, shouting randomly at things we couldn't hear or see. Someone brought it up to the board and they tried to intervene, but when she went and saw someone all her symptoms ceased. So, they stopped sending her to the psychiatrist and allowed her to continue with her studies. No more than a month or so passed and the symptoms came back, but worse. She started coming to classes with numerous injuries and looking crazed.

"In all this time she was by the side of Muggor, who claimed she was fine, just a bit under the weather and he was taking care of her. For whatever reason, they accepted this for a time and didn't take any action. In the end, they had to send her away though, her behaviours became intolerable and she was clearly a threat to herself and others. Last I heard, she was sent to an institution in the country somewhere. Muggor contested this and tried to get the movement reversed, we all assumed he was just in love with her and wanted to be reunited. Supposedly he succeeded again, but we only saw her the once after that and then she disappeared. When asked, he simply said she had moved away but we didn't believe him. We were all making up our minds about him and his ways by this point, knowing something wasn't right.

"What we later found out, was that after he had raised suspicions amongst the professors, unsurprisingly really, they checked his dorm room. They found a large stash of prescription drugs, all meant to treat various mental problems and ailments. With the stash, they also found a notebook. In the notebook, he had allegedly described how he administered these drugs into Jane to see what would happen. He had crushed them up and put them in drinks and food, given her sleeping tablets too and supposedly ground and mixed them with water and injected them somehow into her bloodstream. They said they thought he was trying to find a way to mentally incapacitate someone to the point that they would do his bidding but function normally in society still. It goes without saying that he was immediately cautioned and banned from the premises and all other medical schools, but couldn't do much else as Jane allegedly gave full consent for these 'experiments'. I don't know how much of this is accurate, but if even a fraction of it is true, then I am concerned about everything that has been happening to you. It makes me wonder if your head injury truly is to blame for the problems you have been having."

My head was racing, it was all a bit crazy and yet somehow didn't ring untrue to me. I didn't know how much of the story was accurate, but it made me want to pick up the butter knife from the table and slice the implant out. The area was itching and I could feel my hands twitching. Was it truly possible to chemically make someone lose their minds? If it was and he was somehow doing this to me, how could I stop it? Where does it end? What happened to Jane once he stopped drugging her up if it was really true? My head was pounding and I realised I'd allowed the ice pack to fall on the chair beside me. Dr Smyll was observing me, I felt like I was on show. What kind of reaction could she possibly imagine I would have to this information, to everything at that? It was all just so damned ridiculous. I didn't know what to say, what could I have said? I leaned forward and rested my head on the table and blocked out the world around me.

A banging noise pulled me from my face down position and I looked to the door where the sound came from. In front of the first booth next to the door, the waitress had dropped her tray with all the half-empty plates and cups. I could hear a muffled apology coming from a man crouched down starting to pick the broken shards up, face obscured by the waitress's legs. She ushered him upright bleating about company rules and not being allowed to touch broken crockery with bare hands and he ceded. A lurch in my stomach acknowledged him before anything else. Dr Muggor. My eyes flitted to Dr Smyll sitting in front of me and she was frozen in place staring at a section of wall next to my head somewhere, not turning around to face him yet. He walked over to our table with a confident stride and stopped in front of me with a smile.

"Arnie, fancy seeing you here! I was just visiting an old friend across the road and saw you in the window. I hope I'm not interrupting?" As he said this he looked to my companion, who now slowly turned her head to face him. Dr Muggor offered another smile and extended his hand in greeting, "Nice to meet you, I'm Dr Muggor. I'm a–" pause, "acquaintance of Mr Shack's."

He didn't seem to recognise Dr Smyll and I saw the noted relief in her face quickly covered by a returning smile and reply, "Geraldine, pleasure to meet you, Dr Muggor." She gave nothing away. He nodded back at her and turned his attention back to me.

"I was wondering if we could have a quick discussion. One-on-one?" A pointed look to Dr Smyll in case I didn't understand what he was asking. Dr Smyll caught it and stood up, looking down and brushing her hands down her dress. She started to make her excuse to leave and tucked her hair behind her ears and I felt, rather than saw it, Dr Muggor's persona stiffened and a look of surprise shot across his face. Recovering quickly, he spoke to Dr Smyll again, this time his tone was more intense, "Have I met you before? You look familiar." It didn't really sound like a question and it seemed I wasn't the only one to hear it like that as a hint of fear and apprehension shone in Dr Smyll's eyes.

"No, I don't think so. I get that a lot. I just have one of those faces I suppose!" A tittering laugh a little too high pitched came from her mouth and she nodded goodbye to me and left without looking back. Dr Muggor watched her retreating and a small frown creased his brow.

"Let me escort you home, Arnie. We need to talk in private."

After everything, I had heard from Dr Smyll and the strange encounter between them, I was unnerved and didn't really want to go with him. I was pretty sure that even after all these years he seemed to recognise her. What if he tried to attack me? I was in no fit state to fight off a gerbil let alone a fully grown man with intent. But what other choice did I have? As far as I knew, he thought all I knew was that he was my treating doctor and there was no reason to act strangely around him. Rising up from my seat, teetering ever so slightly and being grateful when he gave me a steadying hand and reassuring nod, I walked back home with him.

****

We entered my apartment without any fuss, my head had been obedient since the seizure, so I was starting to regather myself properly now and process everything. My guard was well and truly up and I didn't know what to make of the news about Dr Muggor yet, but I knew for sure that I didn't trust him for one minute. I just didn't know what to do about it. The most conflicting part for me in this instant, was that a small part of my mind was telling me that we could still be wrong, and everything was just coincidence, that we were jumping the gun. He followed me to the sofa and sat next to me.

"First, I want to check your healing if you can just tilt your head for me." I did and he started probing around checking the tissue surrounding the scar, I only now realised that I didn't have the dressing on anymore and idly wondered when that had come off and where, was it another moment of memory loss or did Sarah take it off for me after we put the chip in? My hair was growing back fairly well too and I could feel him moving it to the side to look closer. A sudden stabbing pain shot up behind my ear and I automatically pulled my head away in response. He pulled my head back with both of his hands with a look of concentration on his face.

"Don't move, I am checking the stitches, one of them seems to be tucked underneath your implant and I was seeing if it was loose." I scowled at him, who just tugs on stitches to see if they're loose and I'm sure after what, a week? They should be more or less ready to come out. "Don't worry, it will either dissolve when it is ready or your body will naturally reject it and push it out as it is a foreign object." I blinked at him, did this mean the implant would be pushed out as it was a foreign object? I asked him out of curiosity, it would make it so much easier if it did.

"No, the implant is specially designed so that your body accepts it as a part of itself." I wondered how in the world they could ever make that work, but clearly, they had.

He carried on, "Tell me how you are, I know Steph hasn't made arrangements to see you yet, but she has been otherwise occupied. How are the nightmares and hallucinations?"

"Have you not been following my progress on your computer?" I retorted with, admittedly, a little bit of childlike huffiness.

"Yes, but I am asking you not what you have been seeing and experiencing, but how you are coping with them. They are very vivid and dark and I need to know that you are managing outside of them and remembering they are not real."

"I am having some ups and downs, I find it difficult to function when I am not sure when something will happen again. It does bother me and I would like to maybe try and get to the bottom of them like I mentioned before."

"I see, I see. Well, just as soon as she can, I'll make sure Steph prioritises you. In the meantime, perhaps write down what you think are key points and you can bring them up to her when she is here with you. It won't hurt to be prepared in advance and get straight to it." Again, with Steph. He had none of the jovial charms that he had before. Now he seemed much more serious, even his voice had deepened.

"Alright, that sounds fair." I didn't know what else to say. I didn't want to ask him about the alteration of the viewing platform and not being able to access the codes anymore. I didn't want to ask if he was a real doctor. I didn't want to push the idea of me seeing a third-party psychiatrist. I really didn't want to ask him what the true significance and intent of this implant was.

He stood and looked around the room and his eyes focused on my computer desk. The screen was still lit as I hadn't turned it off after I used it last, and he wandered over to it, seeing that the viewing portal was active. My stomach lurched, I realised that the note I had made with all the codes was on that desk next to the keyboard. He was bound to notice it any minute. Why did I not put it somewhere safe when I realised he didn't seem to want me seeing them? I kicked myself mentally for not thinking that through even if at the end of it all it was just coincidences and paranoia.

"I see you have left the reading chip in, like I suggested. Out of curiosity can you tell me why you've chosen to do this when you seemed so…hesitant before?" I stood and followed him across the room, frowning a little at the pause and obvious thought he had put in to phrasing the question.

"Just because my partner has been helping me, so she can try to understand what I have been experiencing. Is this a problem?"

"No, not at all. You have a continuous live feed showing each incident. Leaving the reading chip in won't have any negative repercussions, like I said before. As long as your partner knows and remembers she is bound by the same confidentiality that you are." I nodded before continuing, at least he had finally acknowledged that he knew Sarah was aware of the implant.

"Does me leaving it in mean that you have this access instantly too? Also yes, Sarah would not discuss my medical wellbeing with anyone else." I was curious again, I realised that if the chip wasn't in, then maybe he wouldn't see my visions, not that it really mattered.

"We have access to the implant directly. The day I showed you how to use it was just a demonstration. I am directly linked to the implant and so can access it with and without the chip. This helps us if you don't use it for a while and we need to analyse it." I nodded. So, the reading chip was only for my benefit. Even with that thought, I couldn't work out the purpose of that, was it to give me some idea of control? Maybe people would prefer to be able to remove it whenever they wanted but if that only affected when they personally could see the flashbacks then why make it removable? In all honesty, the initial menial interest I had felt had worn off and I had no desire to watch all of the things that caused me so much distress the first time around, I felt like I knew the basics of the nightmares and didn't need to see the scenes over and over again.

"Will I ever have this implant removed?"

He paused and looked at me, I watched his hand in my peripheral view. His fingertips were resting on the piece of paper. His face darkened and he spoke, his voice growing ever more deeper, "Why would you want to do that?" I didn't know how to answer, but my instinct told me to play it cool.

"I was just wondering. But if you say that it can't affect me badly to leave it in, then it doesn't matter, right? It's pretty cool to be part of this and be able to access my subconscious visions, I don't actually want it gone, I just asked for the sake of asking I guess." His eyebrows twitched and my attempt at a smile was faltering. Crap, did I play it up too much? I was trying to take that look off his face. It didn't matter anyway, his whole demeanour had changed and he seemed broader and taller to me now, intimidating.

"Why do you have this list? I thought I told you it was nothing for you to concern yourself with." He was now holding up the piece of paper, the emotion on his face was hard to read but I'm sure I saw something like anger there.

"That was from before I spoke to you, I was just playing around. I like anagrams and puzzles. I haven't looked at it since before you told me it was nothing important to me." His jaw clenched when I told him I liked puzzles and anagrams, and I made a mental note. Then wondered about the validity of my mental notes. I pondered how many things I was overthinking, then shook my head mentally to pull myself out of my internal dialogue. He loosened his stance again and smiled at me, it was disarming. Ideas were pinging through my head and I needed him to go so I could work them out. Then he spoke again, folding the paper neatly and putting it in his pocket and completely caught me off guard with his next question.

"How do you know Geraldine?" My mouth opened and closed again. I felt like a fish caught in a net.

"She is an old family friend, I bumped into her when I was having breakfast this morning. And you?" Damn, why did I ask, I already knew that was dangerous ground. He answered anyway, smoothly, as though he had anticipated such a response,

"She was someone I knew a long time ago, in a different life it seems. Be careful of her, I remember her being a gossip and meddler." The warning he made was clear to me, don't go to her for help with the nightmares and hallucinations, or listen to her input. If he only knew, I had already given it away. Obviously, I would know what she did for a living if she was an old family friend. I resisted the urge to facepalm myself and felt glad he didn't comment on this, maybe he didn't know what she did and I was once again overthinking.

In true English fashion, Dr Muggor clasped his hands in front of himself and mumbled 'right' to himself. He was going, good. I was completely on eggshells around him and he took my note with all the letters and numbers. I knew better than to ask for it back, his mood, although controlled, seemed to switch rapidly. Telling me Steph would be in contact, he showed himself to the door and left. I wondered momentarily to the purpose of his visit and coming here, perhaps it was just a friendly check-up and making sure I did make it back from the café OK. But I felt it was something else. He did say he wanted a one-on-one with me and it didn't really feel like anything too confidential was discussed. Maybe I just wasn't paying good enough attention or he just didn't want any type of audience whilst speaking with me, which in all fairness wasn't a bad thing for a doctor to want.

****

I was answering a few messages on my social networking site, from the football boys who had been asking where I had disappeared to. I rarely used this thing, but as my phone seemed to be failing me I decided to see if anyone had reached out here. They weren't really my friends, so I just wrote a plain 'Been busy' in response to them. They didn't really care, I was just a boozing buddy and they probably missed having the extra head around when it came to getting rounds in. My phone was next to the monitor and pinged up with a message. I opened it and saw it was from Dr Smyll.

'Sorry to have left you so abruptly earlier.
I didn't get a chance to finish talking to you.
Something isn't right, I have taken precautions.
Come by when you can.
D.S.'

Taken precautions? What did she mean? I tapped a message out to Sarah letting her know that if she got back and I wasn't here I had gone over to Dr Smyll's and to come join me or wait for me to get back here. Picking up my keys, I headed straight out and fast-walked to Dr Smyll's. My intuition was firing up that something wasn't right and I knew I had to get there as soon as I could. Unlocking my phone and going back to the message, I stopped in my tracks struck by confusion, it had disappeared. I knew beyond doubt that she had definitely sent that text to me. Picking up the pace again with my instincts sizzling inside me now, I moved faster and felt my thighs protesting at the sudden excursion. My mind raced with thoughts. Why did Dr Muggor react the way he did when I used the fact that I used to enjoy puzzles as an excuse for my interest in the codes? It was indicative of something, I felt certain.

Rounding onto the pathway leading up to her house, I saw the door was ajar. She must have forgotten to close it when she got home. Rapping loudly on the door, I let myself in and called her name. Nothing. Maybe she had gone out then and forgot to close it? I called again to be sure and poked my head into the study to see if she was in there. The sight that met me caused my head to snap back violently and I let out an involuntary cry. Running forward into the room, I fell at her feet. Dr Smyll was in her usual chair but she was motionless. Vomit covered her chest and legs, her head rolled awkwardly to one side with bloodshot eyes staring blindly into nothingness. I saw her sleeve was pulled up and a small rivulet of blood trailed down her forearm leading to a limp hand with her fingers pointing towards the floor. A needle lay discarded, empty. Was she a user? This sweet little lady, of course she wasn't.

Fear caught up in my throat and I backed away, unable to take my eyes away from her. No matter how graphic and convincing my nightmares and visions were, this was real without a doubt, I knew it in my gut. My foot caught the side table and it was pulled away from the sofa's side. Something was poking out from underneath and I bent to look. The label read 'PCG Security Services'. Could this be the precaution she said about? Something inside me said it was. I couldn't stay in the room with her, I was holding back the need to be sick and panic. Grabbing the box, I got out as fast as my legs would take me and ran to the kitchen on unstable legs. Sitting down at the small dining table, I set the box down and examined it through blurry eyes, forcing myself to focus because I knew it was important. According to the label on the front it came with three security cameras, all small enough to hide in inconspicuous places. Although not looking for them, I hadn't spotted any, so she either hadn't installed them or they really were that discreet. The receipt was sellotaped to the top and I saw she had bought them today, not long after she left me in the cafe. She really didn't trust Dr Muggor, maybe she was right about this whole thing. He was asking me about her, did this mean he had done this? He had only left mine a couple of hours ago? But I couldn't see it, he may be strange and eccentric, but I couldn't picture him as a killer.

I choked back a cry again as the mental image of Dr Smyll bombarded me again. A piercing scream cut through the air and I leapt off of the stool, skin prickling. I ran through to the study again and saw Sarah slumped in the doorway, scream faded to a distraught crying. I tried to grab under her arms and pull her away and she threw herself forward, rolling neatly on to her back, throwing up her legs ready to kick whoever had just touched her.

"It's me! Sarah, get out of here please, please come out." I avoided looking at the lifeless form of Dr Smyll, even though I could feel the morbid temptation to look, I don't know what it is about humans. We cannot help ourselves even when we know the impact it will have on us. Sarah jumped up and into my arms and I moved us through to the kitchen again. She was inconsolable and heaving sobs. It wasn't long before she was spent and suddenly stopped, like she slid in to a state of shock. She sat motionless for a time, wordless. I didn't know what to say or do myself. Should I call the police? I asked Sarah and she looked sadly at me, mourning dulling her wet eyes.

"We should call someone to come remove the body. I can't believe she is gone, Arnie, I didn't even know she used drugs. I can't get the image of what she looked like out of my head, it scares me just knowing she is in the next room."

I held her hand and thought for a minute, then decided to vocalise my thinking.

"Sarah, I don't think she did do any sort of drugs." Her head jolted a little, the implication that that small statement had caused her eyes to narrow. "But she sent me a text, telling me she had taken precautions, so she was worried about something. Then I found this," I showed her the security camera box, "and think she may have installed them. They even pick up sounds. But every text I have come through on my phone disappears really quickly, I don't know what is going on. I think I only saw her message because I opened it the moment it came through. I am now afraid, Sarah, we are deep in something and I don't even know what it is."

I could see she was scared and felt terrible for inadvertently involving her in it all. "If you want to go, I won't blame you for a minute. I don't know much about this stuff, but I don't think Dr Smyll's death was an accident, just made to look like one. I want to see if I can find the footage if the cameras are up and running. Hopefully, we will see something that we can hand to the police. But if we call them now and they assume it was just an overdose and nothing more, they will cordon off the house for a while and we won't be able to see or do anything. Plus, we may become suspects. I think I saw her laptop on the desk in the study, I will go and get it. Can you sit here for me?"

She nodded meekly at me, just numbly taking it all in. I had never seen a dead body in real life before and I could barely stomach the idea of voluntarily going back in the room. I was barely keeping it together and forcing myself to function by having a purpose and something to focus on. With my eyes downcast and averted, I made my way across the room and pushed the papers off of the laptop and took it back through to the kitchen where Sarah was still sat staring into space in shock. I don't know if it was all in my head, but it felt like the smell of death clung to me, sunken into my very pores. I unfolded the laptop once back at the table and the screen lit up, I was surprised to see no password prompt although relieved because I wouldn't even know where to start guessing.

Looking at the desktop icons I tried to find one for PCG Security Services. I found it in the bottom left of the screen, double-clicking it, it pulled up a video feed titled 'Live'. There were three different windows, one showing the pathway leading up to the house, one showing the back garden and door and the last one was in the hallway that led to the kitchen, study and stairs. Figured, really, as a professional, it wouldn't do to have any sort of recording in the room that she carried out her work considering its sensitive nature. I quickly reflected how crazy it was that I kept jumping between being rational, to bordering on uncaring about everything, to verging on a breakdown. I had to keep forcing myself to keep focusing on my breathing, but it was unnerving in itself just how well I felt like I was dealing with the situation so far, as strange as that may be.

I looked across the tabs and found the one labelled 'Access Footage'. I entered it and selected the window showing the front of the house. As I moved the cursor the options to rewind, pause and fast-forward lit up at the bottom of the screen. I rewound the clip to the beginning of the recording. Made the task easier her having only bought the recording equipment today I thought darkly. Right-clicking and playing at x4 speed, I waited for the first signs of movement. Dr Smyll only made one appearance and that was moving in front of the camera, giving a short wave then disappearing from view again, must have been checking it was working. Sarah started up crying again and I had a lump in my throat knowing she would never be able to do any of that ever again.

A movement in the top right of the screen caught my eye. I paused the footage to look closer. At the top of the pathway, a petite woman was crouching down fiddling with her handbag. Anticipation, excitement, I don't really know what, caused my heart to beat harder in my chest. Pressing play at normal speed, the woman stood and started to approach the house, head slightly bowed. I was struck by the thought that it looked like Steph. Then I started to think more and more that this was Steph, thinking about her height, size and even the shape of her hair. If it was, why the hell was she here? I didn't want my dark ideas and fears proven right, I didn't want to be involved in this. I turned the volume up so we could hear whatever exchange there was. She arrived at the door and my breath caught in my throat. It was her; it was Steph. Right before knocking, she pulled the hood of her jumper up and over her head, causing most of her face to be concealed.

I watched with bated breath as she lifted one dainty hand and rapped lightly on the door panel. Very soon, Dr Smyll opened the door and she had her usual friendly air around her. She looked at her visitor and bent slightly to peer under the hood and see the face of the person before her. In one neat move, Steph took one more step forward and pulled the hood back. Both women were on the very edge of the camera screen, if they moved even one more step into the house, I wouldn't be able to see them. Dr Smyll just stood and looked at Steph and even with the grainy quality of this footage, you could see the colour had drained from her face. Her mouth opened and we had to strain to hear what she said.

'My God, Jane. Is that you?' I froze, it felt like a block of ice hit me square in the chest. For some reason, when Dr Smyll had told me the tale of Jane and Joseph Muggor I kind of assumed that Jane would have been institutionalised again by this point or dead. I could see from Steph, or Jane's, profile that she was smirking, not for humorous reasons though.

'Geraldine, long time. May I come in?' Dr Smyll was glancing around and a quick flick of her eyes towards the hidden camera showed her fear and reluctance to let Jane in. Perhaps inappropriate, but my mind flicked to the thought of how lucky it was and what good timing she had in installing the cameras. She must have known, this was her precaution, I wondered what made her take such a measure though, had she been contacted by them? Or just the exchange between herself and Dr Muggor in the cafe?

I could feel my mind tugging me away, trying to entice me into thinking about anything but the matter at hand, to pretend it wasn't happening and stick my head in the sand. Fighting it, I felt a surge of anger and sadness as I watched Steph, aka Jane, push past Dr Smyll and pull her in. The door closed and the footage stopped moving apart from some dead leaves blowing around in the blades of grass, getting caught up in little gusts of wind, unaware of what was happening outside of their happy swirling dance. I changed the footage display to the one showing the hallway and rewound it to where you could see Jane and Dr Smyll in the left-hand side just having entered the house. I could just about make out what they were saying, the microphone picking it up better as they moved down the hall.

'So, Jane, this is an unexpected visit. How may I help you?' Dr Smyll's voice had a slight tremor but she was holding her own, trying not to show the unease she felt. You could tell she was trying to make it seem like she was pleased to see her, maybe to direct the surprise visit better.

'Oh Gerry, there are so many things you can help me with. You know I have some trouble with this old thing,' a point at her head and a wiggle of the hips, almost playful, 'and I just wanted someone to talk to. I have heard just how amazing you are and so here I am!' She was playing a game with her and my stomach was in knots. This footage was recorded only two and a half hours ago, which meant Dr Smyll didn't have much time left. I arrived here just less than an hour ago, a window of just an hour and half. My whole body ached with mourning and regret knowing I was just a little bit too late.

'Who, if you don't mind me asking, referred you?'

'Oh, an old boyfriend actually. Really cool guy, Arnold Shack. He said you worked absolute wonders when he was in a bit of a pickle with nightmares.' Dr Smyll's reaction was like she had been slapped in the face, I hope reason ruled and she knew that it was a lie. She was fishing for information. Damn it! I wanted to shout at Dr Smyll, the live breathing one I was watching on the screen, and tell her not to listen to the complete rubbish coming from this despicable woman's mouth.

'Right, well, I can't discuss that in any case. I know the name, but he is not a patient of mine. Just a family friend.' Good, she knew it wasn't true and even in that moment was trying to deter her. I breathed a small, pointless, sigh of relief. I remembered with a jab it didn't matter, none of it did; she was dead.

'Of course, of course. Can we sit down?' I watched them go into the study, the door open and willed them to come back out. The sound was even more quiet now, but the occasional banging and shouting of 'What do you know!' and 'Don't lie to me!' came through on the microphone. I could hear a faint whimpering and then Dr Smyll's voice, unmistakeable came through on the speakers, she was speaking loudly, maybe so that someone would hear it later.

'I know nothing that can help you, nor does he. What I do know is that if you and Muggor continue on the paths you're on, you will pay for it.'

A high-pitched laugh came through and sudden silence followed by the sound of someone throwing up, Dr Smyll I guessed. Jane re-entered the hall and I made out the muttering of 'Meddling bitch' as she rubbed her hands down her front, grimacing as she did so, like what she had just done was just a dirty inconvenience. I watched her pick up her bag from the floor, give her body a shake, then left without looking back. I closed the windows down. We had seen it all now. My cheeks were wet and I didn't need to see the actual event to have it playing vividly in my mind, I was glad the video wasn't from the study. Sarah had her head on her arms, laying across the table, tears running trails down her face and pooling onto the table. We didn't know what to say, so we sat in silence with the now familiar feeling of not knowing what to do or where to turn.

****

We sat in each other's company, silently trying to offer comfort to each other whilst the corpse of Dr Smyll lay in the next room when Sarah held her hand up and motioned for me to be quiet. I didn't know how long we had been sitting there numbly for, it could have been five minutes or five hours. I strained to hear what she had heard. Everything went into slow motion in my mind as I heard the sound of footsteps just outside the house and low voices. It was a man and a woman, bickering with each other.

"If it isn't one thing, it's the next with you, isn't it? How could you forget the laptop, we don't know what she has on us, we have to get rid of it and any other evidence before they find the body." Male voice.

"I wasn't thinking, you know I don't like being the one tasked with disposing of people, I don't see why it should be me and not you." Female.

"You know why, you know your jobs and you get rewarded for it. You know the punishment if you don't do what needs to be done. Now get in there and find that damn laptop. Have you checked in to see where Arnold is lately? Probably not. I question your dedication to me, Jane." Sarah's hand shot up to her mouth to stifle a gasp. We were now hunched behind the kitchen door trying to stay out of sight. I had already worked out who it was, Sarah clearly hadn't.

"No, I haven't. Probably where he usually is, in his apartment. Is he really worth it, he doesn't seem to be responding as well as others have? And he looked for outside help even when you told him not to and lied about it. Hacking his phone didn't deter him." I bit back from saying something, at least that explained that.

"This is no place or time to discuss all this. Get in there and find it, I don't want to see her, I will wait in the hall for you. I want to be in and out as fast as we can, then we will call the police and request a wellness check so they can find her. Hurry up then will you? There is much to be done!" A huffing noise was the only response she gave to Dr Muggor and I heard her stomping across the hall just a few metres away from us. Shit. If they were looking for the laptop it wouldn't take them long to realise it wasn't in the study and they would start to look in other rooms. Panic rising up, I could hear Sarah's accelerated breathing close to my ear. Thinking quickly, I wondered where the door to the back garden was, maybe we could get out that way. Now knowing for certain the lengths these two would go to, I wasn't willing to bank on them letting us go without a fight.

Thinking back to the video feeds, it seemed to pan from the centre of the back of the house, which meant it should be somewhere in this area. Looking around again, I saw a floor-length curtain and breathed a quiet sigh of relief. It was a safe bet that this was the door leading outside. Tugging on Sarah's hand to get her to follow close behind me, I crept around the side of the room, all the while keeping my eyes fixed on the kitchen door to make sure no one came through. We couldn't have much time. Swiping the curtain aside, I almost cheered. Swinging the door open with relief that it was unlocked, we stepped out onto the patio. With a start, I realised we had left the laptop on the table, cursing and having an internal battle with myself, I decided to get it. The more Dr Muggor thought we knew about what was going on the more at risk we were and I didn't know what Dr Smyll had written in there.

Making it to the table in three strides, I grabbed the laptop and turned on my heel ready to run when the voices were suddenly outside the kitchen door. I couldn't breathe, regretting now coming back in to get the laptop. They were talking about looking in the other rooms, and judging by their movements the kitchen was next. Not sure whether I could make it back out of the door without them seeing me, I crouched down and slid under the table, thankful for the plastic style cover that almost reached the floor and an added bonus was it didn't sway from my movement because it was rigid. Good decision, the door swung open just as I pulled my left foot in. I sat, barely daring to breathe, listening to them opening and closing cupboards and drawers, hunting for the evasive laptop. I hoped Sarah was keeping out of sight, from the kitchen window, they would see her make a break for it if they looked at the right time, or wrong time really.

"Jane, did you leave that open?" Damn it, why didn't I close the door?

"No, I didn't even come in here when I came earlier."

"Are you sure, you know how you get when you are under pressure? Unless it was Geraldine?"

"Probably, she was going through menopause or something and needed fresh air, well, she will be lovely and cold now." A dark snigger emitted from Jane/Steph and I rushed with hurt and anger, I barely kept myself in check.

"Alright, let's check upstairs."

I waited until I was sure they had left the room and I could hear the creaking of floorboards above me when I made a break for it. Racing out the door, I scanned for Sarah and she bounded out from behind a bush, her face was tear-streaked and fearful. Giving no time to speak, I grabbed her hand again and rounded onto the pathway at the side of the house and ran, laptop tucked safely under one arm and Sarah keeping pace beside me. We didn't stop running until we got to my street. We stopped at the door panting and heaving for breath. Sarah bent over and I sank to the floor with my back against the wall.

After a few minutes, I realised we looked a bit suspect to any passers-by and imagined a scenario where a police officer stopped by us and asked about the laptop. Unlikely as it may be, we couldn't risk it. Pulling myself up again, I made my way into the building and headed up to my apartment with Sarah on my tail. Once inside, we didn't know what to do with ourselves or even where to begin talking about it. So, Sarah went and busied herself in the kitchen making drinks and I looked for a safe spot to hide the laptop. I figured the bottom of my wardrobe concealed by jumpers was good enough for the time being.

For the meantime, I went back through to the kitchen and saw Sarah sitting slumped on the floor, sobbing quietly into her palms. My heart broke, I sat next to her and cradled her in my arms and we both wept together. It was a good release of emotions and as I thought it, I realised I hadn't had barely anything this afternoon or evening in terms of funny turns or visions. As soon as the thought came, a darker one loomed in, it seemed that if Dr Muggor was indeed somehow causing these effects, then him having been otherwise busy this afternoon would have resulted in him not being able to administer anything. If that was the case, if it was even possible then it could all make some more sense. Nothing seemed far-fetched any more.

"Let's go to bed, Sarah, we will work out what we need to do tomorrow. It is all too raw right now to make a real decision or make any moves. We are safe here, for now at least, they have no reason to know we were at Dr Smyll's house or that we know what happened."

She looked up at me with a slight glint of hope in her eyes and I hoped what I was saying was fact and not just wishful thinking. Keeping her cradled in my arms, I struggled to stand up but refused to let her go and I carried her through to the bedroom, my collarbone protesting with hot stabbing pains as I did so. Laying her gently on the bed, I pulled the sheet over her and stroked her face. Her eyes were already becoming heavy and my heart felt full of love as I gazed at her. If it killed me, we would get through this, I felt it through to the very depths of my soul.

I awoke with a start, for one blissful moment forgetting everything but the sleepiness and the gentle purring of Sarah wrapped up beside me. I looked at the time, 7:45 am. Groaning, I rolled myself out of bed with an effort. Weariness making itself known mentally and physically. My feet hitting the cold floor sent a shock wave through me and with it, the memory of the tragedies that happened yesterday. My weariness faded away to be replaced by heavy sadness and fear, a mentally exhausting combination. I had no real nightmare last night, not like the all-consuming ones I had been having lately, but my sleep had been disrupted by images of Dr Smyll, the discarded needle, vomit, the contorted faces of Dr Muggor and Steph – should I call her Jane now? Probably wise not to. The last thing we needed was for them to know we knew anything at all.

In a rather backwards way, my dream being haunted by real-life events rather than the dark traumatic scenes my mind conjured up was almost better for me. At least this I knew was real and that I wasn't losing my mind. It may not be pleasant, in fact, it was heart-breaking and terrifying to the point I didn't know which way to turn or what to do, almost frozen in a state of shock now, but I knew it was real. Not some crazy hallucination that made me question everything around me and my sanity. It didn't have to make sense, frankly to me, it didn't, but it formed some blanket of comfort to my damaged being.

Having overheard the conversations between Steph and Dr Muggor yesterday I needed to make a game plan, a way to get away from all of this and avoid anyone else being hurt or worse. They had now demonstrated the excessive and terrifying lengths they would go to in order to protect and continue whatever this was. I had to fight it, if what we had learned so far was right. It seemed that they were trying to develop something that could control the minds of people to the extent that they became living breathing puppets. Kind of like the story Dr Smyll had told us about Jane from medical school, if that was the case then I had to give everything I had to not become their next victim.

But it did make me question whether the girl I knew as Steph, the pretty, innocent looking murderer, was actually the one making her decisions? Was she aware of what was going on? Could it be that she did fall victim to Dr Muggor's initial experiments and is now entirely under his control somehow or does he threaten her with madness if she chooses to tell anyone or not follow his command? Did I really care? She murdered someone I had come to rely on and even think of as a friend. A soul that would no longer be there when I went knocking or to indulge my thoughts to. No, I don't think I do care about the circumstances surrounding Steph, aka Jane. If I thought I could get away with it, I would bestow onto her the same treatment she gave to Dr Smyll. And something even darker would be dished to the puppet master, Dr Muggor.

Still perched on the edge of my bed, I rubbed my face and scalp. The pain was almost completely gone from the area around the scar, just a numbed sensation to remind me that all was not perfect. My hair was starting to go soft again and would soon cover completely the harsh mark that I bore above and behind my ear. I felt a hand caress my back and turned to look at Sarah, she laid enshrouded by the white bed sheets, her skin looking a golden tan colour against it. Her hair framed her face and it saddened me to watch the moment she lost her sleepy grogginess and remembered what had happened. Her expression transformed from loving and sweet, with a slight pout, to one with a lined mouth and dulled eyes. Without saying a word, she shuffled up behind me and curled her body around my back and I felt her small heaves against me and heard the small sniffs as she cried quietly. I wrapped my arm around her waist and rested my head on hers, a moment of joined grief, sharing the pain in a bid to lessen it. I felt mine alleviate a little and felt my energy flowing with hers.

Our moment was brought to an end when I heard a loud banging on the front door. I stood, wondering idly who would be coming round and could only think of one person and I didn't want that one person to be here, especially now. I faced Sarah and took her face in my hands.

"Go into the bathroom, clean yourself up. If this is Muggor, he can't know that we know anything, we have to keep poker faces. OK?" She nodded back at me, her trust in me burning brightly in her eyes. I never wanted to see that light fade. She got up and went into the bathroom, closing the door softly behind her. I went to the front door, the visitor still knocking, harder now. I swung the door open and my guess had been right. Dr Muggor stood in front of me, looking worse for wear. He had a dark shadowy stubble and bags under his eyes. He was shifting from foot to foot, to say he looked agitated was an understatement. He didn't wait for an invitation and simply walked straight in and gestured for me to close the door behind him and follow. My heart was beating a steady beat and I swallowed to keep my cool. Obediently, shutting the door I followed him to the sofa. He sat and expelled a long sigh.

"Arnie, good morning. Sorry for my appearance, I have had quite a heavy workload and not had five minutes to myself. You know how it can be." I was a little taken aback, I had half expected him to be a bit confrontational or snidey based on his appearance alone. Was this an attempt at some sort of manly banter, drawing attention to his dishevelled look and making generic bar talk statements to make us more friendly? Let my guard down? I played ball.

"I understand. Life gets in the way sometimes, huh? I have been meaning to call again about that appointment, but the same reason for you goes for me. Are you here for a check-up?" He was looking at me with an unreadable expression. I felt like he was testing the waters, seeing how I reacted to him. I had to be careful here, I was hanging on by a thread. If it was just me at risk, I may have played it all very differently, but I had Sarah to think about.

"Yes, just a check-up. I need to have a look at the implant and just talk through a few things with you." How was he so calm following yesterday's events? You wouldn't ever have guessed he had orchestrated the murder of someone, someone he knew no less. I fought to tamp down my growing anger at these thoughts. "How have your symptoms been? Any events I should know about in the last 24 hours?"

I continued my role as a hapless patient, eager to keep him onside.

"Nothing since yesterday morning really which has been quite a relief. I had a minor moment, but I didn't even have a nightmare last night. Do you know why this would be?" I watched as he gritted his teeth ever so slightly, then he clasped his hands in front of him and looked me dead in the eyes. It was intimidating and I had to dig deep to not shy away from his penetrating stare.

"Don't think too much into it. This could just be a lull. You may have had a temporary rebalance of your hormones which will have, in turn, relieved the level of any hallucinations or visions. I must warn you not to get your hopes up too much, you never know what could be around the corner."

My mouth became very dry and I just stared back at him, fighting to keep my expression neutral. That was unexpected. He wasn't even attempting to make me feel like there was a light at the end of all of this. It seemed he was actually trying to use negative reinforcement on me. If I bought it, it would probably make me more susceptible to whatever he had up his sleeve. So, I just nodded, until I had a plan in place, I would let him think he had the upper hand.

"That said, I would like to assess your injury area if you will allow me to?" I didn't know what I could do to stop him. If he could make Steph commit such a dark unforgivable crime, what would he personally be capable of? I mutely nodded and turned my head for him. He lifted the little hair in the area and I could feel his breath warm on my ear as he inspected it. I fought the urge to cringe away from him. I flinched when a sudden stinging pain pulsated through my scar and his hand came up to hold my head in place. My self-control failed me and I moved away harder, pulling myself away from his grasp. What was he doing to me? I was too unnerved by all my thoughts to even look at him and stared at the TV set, I didn't want my expression to belie my distrust and fear. He cleared his throat and I put on my best poker face and looked back at him.

"Sorry about that, I was just checking on that stitch that was awry before." Looking at his mouth as he spoke, I could see in the corner of my eye him fiddling with his pocket, closing the zipper as he spoke. I think he sensed what I was thinking because he patted it theatrically and carried on, "Just checking I had my beeper on me, I am expecting a phone call from Steph." Believable, I guess.

"No problem, my head is still all over the place really. I don't know if I am coming or going. I apologise if I seem a bit off, I am tired. Is the stitch OK?" He was still watching me closely.

"It is fine, nothing to worry about at all. I want to know you are coping OK, after all, what kind of doctor would I be if your health wasn't top of my priority list?" A small high-pitched chuckle came from him and he stopped it as abruptly as it came. My instinct was screaming at me that this was dangerous territory.

"Now, I saw you the other day in the café with a dear old friend of mine. Funny lady that Geraldine. I know we have discussed her already, but I don't know if you have heard the news?" I felt my spine straighten in anticipation, I kept my mouth closed and waited, letting a questioning expression cross my face. "Word has reached me that she succumbed to her addictions recently and has passed away. Terribly sad news. I just found her again and now she has gone."

He didn't look sad, nor happy. He was completely robotic in the manner he was speaking and acting now. What on earth did he mean about having found her again? He knew I saw their interaction in the cafe and, it was glaringly obvious they were not 'dear old friends'. That was even looking from his perspective where he didn't know that I knew anything about his time in medical school I reacted honestly to his announcement, allowed my feelings at her death to come through, no acting required on my part. My body slumped and I felt my eyes grow heavy and wet.

"I can't believe it. You say she succumbed to addiction?" I had to ask, I needed to know what he would say.

"You are taking it better than I thought. I thought you were closer. You are already asking questions surrounding her death. Don't you need more time to mourn? Come to terms with the news? Maybe you are in shock. I may have something to help treat that, if you feel, it would help?"

I shook my head in response to his barrage of questions and assumptions. No way was I allowing him any more permission to administer anything. He didn't answer my question. But I couldn't push him further; he had to think I had only just found out about her death. My mind shot back to her in her chair, her unseeing eyes sunken into pale cheeks, mouth hung open in a soundless scream. I shuddered, repulsed and sickened by the image. Grief came in stronger and I cried. It was only made worse when I noted a hint of malice in Dr Muggor's eyes. He killed her in spite of the fact she was a human, someone who lived and breathed and had a life, he stubbed it out easier than a cigarette butt. No remorse, all to meet his own ends. Rage bubbled up and quelled my tears and my fingertips tingled with the longing to wrap themselves around Dr Muggor's neck. I didn't need to push further in the end though, he seemed eager to elaborate anyway, tell me the story that he had fabricated about the whole thing. It was like he couldn't resist.

"She had been a user of class A drugs for quite some time – heroin if I am not mistaken – and we all thought she had recovered and ceased the abuse. Just shows us we never really know what someone is going through behind closed doors. If only she felt like she had someone to confide in and trust with this secret."

Wow, he was laying it on thick. Managing to turn it and make it entirely plausible that Dr Smyll and Dr Smyll alone was the cause of her own death, laying out the groundwork so no questions would ever be asked. If I wasn't aware of what had actually happened to her, I would have been inclined to believe him he told it so well. To the point, I was questioning what I saw. I didn't know if I could trust my own mind anymore, but Sarah was with me and witnessed it too, so there was that for reassurance.

No reply was required on my part for a moment as we were interrupted by a vibrating noise coming from his left pocket. He looked at me for a moment, debating whether to answer or not or continue this passive conversation with me. Mind made up, he reached into the pocket and looked at the screen. He excused himself and walked into the kitchen to take the call, I followed him with my eyes and noted he went far into the kitchen so as to not have any interference or be overheard even. All I could make out was a low murmuring and that was with me straining to hear.

I glanced over to the bedroom doorway and saw Sarah poking her head around the frame to see me. She must have been listening from there, probably the better idea, not to become involved in this conversation and for Dr Muggor to not know she was present. I gestured for her to keep herself out of sight and she ducked back out of view just as Dr Muggor came back in the room, absent-mindedly patting his pocket. He halted about a metre away from me and just watched me. Waiting for me to restart the conversation maybe? It wasn't one I wanted to pursue, to be quite honest. My nerves started jangling and I thought what to say, a course of conversation that avoided the subject of Dr Smyll.

As I racked my brain, I felt a tell-tale tingling start at the back of my skull. My tongue felt like it was suddenly too big for my mouth and my vision clouded. My ears had the sensation of being packed full of cotton wool and I tried to focus, pull myself out of it. I could just about concentrate enough to see Dr Muggor gazing at me still, head tilted slightly to one side and doing nothing. I'm sure there was a slight twitch in the corner of his mouth too. Time seemed to slow down drastically. I moved my right hand in front of me and found it was leaden and the movement delayed. I blinked and heard the thud of my eyelids. I blinked again trying to control myself and this time the thud came but the room didn't reappear in my vision, a red-hued light was all I could see with blackened edges. I pressed on harder with my effort and failed. The reddish colour was overtaken by the darkness and I felt myself fall, blissfully completely out of this world before any painful impact.

****

I was on my hands and knees. The ground was wet and mushy underneath me and I couldn't quite make out what I was on. I clambered upright, pressing off my knees to get there, my palms sticking to the fabric of my trousers. Everything was really dark and I couldn't see much past a few metres. I looked at my hands and could see that they were coated in some reddish liquid, I didn't need to think about it at all to hazard a guess about what it was. Somehow, I was becoming hardened to such sights, it felt. It repulsed me, but I didn't freak out as such, like I would have done before. I was still conscious that this wasn't real life.

What confused me, however, was the blue liquid it had congealed with. My sight seemed to be improving every second and I looked back down at the ground and my bravado from a mere 30 seconds before evaporated. I pulled my feet up, wishing I could fly, or hover, to evade what I was standing upon now. I squeaked, bile rising up my throat threatening me with its burning acid. What was underfoot and previously (the thought of it being on my skin and memory of the sensation made me heave) underhand was worse than I could imagine. Or not because wasn't all this concocted in my mind? I tried to tell myself this to lessen the horror perhaps, but it was a fickle effort.

What lay around the floor, covering so much of it that I didn't know what the actual floor looked like, were corpses. Countless hollowed out corpses, the bones were visible but somehow they were without substance. The figures looked like thick robes, morbid coats of skin with gaping wounds and skewed limbs. The part I had just removed my foot from was what was once a face, it now resembled a discarded Halloween mask. Boneless, mouth wrenched open in its terror, glazed eyes seeing nothing but the demise of their carrier. The skin was greyed with blood trickling from each orifice, each corpse that littered the floor around me had this.

As if to make it worse the smell suddenly assaulted me, pungent and sweet, the odour clogged my nostrils like tar and I had to gasp through my mouth to take a breath. As I gasped, a column of dust particles collected from various bodies and tunnelled upwards and propelled into my open mouth before I could react. It hit me with power and I felt my jaw crunch and my head snapped back. I threw my hands out to get purchase on anything, anything to stop me from tumbling onto what lay beneath me but there was nothing but thin air. I fell and clenched my eyes shut, arms wrapped around my head in a feeble attempt at not letting anything more touch me. My mouth was dry and I couldn't even heave any more. I couldn't think about what that dust contained, I just didn't want to formulate the words in my mind and make it fact. I felt the softness of the impact and the warmth enshrouded me. I wasn't breathing, terrified to inhale.

I opened my eyes again because I didn't know what else I could do at this point, I needed to escape. Shock hit me as I saw I was laying in my bed, on my back and drenched in sweat. I looked at my hands and saw they were clean. I sighed a deep breath of relief. Propping myself upright on my elbows, I felt the hint of confusion creeping in, why was I in bed? Where were Sarah and Dr Muggor? The confusion passed when I heard someone moving around in the living room outside my door. I smiled and waited for whoever it was to come in and check on me, thinking to myself it must be Sarah and Dr Muggor must have left already. They must have moved me in here to recover once I'd passed out. The doorway shadowed, but no one appeared there. I frowned a little. The shadow became bigger and then it consumed the doorway. I laid there unsure of what I was seeing or what was happening. Then the very shadow itself seemed to become denser and detached from the walls. It floated towards me, every blink it became more opaque and the edges more refined.

As I watched, wordless and motionless, it became the man, me, the worst version of me imaginable. His face became clear and he was scowling, his jaw hanging off to the right at an obscene angle. He wasn't so much walking as floating and I willed my limbs to react but they refused my commands. My mouth dropped open and in that movement, he shot forward at an impossible speed and his gnarled hands reached out for my legs from below his cloak. I could only stare as they closed around my ankles and gripped tightly, I felt a crunching and grinding and cried out as I saw my ankle bones splinter out from under the skin. He roughly yanked downwards and again bile threw itself up my throat as I watched my feet tear away from me, shreds of skin and sinew where my ankles had been.

The pain was more than I could bear, yet I wasn't blacking out, I was living through it. He discarded my misshapen broken feet and reached back again in no hurry and clasped onto my shins, his acrid odour wafting up to me and he forced me to maintain eye contact with him. I felt something in my groin area dampen and realised I had soiled myself, last of my worries as I was certain I wouldn't be alive for much longer. I truly didn't know if I was dreaming or awake. I felt that to have this conscious thought at such a time didn't have good bearings. All of my muscles were tensed to the point of cramping, which was about all they could do at this moment, awaiting the next crippling action from him, when he pulled upwards instead.

I felt the pillow under my head roll underneath and away and the sheets dragged with my inept arms. I was suddenly airborne soaring towards the back wall near the bathroom entrance. Now free from the trance, I had been trapped in. I closed my eyes and waited for the hit. It never came, I just kept flying and flying and flying until I tried to open my eyes once more and realised I couldn't.

****

I came around and took in my surroundings again, guard up all the way and wariness consuming my being. I saw the underside of my sofa and oddly thought about how I should make an effort to sweep up the debris from under it, I never pay it any mind when whipping around with the hoover. Turning my head, not without protest from my neck, I saw Dr Muggor standing still where he had been. I felt surprisingly with it and coherent, considering on other occasions, confusion was a heavy after effect for me normally. I felt a wash of anger and impotence come over me and in that moment, I was faced with the feeling of defeat once again. Dr Muggor didn't look at all phased by me laying on the floor, nor by what he had undoubtedly just witnessed. He didn't even offer to help me up, just placidly staring at me like I was some kind of entertainment for him. I wondered briefly if Sarah was still keeping out of sight and away from Dr Muggor and if she had seen what happened to me. I hoisted myself up using the sofa arm for support and slid onto one of the cushions. Dr Muggor then followed suit and sat down next to me again.

"How do you feel?" I was taken aback although I shouldn't have been. I think we had established by this point that my actual wellbeing wasn't a concern of his.

"My head hurts, what happened?"

"You had a seizure. Much like I said to you before, you having a period with no events was not necessarily a good indicator. You must learn not to fight it. In my experience in this field, if you allow the changes to happen without trying to stop them, you will find the outcome to be much easier and less damaging to you. I don't know if you are aware of this, but often when the mind experiences a seizure or a blackout, it can create scarring on your cerebral matter. Too much of this and you cannot come back from it or recover to your old self. So, I insist, when you feel this happening to you, whether it be a blackout or a hallucination, let yourself go and flow with it. You may even find it liberating to free your mind to be directed."

"My mind will be directed?" Had he just let himself slip up? I couldn't let that pass, I had to ask.

"By itself, without your secondary conscious mind fighting against it. You have your conscious and subconscious. It is your subconscious that is trying to have its moment when these occurrences happen."

101

Well, I couldn't fathom what my subconscious was trying to tell me apart from making it abundantly clear that I was a self-harming, suicidal being with a desire to see murders and pain. And did that mean the young boy, i.e., me, who didn't even make an appearance in the last vision, was my conscious being? Not far off of what Dr Smyll had said. The thought of her brought back my heavy heart. What had I gotten her mixed up in? If only I had listened when Dr Muggor told me not to seek outside help, she would still be alive.

Dr Muggor had clearly decided his time here was done and he patted his knees and rose up. Giving me a cursory nod and telling me he would be in touch, he left without any further comment and didn't give me any more time to ask any more. Good thing really, I didn't want to be around him. I was amazed at myself for not losing my head (outside of the seizure, obviously) when he was here, I think a lesser person would have. When the door clicked shut, Sarah came rushing out of the room and dropped on the sofa next to me and brushed her hand over my head and down the back of my neck.

"Oh, Arnie, I wanted to come out, but I didn't trust myself around him. If he knew I had been in the room the whole time too without coming out to say something, he would have become suspicious. I couldn't believe he didn't do anything, he just stood there watching you. Did you hurt yourself?"

I didn't bother to answer. I needed to take control of the situation again and myself. I could still feel the tenderness in my legs from the nightmare. The image of my feet being torn off fresh and haunting, I vehemently shook the memory from my mind. I pulled her to me and met her mouth with mine, with a hunger to forget the fear and pain and replace it with me and Sarah, my love for her and our life and get lost in her for a time. She pressed back hard, needing it as much as I did and we threw ourselves back on the sofa and succeeded in getting lost in each other's bodies and movements until we passed out, spent.

****

I awoke sometime later to the sound of tapping. I looked over to Sarah, who was wrapped up in the throw that normally went over the back of the sofa. She was typing away on her laptop, tongue poking slightly out of the side of her mouth, concentration etched across her features. The sweet smell of our love hung in the air and I let out a small sigh and relaxed into the cushions. She heard me and turned to look at me and allowed a small triumphant smile to light up her face. I looked back, questioningly.

"I think I have got it! The codes, I think I know what they mean! They are anagrams! Kind of anyhow. They are just the names of different hormones without the vowels. I was thinking about them and decided to check if they made any sense on Google. Of course, that didn't come up with anything, but then I remembered a puzzle book that my granddad used to have and it was like a crossword and the clues where the words but without the vowels. And that was it! So, once I knew that, it was fairly easy to find them!" I stared blankly at her. My beautiful little genius. I felt if she had cracked it, I could possibly cry with joy. I sat up straight and leant arm to arm with her, looking at the screen. She was in some medical site with descriptions of various hormones and their effects and drugs to combat or aid when you had too much or too little of them. The one she was on was dopamine, currently known to us as DPMN if Sarah was right. I read the paragraph out loud:

'Dopamine!'

'Dopamine plays a part in controlling the movements a person makes, as well as their emotional responses. The right balance of dopamine is vital for both physical and mental wellbeing.

'It is a compound present in the body as a neurotransmitter and a precursor of other substances including adrenaline. Side effects of an excess of this hormone in the system can include but are not limited to irregular heartbeats, nausea, anxiety, headaches, etc.

'High levels of dopamine in the brain are found in patients with attention-deficit/hyperactivity disorder and Parkinson's patients treated with L-dopa, who exhibit impulsive behaviour. Individuals with boosted brain dopamine levels were more likely to act impulsively with a need for instant gratification. People with high levels may experience psychosis similar to psychosis seen in schizophrenia.

'Low levels of dopamine in the brain can often be seen in patients with depression and Parkinson's Disease, this can be due to a problem with the receptors in the brain. Side effects of a deficiency can include but are not limited to aches and pains, loss of balance, trouble sleeping or disturbed sleep, an inability to focus, hallucinations and delusions.'

The words danced around on the webpage and I didn't know whether that was me having a funny turn or the information I was trying to absorb. Sarah waited until she was sure I had finished reading and clicked on the next tab for me to see.

'Serotonin

'Serotonin is made from the essential amino acid tryptophan. Tryptophan deficiency can lead to lower serotonin levels. This can result in mood disorders such as anxiety or depression.

'Serotonin impacts every part of your body, from your emotions to your motor skills. Serotonin is considered a natural mood stabiliser. It's the chemical that helps with sleeping, eating and digesting.

'Low levels of serotonin can lead to depression, anxiety and sleep problems amongst other symptoms.

'High levels of serotonin in the system can cause more severe symptoms such as headaches, confusion, muscle stiffness, high fever, rapid heart rate and seizures.'

I looked across to Sarah, who was mixed between excitement at having worked out the puzzle and concern at what she was reading. I felt quite the same, although more leaning towards a concerned feeling due to the content of what was on the screen. Many of the symptoms seemed to ring fairly accurate on both. And if I remembered rightly, there was still one more code to decipher. Something told me that Sarah already had this one up ready for me to read too. So, what all this meant was beyond me aside from the idea that somehow these hormones were being messed with by Dr Muggor and Steph. I thought back to the paperwork I had found and the title of the page 'Administration of Chemicals' and wished I could see it again and actually have time to read it. I nodded to Sarah to go on to the next one.

'Noradrenalin

'Noradrenalin (NA) otherwise known as norepinephrine is an organic chemical in the catecholamine family that functions in the brain and body as a neurotransmitter and hormone. It is at its lowest during hours of sleep and rest and will increase substantially in times of stress and anger, it is often associated with the 'fight or flight' responses.

'Low levels of NA can cause varying symptoms including but not limited to anxiety, depression, hypoglycaemia, migraines, sleep disorders, etc.

'Having an excess of this chemical in your brain lead to high blood pressure, anxiety, heart palpitations and headaches.'

So, that was a full and fairly in-depth insight into the three codes that we had been looking at if Sarah's puzzle solving skills were correct, which they seemed to be much to my dismay. Not that I wasn't grateful, it was just a lot of information to take in and frankly I didn't understand some of it anyway. Sarah looked at me expectantly, waiting for some input. I didn't have much to offer.

"So, these are the three things that were marked against the times on the screen we used to be able to see. How did you remember the codes?" Paranoia rearing its ugly head for a moment. I knew that she had nothing to do with any of this, but I was so on edge, it made me question the fibres of my own being.

"When we were at Dr Smyll's she had a file on the desktop labelled 'Codes', so I took a picture of it." To show me she unlocked her phone and presented the picture of the laptop screen. That was some fairly quick thinking in a stressful situation, I was grateful for her thinking to do it at all. "I thought you didn't have them written down anywhere anymore and you had said your messages kept disappearing, so I wasn't sure if we would be able to get them again anywhere else."

"That was a really good idea, thank you. I would never have thought of this. We did send it from your phone instead of mine anyway but it is handy to have this in more than one place. Do you know what the other ones mean?" Looking back at the phone, I could see that Dr Smyll had written down all of the information that I had sent to her:

'1645-DPMN/LWR-S1
1915-DPMN/LWR-SRTNN-S2
1930-DPMN/LWR-NRDRNLN-SRTNN-S2
1200-SRTNN-S1
1445-NRDRNLN-SRTNN-S5
1615-NRDRNLN-S1
2315-DPMN/LWR-NRDRNLN-S3'

I looked at the 'LWR' and figured it must mean lower. Judging by the side effects relating to a low level of dopamine, I was getting a lower level of this chemical rather than higher and I had no idea how that could even be possible.

"Well, I think that the ones where there is more than one on a line is where both are somehow in play. But I don't know what the letters and numbers mean at the ends or each one. I think we need to get that implant out of your head; I reckon that Dr Muggor and that girl are using it to mess with all of them somehow. It makes sense. There are times, then the codes for each chemical, what if the 'S' means' strength?" I mulled it over, it fitted and was most likely the meaning for it when I thought about it. So, would 'S1' mean a lower strength whilst 'S5' was higher? I voiced the thoughts to Sarah, who nodded back agreeably. I shifted my limbs experimentally to see that they were fully functioning and reactive. They ached but responded.

I rose up and wandered into the kitchen to make coffee. I glanced back and felt a wave of appreciation come over me as I looked at Sarah's profile. Her delicate face lit up by her laptop screen. My stomach suddenly lurched and I felt like I was going to vomit. I watched as her face contorted and became bloated. Her features became unrecognisable and she turned slowly to me, almost theatrically. My horror rose as her mouth moulded into a thin line and her chin extended out and down, the skin hanging off like it was melting. Her eyes sank into her skull and the sockets sealed over with the waxy skin whilst her hair fell out like a clumpy waterfall down her shoulders exposing dark red patchy skin on her scalp. She reached out her hand and it extended from her to me over a metre long and I recoiled. I threw my hands up to block her advance and she grabbed my hands and held on tight. The warmth of her touch felt like it was burning my skin and I shook my head from side to side, my vision becoming blurred and fuzzy. I stopped shaking my head abruptly, I don't know why but the motion stopped on its own accord and I looked to see what had become of Sarah now. She was standing in front of me holding my hands and completely back to normal, looking at me with unconcealed fear and concern.

"What did you see?"

"You, but not you. You transformed, your skin was melting and you were grabbing me. It was a hallucination again." My voice broke as I spoke, this illness had no qualms about making me fear my nearest and dearest. She was right, I had to get this out of my head. I felt certain beyond doubt that it was the root of all the problems I had been having. I now felt convinced that the accident I had on the bridge should have only resulted in a concussion and a few stitches, if that. Dr Muggor had infiltrated the hospital and used me for his own twisted games. I could see the sadness in Sarah's eyes.

"You weren't here, your eyes were glazed and you were shaking your head around like crazy, shouting for me to stop and let you go." She paused. "But we know more now, we can do this, get away from this. We should go to the police."

I considered what she said. If we went to the police now how understanding would they be when they knew we were at the scene of a crime and didn't report it? Then undergoing treatment with someone even after knowing what they were doing was unlikely to be legal. We would definitely be held liable on some levels if we were even believed at all. No. First, we needed to get this implant out of my head and make sure there was nothing that we could be arrested or questioned for. But this was so out of hand now, I didn't think I cared any more, maybe we should just hand the whole saga over to the police and be done with it. But then how would I get this out of my head? What if they decided I was a local whack job, there was no reason for them to believe me about the chip and implant. Then a spark of inspiration, the footage! I could show it to them and everything else I had and we could prove it. I rushed back to the sofa with Sarah standing behind me and I pulled up the screen to access the videos made by my brain.

'Server not found.'
I frowned, retyped it in.
'Server not found. Contact your administrator.'

They must have removed the site or changed it. What did they know we knew? They were clearly suspicious otherwise they wouldn't have done this, my heart rate accelerated in fear and realisation of what I needed to do next. I needed to stop them from seeing anything more of what I could see. For all I knew they could see and hear everything, not just my 'episodes'. The thought sent tremors racing through me. So, all I had now was a scar and my word that there was a murderous duo running around town trying to control people with the use of chemicals. Chemicals that I didn't really understand nor have an explanation for how they were dosing me with and an implant that I surely wouldn't even get a chance to prove I had because they'd turn me away as someone with crazy ideas. I could feel Sarah's energy behind me, antsy and unsure. She sat next to me and rested a hand on my knee and we both just stared blankly at the screen wondering what we could do next.

****

Later that evening, we were still sitting on the sofa, dinner plates on the table, one half-eaten and the other cleared. I had no appetite. The TV was off and we had discussed everything again from the beginning to where we were now but it brought us no closer to working out a plan of action, and left me feeling like we had wasted the time saying the same things all over again. I had had a few moments where everything was coming in and out of focus but no real hallucinations or loss of conscious being. I felt completely on edge and sure my heartbeat was in my throat at points. I could even feel thudding it in the soles of my feet when it got a bit stronger. What we couldn't fathom was the purpose of it all, was it just something to say he could do it? Look at me, I'm a clever man who did something no one else could? Control was something some people couldn't let go of and Dr Muggor was taking it all the way to another level. I just didn't know what conclusion to draw. But there was no denying he was intelligent, simultaneously impressively and scarily so.

I stood, anxiety pulsing through me and making me feel like I couldn't sit any longer. I started pacing back and forth on my fizzing calves, rubbing my head and chewing my bottom lip. I had to make a decision and it was one I didn't want to have to make. But it was step one of escaping this. I needed to get this implant out of my head no matter the cost. It was taking over everything in my life; ever since I had it, everything had gone to shit and I regretted ever feeling so hateful of my previous calm and working lifestyle. In all fairness, this had made me feel like I could pursue something different in life now though rather than stick to a job I hated. Once this was over that would be one of the first things to change and stop wasting my time with.

Decision made, I had to just throw myself at it in spite of how it sent shivers down my spine and made my teeth ache. Home surgery was the only way. In one fluid movement, I made to put both of my hands down on to the back of the sofa and found my hands slipping through the backboard and fabric continuing downwards towards the ground. Because I had made to do it with gusto, I had too much forward force to slow myself down.

A shouting started up somewhere near me, almost right into my eardrum and a buzzing irritated me. It grew stronger and I seemed to be falling in slow motion acutely aware of various things happening around me. I peered to my right and saw the little boy standing in the kitchen doorway with a hand outstretched as if to help me. I extended my own but it was too far for me to reach. I let out a frustrated roar and finally hit the floor. A multitude of voices bombarded me from invisible sources. Full incomprehensible conversations nattering in my ears like you would hear in a crowded restaurant. I fumbled to sit upright again and the room swayed around me and my tongue tasted metallic. I had a renewed throbbing in my collarbone injury.

Sarah came into view and I heard a secondary shouting, but it was coming from my own head, I wasn't sure if it was coming out of my mouth though. It sounded hollowed and far away yet somehow close. A crashing wave sound ran through my head and all at once everything went deadly silent. Sarah came fully into view and I looked at her, waiting to see if anything else was going to happen. I seemed to be alright again barring the scolding pain in my skull joining the pain in my collarbone, and wooziness. I waited to regather a bit of my strength before speaking again.

"Get the implant out. I want you to do it. Help me. Please." My voice was barely above a whisper, but I could hear the determination in my voice.

"But what if it goes wrong? You said it was somehow attached to your brain?"

"Take out the main section, the wires that they said extended out of it don't need to be touched. As long as we don't actually touch those, we should be OK. If not, well, I don't see any other way."

Her eyes danced with tears and fear, but she nodded anyway. She knew my mind was made up and if there was anything I was known for, it was stubbornness and will.

"We need to get some stuff from the hardware store, pliers, wire cutters – the really fine ones – and a craft knife or something. And drugs, bring me all the painkillers."

Obediently, she stood up and helped me back to my feet, holding her hands out cautiously as I moved back on to the sofa. I laughed to myself a little, that was karma for trying to be a little bit active, even if it was just pacing. Sarah smiled back at me, but it wasn't a genuine smile, she was unsure and frightened and I couldn't blame her for a second. If we got through this, I was going to marry this girl.

I watched her as she turned to leave, picking the keys up off of the coffee table and slowly making her way out the door. I leaned my head back into the pillows and stared at the ceiling. I was jittery, I couldn't even sit still and yet didn't dare to attempt to move around again. Tapping my feet, I waited impatiently for Sarah to return. In this day and age, when someone was waiting for something or even had a spare thirty seconds, a smartphone would be whipped out and social media sites perused. That never caught my interest and I didn't have any games on my phone. I didn't want to call or message anyone, I didn't want to pull anyone else into this and I felt like they were watching all my phone calls and messages.

Flicking the TV on I stared at the screen, it was some American sitcom that was vaguely funny but only if you were in the right mood. I watched it without really seeing it or absorbing it. I kept picturing everything in my mind and mostly it was the image of having Sarah cut into my head that was consuming me. I trusted her and hopefully, she could look at it like one of her recipes, cutting a chicken fillet or something, God knows. But she had deft hands and I trusted her not to go wrong, I had to, it was my only choice. I half wondered what the reaction of Dr Muggor would be if I called him and asked him to extract it, but I didn't have any hope in that and it would invite too many questions. The TV carried on in front of me, and I got lost in the swirling thoughts in my mind, letting them somehow meld with the background noise of the show. It felt like even one more minute was too long to wait for Sarah to get back and take this implant out.

****

By the time Sarah returned, I was going out of my head. Now I wanted it done, I wanted it done now, was the mantra going through my aching head. Over and done with, the sooner the better. It was going to hurt and it made me apprehensive, even more so when I considered the implications if it went wrong. I'm sure when it came to anything cerebral, it was easier to cause lasting or permanent damage than to fix it. She came through the door with a plastic bag full of stuff, chewing her lip deep in thought.

"OK. I have thought about it all and the most important thing for me would be to have a calm and steady mindset. So, please try not to stress me out before I do anything and not whilst I do it. I have a lot of painkillers, strongest I could get, but that won't change the fact that it will hurt. I'm scared of hurting you, Arnie."

Her bottom lip quivered at this point and I stood to comfort her, I understood where she was coming from. It wasn't a selfish thing that she was so upset to do this, it all stemmed from a concern for me, but I will admit a part of me wished for her to be a bit harder. At least she would be strong and not belie the emotion she was feeling, my own feelings were overpowering as it was. I moved her away from me and gave an chummy clap on both of her shoulders and we both shared a moment of understanding and bonding.

"Right. It's now or never, I don't know that I will have the balls to do this at any other time," I said it with a hint of humour to lighten the mood for the following events. She gave a small smirk, visibly straightened and pulled herself together and carried the bag through to the bathroom. It made sense to do this in the bath; I wasn't expecting a large amount of blood as it shouldn't be that deeply imbedded, but still, I'd rather any mess it resulted in was contained to somewhere easy to clean. I followed her, ignoring the heaviness in my footsteps. I clambered in the bath, rested the side of my head against the tub and waited with my eyes closed, willing myself to have the power to get through this without backing out. It was for the best, I chanted inwardly. I imagined Sarah was doing much the same.

"Ready?" She paused waiting for a response and when she realised I wasn't going to give one, she spoke again, "I don't know why I said that. I know you are, but not. I'm just going to do it, OK? OK. I'm just going to talk when I need to, you don't need to reply."

I could hear her muttering under her breath, then braced myself as I heard her count down three, two, one. In the first moments, it wasn't so painful, more just like intense isolated heat. Then it felt icy cold and I could picture my skin folding away neatly from the knife. My hands were clenched and my feet were almost cramping I was tensing so hard. I pulled my bottom lip between my teeth and bit down, trying to ignore it and put myself somewhere else in my mind. I heard the sound of the knife hitting something, and felt the resistance. I was already fading to somewhere else, knowing that Sarah was so close, yet she seemed a million miles away.

I lost myself and it felt almost like meditating. Scraping noises and vibrations rippled through my eardrum. I felt something panging and didn't want to think about it. The pain was like background noise, present but not my own somehow. The panging sensation increased and my vision shot blood red. I couldn't see and there was a screaming sound. My head rose and thudded against the bath side of its own accord and I heard the clattering of something metal falling to the ground. I tried to lift my head again but it was held in place, invisible hands restraining me and preventing my movements. The weight increased and before I knew it, once again I was fading into oblivion.

****

My vision focused and I was somewhere I felt I had been before although I couldn't place it at first. Lush green meadows surrounded me, rife with floral splashes of colours in the forms of daffodils, lavender and posies, I think they are called. Two buildings to my left, one a beautiful scenic cottage, the other a derelict abandoned shack. A paddock in the near distance with what looked like horses or ponies, I struggled to tell as they seemed to be like in an abstract painting. The large tree stood proud at one corner with an old-fashioned park bench tucked away at its base. The feeling of serenity soon dispersed when I realised with a jolt where I remembered this place from. This wasn't based on a memory of where I had physically been. I knew what happened here.

My heart rate accelerated and my spine tingled painfully. I made a fast decision, I would get as far away from the buildings as quickly as I could, then hopefully I wouldn't have to face what I knew lay beyond those doors of the derelict shack. I tried to walk and found unresponsive legs, however, I seemed to have the ability to float instead and concentrated on making the movement direct towards the tree. I could see a figure on the bench again, gaining more clarity the closer I got. It was small and it was with some relief I realised it was not the cloaked man, it was the boy, I must be doing this right then.

I mentally pushed harder and I kept getting closer. The boy came into full view and his angelic face screamed innocence and trust. He reached out his hands to me to come to him and I was trying to oblige. I blinked and found myself stood in front of him all of a sudden. He looked up at me imploringly and wordlessly pointed back towards the abandoned building. I followed his point and shook my head, "I will not go there or allow you to be taken there. I will do everything I can to protect you."

He looked back at me blankly and gestured again. I shook my head again, confused. His face contorted in what I thought was frustration and I half anticipated a tantrum to ensue. But the contortion rapidly went beyond a scowl and pout, his face elongated and stretched upwards until it became no more than maybe two centimetres wide and absurdly long. His mouth was open in a howl, and the noise was similar to the sound of screeching brakes on an old car. I watched in horror, motionless and unable to process what I was seeing. His body followed his face and he towered above me, like a string and in an even more surreal twist, his string-like body exploded into confetti type material that showered down over me. I tottered backwards in shock, no idea what was happening but sure it wasn't good. I knew I had to move further away. I made to move forward again and felt something like a lasso hoop around my neck and it yanked me backwards. I launched myself backwards off my feet trying to go with the movement to lessen the likelihood of my neck being snapped.

Thudding onto my back I gasped for breath and rolled instantly onto my front trying to grab the rope. There wasn't any, but even as I acknowledged this, I felt it tighten and it pulled me again with more force towards the buildings. I kicked my legs out to halt the process and realised although the noose was fastened around my neck, my breathing wasn't affected. Come to think of it, I didn't appear to be breathing at all.

I blinked and was suddenly outside the buildings, terror building up in my body trying to work out how to stop myself going in the shack. Terror turned to surprise as I was dragged to the cottage, the door stood ajar with an inviting air. The pull stopped and I managed to stand back up. I turned and looked at the cottage properly, it was exactly as I had envisioned previously. All I could see was the front room and reception area, but it looked cosy and warm like somewhere you'd visit your nan and she would be in a corner somewhere knitting with a blurry TV blaring out some game show.

Not really consciously, I went into the cottage although not minding this too much as I didn't feel at threat coming in here. The door swung gently closed behind me once I had cleared it and I looked upon a huge fireplace taking up most of the wall with red bricks surrounding it. It looked like it belonged in a rich person's mansion with a dog lounging on the mat in front of it and red leather armchair to the right laden with a tartan style throw. This one didn't have that, it had a mat, but in front of it was a plush sofa that looked like you could sink into it and willingly stay forever.

The room wasn't so big in spite of the size of the fireplace, but there was pine furniture dotted around and a doorway that led off to the right. I wandered towards it, curious as to what else lay in here, *It can be an inspiration for future home décor*, I thought, a little amused and not sure why. I went to turn the brass doorknob and it swung outwards before I had a chance. It opened into a hallway, scattered with various ornaments on tables with spindly legs and paintings of animals. It looked like a farmhouse layout. Directly in front at the end of the hall was a set of stairs and I don't know what, but something drew me towards them with the picture in my mind of finding a room with a big four-poster bed (because I'm sure a place like this would have one) and having a rest.

I walked up the stairs, comfort drawn from the creakiness indicating this house had been lived in and loved. I reached the top and rounded on to the landing, the floor was all laminated wood with a carpet runner down the centre, the colour of deep indigo. There were two doors to my left, both closed and I felt no desire to explore them. The room that was sending out a silent beacon to me was the third door up, just past a small bedside table with a wall-length mirror behind it. I headed towards it and glanced in the mirror, strangely at ease and almost enjoying this. I kind of looked like my old self, with a slight jolt I saw my hair was now black and my teeth movie star straight and white. I pulled a face at myself and found I just looked strange and didn't recognise myself nor like the changes, so I moved on, the shock not as much as it maybe should have been.

I came to the door I wanted and again, it opened of its own accord and I drifted in, the door neatly slotting back into its jamb behind me. The room was how I expected. Deep carpets lined the floor corner to corner, a warm reddish colour. The four-poster bed I had envisioned stood in the centre of the room with just the backboard touching the wall, cabinets each side. Lit candles created a serene atmosphere and I half wanted to see a woman sitting at a reception desk in the corner talking in a whispery tone that I would be seen shortly for my massage. Instead, there was a magnificent tall wardrobe, like the one you envision when reading *Narnia*. Bean bags made up the rest of the space on the rug laying before it and I wanted to jump into them but resisted.

In the far right corner sat a large bookcase stuffed with a huge variety of books, all dusty and ancient-looking. I stepped forward to inspect them, they piqued my interest. As I pulled one out of the row, dust spewed up and I coughed a little. It hung around the air and made my eyes mist. The title read, *'Psychologies and Habits of a Broken Mind'*. *Strange title for a book,* I mused. I scanned the rest and they all revolved around the theme of psychosis and mental ailments it seemed. I pulled another out, unsure of what possessed me to do so. As it came away, I heard something click and second cloud of dust rose up much thicker this time. It consumed my vision and nostrils. I batted my hands around my face trying to clear it and hit something hard.

Jolting back, confused I looked to see what I had hit. The dust dispersed a bit more and I felt my stomach drop painfully as I looked into the pitted eyes of the cloaked figure, a scarf of sorts concealing the lower half of his face. His charcoal eyes bore into mine and I stared back, in shock. He slammed one bony fist into the bookcase and they all scattered around the room with the force. He tilted his head forward towards me and it sounded like he was speaking to me. I strained to make out what he was saying.

"You cannot win this way. You know your mind. Your weaknesses. You will lose. Give in now or you will face an life of eternal pain and misery."

I was confused and stared back at him, appearances aside he now seemed more human again, actually trying to communicate with me. He didn't seem to appreciate the lack of response and he pulled down the scarf exposing pallid grey skin and a mouth like a dark cavern.

"You will lose. There is no hope. Seek yourself in the darkness and you may have some rest, but you are now doomed for always!" His voice kept rising into a shout. His cavernous mouth not forming the words properly and it bizarrely made me think of badly dubbed TV shows. I shrank back, not particularly afraid but very much not at ease. In my movement, the room shifted off-kilter and I felt myself go off balance. I put my hand out to the bookcase to steady myself and waited for my vision to right itself again. Once it had, I looked back to where he had been standing and I saw he had gone.

I looked back to the bookcase and was surprised to see it wasn't there, my hand was actually resting on the back of a chair. A chair I recognised. My tummy turned as the realisation sank in. It was Dr Smyll's chair, the one she had always sat in when we went over there. I didn't want to look but my willpower didn't hold. As I looked down, the chair slipped away from my grasp and span slowly around. Fixated, I couldn't look away. There in the seat sat the shrunken form of Dr Smyll, her skin a greenish colour now, her face resembled that of a mummy, barren eye sockets and hollowed cheekbones, mouth gaping open. Her body had disintegrated so much she looked half of what she had been before in life. My stomach churned again as I watched, her mouth started to twitch, then began popping open and closed like a fish out of water.

I heard the grinding of bones that were without the muscles and cartilage that prevented them from touching each other. A low mewling started up and I took a step back. Fear stabbed into me as her head snapped towards me as I moved and I quickly realised her unseeing eyes depended on her hearing for direction.

She tilted her skull to the side and listened for anything more and I stayed still, breath bated. It didn't work. She moved in something like snapshots. I didn't really see her move but my vision went black like blinking for a split second and she had suddenly moved, I was literally in a horror movie. I was pacing backwards faster now, but she gained on me in the flashing movements. I couldn't breathe, too scared to take my eyes from her advancing corpse.

In a heartbeat, she threw herself towards me, her hands grasping each of my shoulders with surprising strength and propelling me to the ground. She landed on me with a thud and her face was a mere few inches from mine. The stench was unbearable, and she was too strong for me to remove her, I was at her mercy. She opened her mouth again, the mewling restarted then abruptly stopped. I watched as a small patch of her cheek became shiny and wet. Before my eyes, she transformed back, from death into life. Her skin plumped up and gained a rosy hue, eyelids dropped down from the loose skin around the sockets and she blinked. When she reopened them, she had eyes again. Her hair regrew and fell around her face. She was crying now.

"Arnold, you are not too late. Don't give up hope yet. You will find the way. You will escape this. But you must know, he knows."

I drew in a deep breath again, and with a piercing scream that caused my eardrums to sting, she dissipated into nothing but dust, coating me. I relaxed my head and lay back and everything faded off and I knew this was the end of this dream and gratefully allowed it to carry me away.

****

As I came to, I groaned. My body was aching like crazy and I had a deep searing pain in the side of my head. I tenderly put my hand to it and winced. There was something rubber over what felt like a deep wound and it took a second to realise it was a plaster, and remember that Sarah had been trying to remove the implant. I looked around for her and she was sitting on the toilet seat, head in her hands and shoulders moving with a silent cry. I grumbled to get her attention, lacking the energy to form words yet. She looked up with a jump and skidded across the tiles to me and started smothering my arms and face in kisses. Her crying wasn't silent any more, she was letting out great heaving sobs. She was trying to speak but only succeeded in gasping for breath. She pushed her head into my arm that was hanging over the side of the bathtub and tried to calm herself down.

"I thought, I thought you were dead." She started up again, face crumpled and soaked with sadness. "You, you had no, no, no heartbeat, Arnie. I couldn't feel it. I thought you died!" She was completely distraught struggling to speak, and with a great deal of effort, using strength drawn completely from within I pulled myself out of the tub, more sliding and thumping ungracefully than anything else really and thudded down next to her. I put my head, the uninjured side, on her lap and she cradled me. She was saying over and over again, rocking on the spot that she thought she had killed me. All I could think about was whether or not she had gotten the implant out. I mumbled the question to her. She shook her head, looking disheartened.

"I couldn't, you blacked out and started fitting. You were shaking and thrashing around so much that I couldn't do any more. I'm so sorry, I'm so, so sorry." I stroked her leg in response and lightly shook my head, the movement making me want to vomit. It wasn't her fault. There was only one person to blame for all of this and it certainly wasn't her. I needed painkillers; I could barely see for the pulsating pain rippling through my skull. I told Sarah and she gently lay my head on a dressing gown and rushed through to the front room for a drink and pills. I lay for a couple of seconds assessing my condition. I looked up with just my eyes when I heard Sarah re-enter the room.

"What are you doing?" she asked, confused.

"What do you mean?" I was equally confused. What did she mean? I was waiting for her to come back.

"Why are you laying there again, Arnie? Is your head hurting again?" I stared blankly at her. What on earth was she talking about?

"What do you mean?" I repeated. "You went to get me some painkillers and a drink, I was waiting for you." Her face told me that what I was saying was strange.

"We did that. That was hours ago, Arnie. You took the painkillers, we sat for a while, then we watched some TV, spoke about what we would do next. Then I went to make us coffee and you wandered off. I thought you were going to the bathroom. Don't you remember?"

Frustration bubbled up inside of me, ready to erupt and overflow like an active volcano. No, I didn't remember and now thinking about it although present, the pain in my head was largely numbed. I sat upright and tried to control myself, I wanted to scream and lash out. At this moment, I just didn't understand anything. It was all failing so miserably. We had a small moment where I felt like it could start to improve and now it seemed to be getting worse again.

I thought back to the nightmare I had whilst unconscious in the bath, the cloaked evil version of me trying to talk to me, like a warning, but not quite, and Dr Smyll. And the boy. I almost forgot about him. It didn't seem like a good sign that he exploded in front of my very eyes, but seemed to fit with the way things were going. I felt like I was losing and my entire brain was clearly aware of it. I ran through the whole dream with as much detail as I could remember, and Sarah sat cross-legged on the floor in front of me, patiently listening and taking it all in. She reacted strongly when I told her about Dr Smyll making an appearance. Perhaps for that part alone it was a good thing we couldn't watch this back. When I was finished, she started talking straight away.

"I think you are right. The boy going is not a good sign. Dr Smyll telling you that you will be alright and get through it but warning you he knows, that must be about Dr Muggor. The cloaked man was telling you he was winning, I think, but not in a good way, he is a part of your subconscious and will be aware that if you lose yourself completely, even his personality won't be able to have any control over you or your mind. It would be easier if we could still access the database with the visions on it, then we can look properly. And what does Dr Muggor know? Everything?" She gasped and a hand came up to her mouth. "We can't access the database, but he can. He will now if he didn't before! He knows what you see and hear. So, even things he can't see outside of the visions and blackouts will sometimes show up in them and he will see them and know something more."

She started to look panicked, overwhelmed. I felt it too. I hadn't thought of it like that. Dismay coursed through me. I just looked at Sarah, feeling the full weight of my emotions heavy on my face. I didn't need to say it for her to recognise I felt hopeless. She skirted over to me and looked deeply into my eyes.

"The only way we can do this is if you have faith, you need your strength. We are not giving up. We can't. I can't lose you." I nodded in response although not really feeling it. I imagine she knew this but took it as a better sign than me crumpling and giving in. I held my hand out to her for her to take to glean some comfort of sorts.

A bolt of fear shot through me when I saw my hand was mangled. Bone and sinew bared and the skin torn off hanging down over my wrist. It looked like some gory prop from a horror movie. With a blink, it passed and I shook the image from my mind again. I couldn't do this. I knew I couldn't. I couldn't live in this state any more. What was little over a week felt like a lifetime and I couldn't do another one. Sarah said she couldn't lose me, but in reality, I think that she would be better off without me, without all this. This was a burden no human should have to take on or feel obliged to. I was losing it more with every passing 'attack' and didn't know when I would have one that would send me completely over the edge, it now felt more so than ever that I was losing my grip on reality.

Sarah took my hand and caressed my palm, a frown lining her brow. I was just glad she couldn't hear my thoughts or she would have dismissed them and I know it. I didn't need to be argued with about how I felt, I felt an odd sense of inner peace as I came to my conclusion.

"Do you know what I think I need right now?" I asked, letting my tone almost sound carefree.

"What? I'll get it just tell me."

"I would love to have a curry. I am so hungry; I haven't eaten much lately. I don't want to think about any of this right now. I need some time where I can relax and hopefully not have any crazy hallucinations or blackouts. I don't want to leave the house though. Can you get us one?" she frowned again ever so slightly.

"We can order in if you want? You should have the take-out menu in one of your kitchen drawers."

"No, I don't want to eat from that place. I want it from the Taj Mahal place in the centre of town. They don't deliver to here."

"I know you are having a hard time, but can't we just get one from the one we usually do, it is lovely there and easier?" She could've been pouting with the tone she had. I knew I was being pushy and probably sounded out of line, but I wanted her out of the way for a while.

"Please, Sarah, I just fancy something a bit different to what we usually have. It's just this once. Can you do it for me?" I hated to say it like that, being the needy boyfriend who made someone feel like they had to do something out of obligation through being with you. I knew it wasn't in my character, as did Sarah, but what worked in my favour was the fact that I had not been myself lately and my character was questionable at any given moment. She bowed her head slightly, almost in defeat and I felt bad but stood my ground. It was all for the greater good, I told myself. She asked what I wanted and stood to go. I called her as she got to the door and she turned to look at me.

"I love you, Sarah." My heart warmed as I saw the side of her mouth twitch upwards and her eyes softened. She nodded at me.

"I know, Arnie." I let out a little laugh, nervous laughter maybe, I don't know. And with that, she left pulling the door to behind her. As soon as I was sure she was gone, I sprung up. She should be gone for at least an hour, which wasn't a lot of time if I dawdled. I wasn't going to be dramatic and leave a note. It was pretty obvious why I was doing what I was doing. Grabbing a glass from the counter in the kitchen, I filled it to the brim with water. Shaking my head, I emptied it into the sink and opened the cupboard next to the fridge. I had something better in mind.

Pulling out a bottle of whiskey, I poured it into the glass, my last drink should be a good one. Fetching the packets of painkillers, I took myself through to the living room and locked the front door, sliding the lock across so Sarah couldn't get back in. I calmly walked back to the sofa and took my seat. My final place of rest. I didn't feel afraid, just accepting and ready. Popping open the wrappers, I counted out fifteen. That should be plenty. I looked at the label, Paracetamol, 1000g. Yes, that should be plenty. I sniffed my drink and swirled it a little appreciating the way the amber liquid span and centred into a whirlpool.

Flicking on the TV, I tuned into the Discovery Channel, I could drift off with a bit of David Attenborough, there were worse ways to go. Settling into the cushions, I span sideways and propped my feet up. I closed my eyes for a brief second, allowing myself a reflective moment and again felt the wash of calmness and surety that I was doing what needed to be done come over me. I decided there was no point in delaying any further and took the first three pills at once, washing it down with a healthy sized chug. The whisky scorched my throat and I let out a little burp. I took them in threes until they were gone. Doubt niggled me, not at what I had just done, but if I had taken enough. I took another five to round it up to twenty. Twenty thousand milligrams of Paracetamol. Soon I would be asleep, but really asleep with no nightmares to haunt me. Free. As a result, it would relieve Sarah too. It may not take away what happened to Dr Smyll, but it avoided anyone else who tried to help me meet the same fate. Fate. The word stuck in my mind. Why? Fate. There it was again, lighting up like a Christmas tree, so luminous I could literally see it in my mind. What about the fate of others? If I died, Dr Muggor would simply seek another person. Then they would go through all of this. Damn it, I didn't care. I had paid my dues. But I did, I did care.

Panic struck me now. Shit. Is this what people normally did when they wanted to top themselves? Is this the doubt they suddenly have when they change their minds? I doubt it, mine was a bit more than that, I think. If I went, I actually risked more people's lives and wellbeing. When people get stuck with doubts pre suicide, I assume it was only really relating to the fact they wanted to live in the end. Most people did it as a cry for help, in fact, praying someone would come to their rescue at the very last minute. I wouldn't have that. I still had at least 45 minutes until Sarah would return. Sarah. She could do it. I will go now and she can get Dr Muggor arrested because they will do a post-mortem on me and find the implant.

My panic subsided and I returned to a state of calm. It would all be OK, I didn't need to be here. My happy state didn't last long. I felt acid bubbling up in my stomach and it crept up my throat. I grabbed at my throat trying to stop it. My stomach started to seize and I doubled over and a fizzing sensation started in my extremities and grew into a burning that spread down my arms and up my legs, I felt sure that although I couldn't see it there was a fire coursing all over my body. I screamed out in agony; my head pressurised to the point I thought it would split in two. The pain increased exponentially and I passed out from the sheer intensity of it, the blackness swamped my vision and my last thought was I was glad that it was finally over.

****

A distant beeping sound roused me into a semi-conscious state that highlighted to me a deep pain in my stomach and skull. A bright light was beaming into my eyes, my eyelids being prised open by someone I couldn't see outside of the offensive glare. I heard a clicking sound and some murmuring. I squinted my eyes, pupils burning. As they adjusted, I was swamped with a feeling of déjà vu. I was back in the hospital bed and could feel something rubbing against my hand. Turning my head, I looked at who it was and for a moment didn't recognise her. Sarah was sitting on the bed next to me, her tear-streaked face downturned and hair knotted up into a bun on the top of her head. She looked up when I twitched my finger. I didn't know why I was here, I couldn't remember.

For a strangely blissful minute or so I allowed myself to imagine that the last thing that had happened was I was on the bridge heading to get some lunch and had a fall. Nothing happened since then. A man could dream, couldn't he? But I knew better really. Little bits of the puzzle clicked into place and I remembered sitting on my sofa, drinking my whiskey, downing the tablets. The intense pain, ironic really, painkillers causing that. I felt disappointed, I failed even at that. How did she even get back and into my flat in time? Sarah was shaking her head at me, bottom lip sucked between her teeth trying to contain an emotional outburst at me. She had every right to be angry, but she should also understand. I think it was a sense of understanding that was stopping her from losing her temper with me. I cleared my throat to see if I could speak and found something blocking it. I started to choke and Sarah's eyes widened and she shot up to her feet.

"Excuse me!" She was waving her hands and calling out of the open door at people passing outside the room. "Please! He is trying to speak! He is choking!" I heard a maniacal beeping start from the machinery to my right, my heart rate accelerating. A nurse came rushing into the room and pressed a few buttons calmly but at no slow pace. Then she lifted my arm and slotted a needle into an IV and I drifted off again.

****

This time around, I came to with more sense to my whereabouts and didn't feel so confused. I had no idea how long the nurse had knocked me out for. I reached up to my mouth to feel the tube that had choked me before and felt it had gone. Sarah was asleep in the armchair next to the bed, curled up in a ball with a wiry moth-eaten blanket covering her legs. I didn't want to wake her, so I tried to prop myself up a little, my lower back muscles felt like they were in spasm. My body groaned with the effort and I grunted. Sarah woke up with a start and moved over to help me, not even slightly awake. She pushed the pillow further down my back and found the remote for the bed. With a couple of clicks, I was sitting upright and more comfortably. She groggily blinked her eyes and rubbed her face forcing herself back into wakefulness.

"Arnie, what are you doing to me?" She gave me a small smile, "I'm going to have start dying my hair all the greys you're giving me!"

I laughed a little, appreciating the attempt at levity. But the small high didn't last very long, "Seriously, Arnie, what did you think you were doing? This isn't the way. If you had succeeded in committing suicide, Dr Muggor would have gotten away with all of this and found someone new."

I shook my head, feeling my eyes bouncing in their sockets and explained to her my thought process, about how the post mortem would have solved it all. She looked sadly back at me.

"You know they don't do post mortems unless it is under suspicious circumstances. You were sat with half a pint of whiskey and an empty packet of pills. It was pretty obvious that it was your doing." Again, bubbles of frustration climbed up inside of me. "The take-out place was closed, so I turned around and came back and couldn't get in, then I realised something was really wrong. So, I knocked on your neighbours' door and they gave me the spare key. We were almost too late." I had forgotten I'd given a spare key to Mrs Tempera when I went on holiday a while back, she looked after my place and an old plant she had gifted me, long dead now, not that she had to know.

Now in the cold light of day, I could see that it wasn't the best way out, just the easiest. For me and me alone. They do say suicide is a selfish act and they are not wrong. You can justify to yourself at the time that it will benefit everyone, but I read a saying once which seemed pretty apt to me now, 'Suicide doesn't take the pain away, it just passes it to someone else.' Still, I was adult enough to admit a bit of me still wished I had succeeded. We sat and spoke about it for a little while and only stopped when a painful grumbling started up in my stomach. I wasn't allowed to leave the room until a psychologist had been in to see me, so Sarah offered to run down to the cafeteria on the proviso that I didn't attempt anything foolish. I had had my moment, I didn't intend to repeat it. She left the room and I sat and mulled over my thoughts. I was oddly relaxed, all things considered.

I hadn't had any mad moments since coming round and I didn't know if that was down to me being in here. I had thought that somehow Dr Muggor was controlling that in some way, but he wouldn't know I was here, would he? If he did, it would make sense to not cause me any hallucinations or effects and with that thought came tumbling despair again. I sank deeper into the pillows and for what seemed like the millionth time tried to find away from all of this.

My brain scanning was brought to a halt by a short man entering the room, clearing his throat and absentmindedly tapping the orange clipboard in his hand.

He introduced himself as Dr Mercer, my in-house psychologist. With a wry grin, he told me not to worry, it was just routine. As it was my first attempt (and presumably last, he added with another upwards flick with the corner of his mouth), he just wanted to ask a few questions and he would leave me to rest. I nodded my consent and kept in my mind to not say much for fear of drawing him into this mess that had become my life.

"First things first, do you have a history of depression?" I shook my head in response. No need to indulge anything there.

"Good, can you tell me the events that led you to believe that suicide would be your only option?" It didn't sound so much of a question as a demand. I took a deep breath and started to speak.

"Well, I hate my job and don't know how to find anything else." He nodded knowingly at me. "Me and my girlfriend have been having a lot of arguments recently and I think we are close to breaking up." The nodding increased and he scribbled on his notepad. "Then I had a tumble and hurt my head," I gestured to my injury, "And nothing felt like it was going right. I was so unhappy, I felt like a failure. So, I decided that it would just be simpler to not have to deal with any of it at all."

Dr Mercer's nodding was almost enthusiastic, he was probably over the moon that I was such a textbook case. He spoke to me again, "Right, I can understand all of that, it is a lot to be going through at once. I see you were admitted recently, I assume that was for that?" He pointed the nib of his pen at my head and I mirrored his nodding from earlier. "OK and do you still feel this way inclined now you know the implications of such an action? I see your girlfriend was very distraught and you don't seem to be ready to jump any time soon. If it is of any use to you, I don't think she will be leaving you. She clearly loves you a great deal. Let's make a deal amongst men, shall we?" I felt one of my eyebrows shoot up, questioningly. What kind of psycho-babble method was this? "You give me your word that you will change your career path to something you enjoy more, spend more time with your family and girlfriend and be patient with your healing time. We all get injuries, it isn't just you. You are not the only person in the world to feel like you are suffering." Was this supposed to be helping me? I didn't want to point out the fact that actually, I was pretty sure I could be the only person in the world going through what I was, but that would be giving up information that I couldn't share.

"Yes, Dr Mercer, it was a moment of weakness on my part. And frankly, the pain of the overdose was more than the pain of life." There, that should do it. He looked at me for a second more, assessing. It was a winning statement, his mouth quirked and he nodded and said goodbye, stating he hoped he never had the need to see me again. Once he had gone, I mused over his method, not comforting but blunt and I imagined that had more of an impact on people than being mollycoddled. I quite liked him, actually.

Sarah came back in the room a couple of minutes later brandishing sandwiches and crisps and two piping hot cups full of the swill they call coffee. The machine stuff was never good, but passable when you needed a caffeine hit. I thanked her and broke into the cellophane wrappers, cheese and ham sandwiches, gourmet grub. Tasteless and I imagine lacking in any sort of nutrition but it was food nonetheless. Sarah just nibbled at hers, without any appetite. When she put it back in the package, half-eaten, I took it from her and ate that too. She wasn't paying much attention, seemingly off in her own world.

"What are you thinking about?" I asked.

"What we are going to do? I think we need to confront Dr Muggor. Maybe if we threaten him with going to the police or exposing him to the medical world, he will stop?" I didn't know. Maybe it was plausible, especially the part about exposing him to the medical world. They were a group more likely to listen to what we had to say and if, like Dr Smyll, they had heard of him and his previous antics, they were also more likely to believe us and help. Bringing one person into the mix was dangerous, but he couldn't clear out a whole bunch of them surely. There was more strength in numbers.

Revitalised, I pushed myself further up and voiced my thoughts to Sarah, who looked wary but on board. My time of weakness was over, I needed to stand and fight and if I couldn't get this implant out I would damn well make sure Dr Muggor did. Feeling like I didn't want to be here anymore, I started to put my legs over the side of the bed just as the nurse came wandering in for check-in. She hurried over and scowled at Sarah for not stopping me, who merely threw her hands up in mock abandonment. The nurse's jowls wobbled in annoyance and she directed it at me.

"What do you think you are doing? You need to rest."

"I want to leave; I want to discharge myself. The psychologist said I was fine and not a risk. Did he not relay this to you?" With a small pout, she lifted the sheet of paper on the orange clipboard that he had left at the end of my bed.

"Fine, so I need to make sure you are of sound mind to make this decision."
She turned to face Sarah, "Will he be under your care once you leave the premises?"

"Yes, he will, we will go home and I will make sure he drinks plenty of fluid and remains in his bed for the time being until I deem him adult and human enough to make the decision for himself to be allowed to leave it." Her tone dripped sarcasm, she clearly hadn't taken a liking to the nurse, I couldn't blame her, she wasn't the friendliest. The nurse huffed in response.

"Very well." She then busiest herself removing the IV drip and disconnecting the various medical equipment and once done told me I was free to go once I had signed the form. I did so and she left. Sarah giggled to herself and I frowned at her.

"That wasn't very nice, she was just doing her job, Sarah." I scolded.

"I know, but don't do the job if you are going to be snotty with patients or their 'carers'," she retorted. I shrugged back at her. Fair point.

****

We gathered our stuff and slowly walked down the hallway; my body not quite ready for any fast movements. We nodded our thanks at the reception desk in true English fashion and exited into the street, just barely missing a small figure who hurried past with a large black coat and face concealed by a baggy hood. I shook my head in annoyance at the rudeness of some people. We meandered, hand in hand, just heading in the vague direction of my place. The chill in the air gave me a new sense of alertness and I felt like I could see and feel everything. We were passing a small lot to our right, the chain link fence on its perimeter had seen better days.

A small movement by the side of a skip inside the lot caught my eye. In that second, my mind shot back to the small figure who practically barged us out of their way and a very delayed recognition shot through me. I had seen that coat, with the hood pulled over in that same fashion before. Surely what I was thinking was not right, my mind had to be playing tricks on me again. There was surely no way they could have known I was in the hospital, I hadn't had any episodes in there and my phone wasn't with me. But the thought persisted. I stopped and stared where I thought I saw the movement. If the person in the hospital was who I thought it was, then this could only be the other one of the pair. I know I wanted to speak to him and confront him, but I didn't have the strength, nor knowledge of what I would say yet. Whatever it was, I couldn't see it anymore. I thought I had seen the figure of a man run behind the skip as we approached. Sarah nudged my side, staring in the same place as me. She kept her face still, muscles barely moving and spoke in a way that I could only hear and see.

"I saw it too, Arnie. It isn't you if that is what you were wondering. I think we need to get out of here, I have a bad feeling." Almost theatrically, I turned to face her, gave her a big kiss and threw one hand up.

"My mind is playing those tricks on me again, always seeing things, let's go home and rest," I said it loud enough that it could be overheard if Dr Muggor was there within earshot. If that had been Steph, aka Jane, going into the hospital, it will have been to scout for information and see what happened and what had been said.

I turned on my heel again and Sarah followed suit. A small bout of adrenaline spiked with fear coursed through me and gave me more energy and numbed the deadened feeling in my limbs. We picked up the pace and strode along. Every now and then I would stop, feigning a cough or head pain and bend or lean against a wall, using the opportunity to glance behind us. We didn't really speak, paranoia keeping our mouths shut until we knew we couldn't be overheard by anyone. I hadn't seen anyone tailing us but that didn't mean they weren't there hiding behind some corner. It seemed excessive even to my own ears, but I didn't know which way was up anymore. We kept walking until we rounded on to my street and stood in front of my door. We hadn't been walking fast but I was short of breath, vision getting spotty. I scrambled in my pockets to get my keys out and fumbled with them in the lock. I started to push the door open and pulled my hand back abruptly when it melted through the wooden panel.

"Ha!" I jumped. Looking to my right, there was no one there. Shit, I had to get it together. My hand seemed to have reformed, so I pushed the door again and walked through. Something hindered my steps and I looked down, confusion pumped through me when I saw my legs seemed to have fused above the knees, leaving just enough room at the bottom that I could waddle, like a penguin. I patted them and watched the fabric fall apart under my touch and my legs separated again. I clapped my hands, hoping the shock of the noise would stop this medley of hallucinations. I knew that was what they were, but it was terrifying nonetheless.

Sarah was pulling my forearm and I followed her, now closing my eyes so no visions could halt my progress further. She led me to my front door and took my keys that were still clasped in my hand. She took me in and sat me down, only then did I dare to open my eyes again. A small sigh of relief came out involuntarily when I saw that everything looked normal again. Sarah was keeping an eye on me as she moved around, poking her head out of the kitchen window every minute or so whilst she made drinks. When she came back through, she picked up her laptop and fired it up.

"I am going to find who was in the same classes or year as Dr Smyll and Dr Muggor. Then we can find a list of names of people we can contact if we need to. We need ammunition when we speak to Dr Muggor and this will be some." I nodded at her. I was drained again and I reflected once again on how lucky I was that Sarah was helping me and sticking by my side for all of this. I truly couldn't have gotten this far without her.

"Do you remember if Dr Smyll ever said what years she was in medical school?" I shook my head, I had no idea, it had never been mentioned as far as I could remember, not really something we would have discussed.

"Why don't you look up her credentials on there, there must be a medical database somewhere that we can see and it should have at least a graduating year. Otherwise, you could ask your sister?" Sarah shook her head at me.

"I won't bring anyone else into this, but finding a graduation year is just as good." She set to work, typing away with me just watching over her shoulder, seeing if there was anything I spotted that she may have missed. After a while, she came across a page, which was actually dedicated to Dr Smyll herself and her services. See, this is where paying for advertisement services comes in handy, this page should have been one of the first ones we found when we typed her name into the search engine.

Scrolling to the bottom of the page and neatly avoiding studying the photo of her smiling out at us we found what we were looking for. There was her graduating class and year with the name of the school too, plus all the follow-up courses and qualifications she had to her name. She had been a busy lady by the looks of it. We wrote down all the information we could and then looked up the graduating class in the search engine. A list of names came up and we jotted each one down. All of these doctors should have some recollection of Dr Muggor if the rumours that Dr Smyll had told us were true.

Feeling positive, we then started to construct a plan for how and when we would speak to Dr Muggor and tried to think about each outcome that could happen and what we would do. After what felt like many hours, we felt we had done as much as we could and decided to settle for the evening. Bodies heavy and tired, we plodded through to the bedroom, the suicide attempt feeling like a million years ago, and laid down in the sheets. It didn't take us long, I heard Sarah's breathing deepen beside me and very shortly after mine matched hers and I fell into a deep slumber.

****

I was running, legs pounding down onto the concrete below me, pains tearing through the soles of my bare feet as small stones and rubble skidded underfoot. I didn't know where I was running to, nor what I was running from. But I had no control over the motion and could only pump my arms to keep my balance and try to inhale enough oxygen to stay conscious with the panting that I was doing. Everything around me was dreary and dark, ominous clouds loomed low in the sky threatening me with their icy cold contents. Darkened buildings created shadows that crisscrossed in front of me. Every shadow I ran through, I felt the temperature drop a little giving me goosebumps up my arms and legs. I felt it before I saw it, a huge rock in the middle of the road that seemed to appear from thin air. I smashed into it with full power, shins splintering with the impact. I propelled over the top of it and thudded neatly onto my back the other side. Winded, I was glad of the respite from the running.

Something jagged was digging into my ribcage and I rolled myself away from it. Taking in my surroundings, I noted I had fallen into a crater of some sort, like a really big pothole longer and wider than my entire body. On all fours, I started to crawl out of the pit. As I reached the edge, I felt the ground below my knees start to give way, in slow motion at first. Then like a landslide, it picked up speed and the stones started to slide backwards away from me. I grabbed for the edge more frantically after seeing in my peripheral the hole getting deeper and darker behind me. I made it by my fingertips and by this point, my body was extended backwards with my feet dangling over an abyss. Panic pulsing through my veins, I clenched to what little surface I could, feeling the skin of my fingertips ripping.

Just when I thought I couldn't hold any longer, two hands reached down and clasped around my wrists. Gratefully, I let go and turned my own to grip onto theirs. Not caring who it was, just knowing that they had just saved me made me like them automatically. I was hauled up over the edge and rolled over three times away from it to be certain I wasn't at imminent risk of falling again. I sat upright and looked for my saviour, but there was no one here, just the same dusty landscape that I had been running through. I scoured the area with my eyes and saw nothing moving, the odd flickering in a dark window on the surrounding buildings, but I put that down to my eyes playing tricks on me. There was no way that anyone could have got into one of those buildings and climbed several floors in the time it took for me to sit up.

Shaking my head to myself I rose to my feet, my shattered shins forgotten. I peered over the side of the pothole I had been in and watched a few pebbles fall down it. A sense of vertigo threatened to unbalance me and I tensed my legs to reassure myself that I was standing upright. The hole had now become bottomless it seemed and reminded me of the one I had envisioned when I read the story of *Alice in Wonderland* as a child. It was wide and unforgiving and I absently wondered if it reached all the way through to the other side of the world.

As the thought formulated in my mind, I felt something tickling the top of my neck. I swung my head around feeling the presence of something bad. I didn't get to turn all the way around when I heard the voice of Dr Muggor bellowing, "You don't have to wonder such things, my boy!" and I was shoved roughly in the back, sending me careening over the edge, arms and legs flailing for purchase.

I was now falling. The further down I got, the wider the hole became. Strangely, I could still see, the pitch blackness that I had looked down into was now just a dark brown colour and I could make out all the marks on the walls but still could not see an end to the pit below me. I was screaming, high pitched and terrified. I don't know how long was falling for when I realised I couldn't scream anymore, in fact, I had ceased to without realising. I was falling in silence with my mouth open in a soundless shout, just an utter terror encompassing me, waiting for the end.

Shortly, what could have been twenty seconds or thirty minutes later, I don't know but it was long enough for some of my intense fear to abate, I noticed a very dim light was feebly flickering away somewhere below me. I moved to face my belly to earth and stared at it. As I watched, it increased in strength and I had a strange thought about how nice it was. The realisation then hit me that if that light was getting bigger and brighter, I was actually reaching the bottom. The fear that had faded off now came back full force and I started frantically waving my arms around again, not sure what good it would do but felt like I had to do something.

With nothing more than a blink, I suddenly touched down on the ground, featherlike. I felt completely disorientated. The source of the light I had seen was coming from an old lamppost, rusty and black with the little windows, like from an old street. I appreciated its beauty for a moment and reflected on how bland our streetlights were nowadays, grey, tall and nothing great to look at. We used to take such effort in creating attractive towns, now it was all commercial and industrial. There was only one direction I could go from this clearing and it led straight down a dankly lit tunnel. Old fairy lights lined the walls, dim and cloudy with age. It looked like an old mine shaft. I could hear a clanking coming from somewhere down there and for no reason other than curiosity headed in its direction, pulled like a moth to a flame.

Gravel crunched with every step I took and the closer I got, the more aware I was that I should probably be a bit quieter. Instinct told me that I didn't want to alert anyone to my presence. I thought about what the noise could be and found myself slowing down. What if it was something waiting for me? They knew I was here, of course they did, I was pushed down here. I felt certain that the voice that had shouted at me was Dr Muggor's. I thought about what Dr Smyll had said to me, her words were that he knew. Or it could even be the cloaked evil version of me. I felt a small pang of hope when I thought it could be the little boy, that all hope was not lost and he hadn't completely vanished since our last explosive encounter.

A low humming noise started up close by just around the bend, I could see an amber light glowing up the wall in front of me. The humming was coming from a male, it sounded like, and the tune was one I could place in a childhood memory, a nursery song perhaps but I couldn't think which. I reached the turning and hung back for a moment. There was nowhere else to go, I had no choice but to carry on or remain in limbo and for some reason I couldn't do the latter. The humming was louder now, the person singing wasn't that far away. I was toying with the idea of heading back to the clearing when a voice carried over to me.

"Arnold, why so hesitant? Accept what must be accepted. Embrace what must be embraced. You still believe you are your own being…" I was shrinking back, but the knowledge that I was trapped down here acted like concrete in my feet. I heard crunching and the shadow cut through the amber glow. Then in front of me stood Dr Muggor. He was wearing a medical robe and had the instrument that listens to your heart wrapped around his neck, stethoscope, I think? Not that it was relevant. He even had a small clipboard clipped to his pocket, like he was ready to go and do rounds at the hospital. He looked like the first time I saw him, together and neat. His twitchy persona was now that of a confident man, standing tall before me, exuding power.

He spoke again. "You still believe you are your own Arnold, but you are not. You are mine now." I shook my head at him, reminding myself that this wasn't reality, although it felt like it. This gave me more strength and backbone.

"No, I am not. I am not yours. You will leave me and everyone else alone. You are twisted. What do you even want?"

"What do I want?" His eyebrows wiggled at me and his mouth twitched. "I will have my own following. I will be able to create an…" he paused thinking, "army, yes, an army. Think about it. If everyone is willing to do exactly as you command, without whining or having 'rights'," he emphasised by doing the quote marks with his fingers, "we can have something that can best be described as human robots. It is a perfect system, a perfect world. Our society would change for the better with those in power being able to actually control the masses and not have to deal with such nonsense as civil unrest and uprisings. It is for the greater good."

I didn't know what to say, I was aghast. My mouth was hanging open in surprise. This wasn't just a few people he was talking about controlling but thousands, hundreds of thousands even. "All I have to do is break the spirit of people and with carefully measured electronic pulses directed into the correct nodes of the brain, I become their brains for them. I control what they think, see, how they behave."

"That is just wrong!" I shouted. "You can't do this, you won't get away with it."

"That, my boy, is where you are wrong. How do you think I am here with you now? You think this is your dream? You think that anything you have been seeing has been a vision of your own making?" I was confused, he sensed it and continued, clearly proud of his work. "I fabricated all that you see, right now, all the visions have been experiments to see, which you react to most strongly, which are the best to break your mental strength. I have to give you credit; you are not an easy one, your own memories and underlying problems have certainly contributed at times to your visions. The implant in your head is a cleverly manufactured device that sends the small electronic pulses that I mentioned before, it transmits them to the right places causing certain hormone levels to increase and decrease resulting in your mind entering a very vulnerable state, which I then intercept. On the odd occasion, I have to inject a small dose of lubrication to the implant to prevent your skin from rejecting it and pushing it out." So, that was what those sharps pains had been when he was inspecting the injury site. "But with time, I will find a way around that where such a hands-on approach won't be necessary." He laughed suddenly and I jumped. "You wouldn't believe the excitement I felt when I thought you saw me putting the needle back in my pocket the last time!" He laughed again, high pitched and cutting. This man was truly a lunatic.

"I will tell people. I will let them know what you have been doing. They will stop you, even if I can't on my own." His pealing laughter increased and he grabbed his stomach in an elaborate show of how funny he was finding this.

"No, you won't." The laughter abruptly stopped and his face grew serious. Dark. He bowed his forehead closer to mine and grabbed my chin with his hand so I couldn't look away. "All it would take is a small press of a button, Arnold Shack. And your life, everything you have and ever were, could be, will be erased. It is more effective than the electric chair, you see?"

He tugged hard and my body followed my head, round the corner. There was a chair in the centre of what could only be described as a cavern. A single wide metal table sat against the wall. The chair was the same as the one in his office and there was a person sitting on it, a young man who, as my eyes adjusted to the brighter light in here, was a spitting image of me. He was strapped down so he couldn't escape. Tears streaked his face and he looked at me with a pleading look in his eyes. He had been gagged as well, so he couldn't speak to me. I looked again and saw the little scar on the cheek and sickness threatened me when I saw that it was actually me, I was looking at myself.

"What do you think? This Arnold wants to tell people what we are doing here before we are ready for the world to know. Shall we show him what happens?" he spoke in a singsong voice. This was all a game to him. The other me was shaking his head frantically in the chair, he didn't have to speak for me to hear him begging. His voice seemed to penetrate my brain telepathically.

"Don't! Please! Please stop him, don't tell anyone. Submit and it will all be over! Living under control is better than dying like this!" I wondered briefly if I believed that but not for long as I couldn't handle the idea of seeing anyone hurting like this, it was more terrifying when you were watching yourself. I looked to Dr Muggor, who was watching me expectantly, his eyes burning into me with a manic glint.

"Leave him, please," I begged, voice barely above a whisper. Dr Muggor wagged his finger in front of my face, shaking his head with the motion. He turned away from me and I leapt forward to the side of the other version of me strapped into the chair.

Before I had even touched any of the restraints, I heard Dr Muggor clearing his throat behind me. I looked to him and he was holding his laptop and with his index finger, tapped the enter key, then a large smile erupted onto his face and he gestured with his head to look at the man in the chair. I didn't want to but had to, I looked to him. His eyes suddenly glazed over and his back arched, restraints barely holding him. Saliva speckled with blood started to trickle out of the side of his mouth and with his head thrown back, I could see all the veins in his neck fighting to break loose of his skin, deep purple and blue they pushed outwards forced by an invisible pressure. His legs bent at an impossible angle and I watched in horror as his unseeing eyes flooded with blood and they overflowed down his cheeks congealing with the tears. With a hard jolt his body slumped, the fight finished. My shoulders weak, my head bowed, I looked back at Dr Muggor, who was observing like it was nothing more than a daytime show to pass the time, he almost looked disinterested. I couldn't find my words.

"Is he…" I managed to mumble.

"Dead? Yes." I held back a cry, I was at his mercy. "Time to go, Arnold. Bye-bye." The last thing I saw was him giving a childlike wave of his hand and the room faded into darkness.

****

The darkness lifted surreally and with some confusion, I realised I was at home in bed. What had now become normality for me was waking up with sweat-drenched sheets, but normal or not, it wasn't welcome. I peeled the sheet away from my legs and sat upright, cradling my aching skull in my hands. It all went far deeper than we had ever imagined and although just yesterday I was prepared to take my own life, the threat of him taking it from me in such a brutal way terrified me. I didn't want to die now. I had had the shock I needed to stop me feeling like that. In spite of the threat he made making me watch my own graphic demise, it only fed my desire to crush him into the ground. I wanted to watch his life force seeping away from him for all the hurt and damage he had inflicted on people in his insane attempt to control them. It was essentially killing a person, their very being but leaving the vessel that carried them live to carry out his bidding.

I wondered where he was. I wondered if what I had dreamed was actually him talking to me or if it was my imagination. I couldn't discern between the two anymore. If I had imagined it all inside my head, then it shouldn't be too much of an issue, however, he could watch it all back and I imagine he already had. So, that idea went out of the window anyway, that dream gave everything away even if he hadn't actually projected himself into it. There was also the element that he gave a lot of information, information that I was certain that I wouldn't have had buried in the back of my mind. I was just talking myself in and out of it, not sure. I settled on the idea that he had actually been present in my dream, it made more sense, even though in reality none of it did. From the very outset, this whole thing sounded like a bad story, not believable even to me, who was going through it first-hand.

Sarah stirred behind me and sidled over next to me, yawning as she did so. It caught on like a virus and I joined her, the big gulp of air expanding my lungs and relaxing my tensed body just a little. She rubbed my back and asked what it was, why was I so tense, well, outside of the obvious. I started to tell her about the nightmare, vision, hallucination, whatever it may be called, trying not to leave out any detail. Even though dream Dr Muggor had told me it was all of his making, I didn't want to miss anything out in case it should be significant at some point and I forgot it. At some point whilst I was talking, Sarah took my hand and moved it onto her leg and put her own hand firmly atop of it. She didn't interrupt, so I kept talking. By the end of it, I was in tears and emotionally exhausted. Concern was written all over her face and before saying anything else, she lifted my hand that she had moved earlier and showed it to me. It had scores and scratch marks all over it tracing up my arm.

"What was that from?" I asked her, her lips pursed at me and her eyes grew sadder and more concerned.

"You did that whilst you were talking to me, I didn't think you had realised, so I stopped you. Talking about it was stressing you out even more. It is a sort of tick, my cousin used to scratch himself without realising any time he was under stress."

I felt myself lose grip a bit, my head was washing with a multitude of thoughts and feelings. I was almost sick of thinking about how tired I was of all of this, the fear, sadness, anger, loss and utter dismay. I wished I could go back to the day it all happened and just sit in my dingy little cubicle in the office, drinking the putrid piss water they call tea and lose myself in the mindlessness of television shows and pub banter and not have gone out and over that damn bridge that day. I never even found out what happened to that boy, nor did anyone ever follow up with me about the thugs, just yet another event in this society where they didn't have the time to deal with what they would deem a trivial matter.

I voiced my thoughts to Sarah, who nodded sagely back at me and mumbled, "I know, me too." I had to come up with another plan, a way to handle this in a way that Dr Muggor and Steph wouldn't know what I was doing. But the slight glitches in my mind were coming and going so frequently now, even just little things like the impression of something zooming in or volumes increasing and decreasing, that if they could see everything whilst I was having them, they could see and hear just about everything going on now. But could they hear my thoughts? Was that crazy and a step too far to think that?

"No, that's not crazy, I mean, all of this is out of this world, insane, but in light of everything that doesn't seem at all far-fetched to me now." I jumped, I hadn't realised I'd spoken aloud. But it helped to hear some reassurance that she thought it could be possible too. I shook it off. "Look, we need to work out a way to communicate outside of these times when you are having a 'hormonal imbalance'." She paused and frowned at me. "But, I have to grant, it is scary how they are controlling the chemicals in your brain by sending electrical pulses. Scary, but damn clever." I nodded back at her, there was no denying that fact. If it wasn't happening to me and not for such dark purposes, I would have congratulated the person who had managed such a feat. "How are you feeling right now?" I shrugged and thought about it, everything seemed to be in order. Then inspiration struck me.

"What if you have a sheet with the alphabet on it when I'm not sure how I am feeling and you point at the letters and I will keep my hands out of my line of vision and signal to you when you are on the right letter? Then rather than going through the rigmarole of spelling out everything I'll do it shorthand, so to speak?" She pondered this for a second and then spoke.

"That is a really good idea. I won't react either. I will write down at random times so even if your brain is 'recording' they won't see what you are signalling for. Does that sound good?" I nodded again, feeling like a schoolboy trying out a new thing and being positive about it. It wasn't the best method maybe, but if it worked, how could we knock it?

The room suddenly swayed and I felt drunk, the sensation of my body waving side to side bringing about an instant sense of motion sickness. I looked to Sarah and watched as her face bloated outwards then inwards again, becoming rodent-like in its appearance. Then an indecipherable shouting came in my head, my tongue felt fuzzy and too large for my mouth, making my lips tingle like I'd just eaten a tablespoon of sherbert. I felt the desire to stand and stomp my feet and smash my fists into the nightstand. I could picture so strongly in my mind, picking up the lamp and launching it at Sarah. The image and feeling was so clear in my head that I could have been doing it, I could even envision the shards of china spraying out after it hit even though I was not moving at all. It was like watching an alternate reality, with the current reality seemingly paused and unaffected.

In my head I was swinging my legs around, feeling the pain and impact with every surface I collided with. No restraint, full-bodied kicks and punches to everything, then I could see myself picking up a pillow and putting all my being into a roaring scream, the fabric coarse against my face, inhaling the fibres. Sarah was staring at me, unsure of what to do as I stared blankly at her not doing anything whilst these images ransacked my brain. I could hear that crazed laughter again and realised that it was coming from me, as soon as I did, the contained vision abruptly stopped and with it my laughing.

Pain suddenly shot through my skull and I grabbed at my head trying to push the pain away like it was a physical being, trying to contain it or stop it, anything. I just needed it to stop. With that wish, as simple at the thought itself, the pain vanished. I blinked my eyes hazily, feeling half asleep, but now a feeling of full consciousness was pulsing through me again. It was almost too much to bear. I stood without caring if I fell. I started to pace on wary legs, my upper body and lower body seemed to be two different entities at this point, my legs lethargically lagging behind my torso, which was pumped and stressed.

Forcing myself to clear my head, I moved through the kitchen and flicked on the kettle. Sarah trundled in behind me, aware that I wasn't in a particularly coherent state, just winging it until the phases passed. I was grateful she didn't interfere and just hung back leaning against the counter. I set up the cups and put the coffee granules in them. Each move was measured, precise. I was pushing myself to keep it together. The boiled water followed and it went OK. Taking it step by step. Moving away I felt a flush of relief. I had no funny turn for at least a minute. I wanted to cheer.

Sensing the triumph I felt, Sarah spoke up, "If you are OK, I'm going to pop to the craft store and grab a big board and notepads. There is nothing lost in trying the method we said about with the pointing. It feels like Dr Muggor and Steph are always ahead of the game. Do you need anything else?" I was hungry and didn't want to bother cooking and didn't feel like it was fair of me to ask Sarah to cook after all we had been going through. What I fancied was a fry up from my favourite café, it was en route.

"Yeah, if you are heading that way, can you grab us some breakfast from the Breakfast Café?" Her eyes lit up at the prospect of a fry up. Good food has that effect on people. She cradled her steaming mug in between her hands and sniffed the strong aroma of the coffee, a surprisingly calm aura surrounded her.

"Of course, that sounds good to me. I was thinking, Arnie…" she waited until I turned to look at her again instead of pushing the few spilt granules of coffee into a small pile with my fingertip, "when this is all over, what do you think will happen? Do you think you will have problems after this? Do you think we will be able to get him to remove the implant? What if, if we could somehow get to it, we destroyed his computer and all and any hard drives we can find? If we incapacitate him somehow, by getting him arrested, I guess, and destroyed everything, he shouldn't ever be able to control your mind again, even if he ever got out. I don't know what the chances of us getting the implant out of your head are. Judging from the dream you just had, it looks like he isn't willing to let this go. Or maybe it isn't even possible? I tried and you had a massive seizure." She was speaking very matter-of-factly like she was addressing someone who needed someone to go easy on them but had to know hard facts. I suppose that was me right now, even if I didn't want to admit it.

"I don't know, maybe he won't remove it no matter what we do, but you are right. Frankly I wouldn't trust him to, it would be a perfect opportunity to control me more if anything. If we can remove his ability to access it and make it function, it will be the next best thing."

Once I'd finished speaking, I let out a heavy sigh. She reached forward and stroked my bottom lip with her thumb, then tiptoed to plant a soft kiss in the same place, I felt a small smile crease my lips and a tingle where her mouth had met mine. She placed her half-drunk coffee on the side and clasped her hands together. So very British. It was the unspoken version of a slap on the knees and exclaiming, "Right!", she grabbed her bag and waved goodbye to me. I stayed in the kitchen swilling my coffee around watching the small bubbles spin and pop. I needed darkness right now, not because I felt depressed, although depression did have some hold on me at the moment, but because I didn't want to think or see anything. I reached over and closed the blinds over the kitchen sink and closed the door to the kitchen. I shut off the light and slid down the wall onto the floor, not paying any mind to the cold tiles. I rested my head against the faded yellow wallpaper and closed my eyes, allowing my mind to wander where it so desired.

****

Sometime later, I woke due to the pain pulling up through my shoulder and neck. It took a moment to remember where I was and why it was so dark. I had fallen asleep slumped against the wall, funny. I hadn't felt tired, but then that was happening a lot at the moment and I shouldn't have been surprised. But a perk was I didn't remember having any sort of dream or nightmare, which was odd. I had no concept of time in here, so I rose up and flicked the light back on, looking to the clock next to the window. 7:45 pm. Jesus, I had slept hours.

Where was Sarah then? Surely, she would have woken me up and moved me? It can't have been long before midday when she left to go to the shop. My stomach rumbled, politely reminding me that she had also gone to get food. Self-doubt racked through me, I wondered if she had decided to leave me, not face any of this anymore. The more we had tried to fix it or change it, the more hopeless it had all seemed. I couldn't blame her. An instant feeling of certainty that this was in fact the case swamped me. Of course that would be what had happened. Sadness hung like a black veil over me. Then like a flick of a switch, I felt like I was talking nonsense to myself. Of course, she wouldn't have left me, she wouldn't leave me like this. If she had she would have at least spoken to me about it. I wandered into the living room to collect my phone and see if she had messaged me. The green light was flashing on the top of the screen to indicate a message or call had been received but missed. I unlocked it without much hope considering the track record I had with this phone and the recent discovery that it was being hacked. My lack of hope was correct, there was nothing on it. Whatever had been received was gone.

Something caught my eye in the corner of the room by the front door. I walked over to check it out and felt a wave of worry come over me. The door was closed but trapped in the bottom corner was a small strap of fabric, not unlike that on Sarah's bag. I opened the door and sure enough, her bag was discarded there on the floor. There was no way she could have dropped that without realising it and not come back for it. She had keys, she could have come in and out again without me realising if that was her intention.

My earlier thinking about her having left me went away completely and was replaced with one of growing dread. I pictured Dr Smyll in my mind and my throat blocked up just thinking about the possibilities. He had warned me. But I hadn't done anything. My eyes darted around in growing panic and I noticed something red smeared on the wall, my heart seized thinking the worst had happened. I looked closer at the stain and saw that rather than the red of blood, it was orange coloured. I sniffed it and found it was some sauce from baked beans. So that could only mean one thing, she had come back like she said she would, but something happened here at my front door. Something caused her to drop her bag whilst opening the door and hit the bag with the takeout against the wall. Knowing something had happened to her whilst I was so close and yet unaware of her predicament sickened me. A million awful pictures conjured up in my mind and I didn't want to consider any of them as possible. I would much rather have believed the more innocent (in comparison) story of she came back, saw I was asleep, got angry and ran away, launching her food at the wall in a huff. But of course, I knew that wouldn't be true. I cursed myself again and blamed myself for having fallen asleep. If I had been awake, I would have heard her coming in at least, then maybe heard whatever else was happening and helped.

I considered it for a moment, I hadn't been tired, so why did I fall asleep on the floor of all places? This happened to me a lot, then it dawned on me that if Dr Muggor wanted to, he could increase whatever hormones induce sleepiness and cause me to nod off at will. If he wanted me out of the picture, that would be an easy way to do it. I was barely holding back a full-blown panic attack, knowing that at this moment, it wouldn't help anything. Grabbing my phone back off the side and slamming the door behind me, I forcibly tapped in Dr Muggor's number and waited for the dial tone, nervously stepping from foot to foot. It connected and I felt the pulse in my neck quicken. It rang just once before the line went silent. Only a distant crackling indicated to me that someone was on the other end.

"Hello?" I tried to keep the quavering out of my voice.

"Hello, Arnold, my boy." I wished he would stop calling me that, and very quickly remembered the words from my nightmare, it was like he was taunting me. "How can I help you?" My blood boiled, I knew he was behind Sarah's disappearance and he was so blasé about it. I wanted to scream at him.

"You know damn well how you can help me." Anger bit through my tone, making each word sound clipped.

"I'm sorry?" I could picture the look on his face, feigned surprise and innocence, it fed my rage. "What do you mean? Are you having trouble?"

Doubt niggled at me once more. Maybe I had imagined the whole saga in the dream and he hadn't really projected himself into my subconscious mind? But even if I had made it up, it didn't change everything that had happened before, or did it? What if I imagined the whole thing? I stopped, confusion rattling through me painfully. It was a physical sensation and I tried to shake it away. I looked over to where I had discarded Sarah's abandoned bag on the sofa and restrengthened what I had been thinking about before, ignoring my ever looming doubts.

"You took her! What have you done with her? If you hurt her, I will hunt you down and kill you with my bare hands!" My voice was now shrill and I didn't care.

"Arnold! Took who?"

"Sarah!" I bellowed down the line. "You are playing all these sick games and I am done! I told you already in your stupid damned dream, the one you made me have, I will do what is required of me, just don't hurt her, bring her back to me." My voice broke, unable to continue. Silence roared in my ears as neither of us spoke. I wondered if he was still on the other end when he cleared his throat, making me jump.

"Is that what you think is happening? Surely you can hear the absurdity of what you are insinuating?" His tone was silky smooth, as though he was talking to a distressed dementia patient who thought it was 1972. Doubt reared up again and I lost my footing. The confusion raging through my head was making me want to cry. "Arnold, are you sitting down?" I shook my head at the phone, then when I realised he couldn't hear that I mumbled no. "Maybe you should be." Fear pumped through my veins, what was he going to say to me, was she hurt? Was she in on it all? I perched on the edge of the sofa and waited.

"We have spoken about this before. But I will tell you again, much as it pains me to do so. Sarah is dead, Arnold." A piercing ringing filled my eardrums and everything lost focus. I felt my stomach drop and I gagged. "She died in a hit-and-run over a week ago. When you found out, you lost all sense of reality when you realised you'd never see her again. Started talking to yourself, insisting she was there with you. Fabricating scenarios and conversations to help yourself cope with grief. You became fixated on the idea of an adventure that you two were in together and I was the bad guy. This, unfortunately, was what I warned you about after your head injury, the lines of reality can become easily blurred."

I tried in vain to absorb everything he was saying to me. If what he was saying was true, then he wasn't the enemy, he had been trying to help with the implant and meetings. If she had died a week ago, it would have been about one or two days after my head trauma, which then meant that everything, literally everything after that was not true, a fabrication in my own mind. I collapsed into the sofa, sobbing. My phone was forgotten about, fallen to the floor and discarded. I curled myself up in a ball and wept, allowed my emotions to heave out of me in great wracking waves. I lay in my pit of pity, for what felt like hours. As I lay there, a multitude of phases came and went but I was so spent, I didn't move. I allowed the sofa to sink underneath me and the TV to flicker ominously. I didn't care when the walls of my flat curved and split with licks of fire climbing them scorching wispy patterns into the paint. Even when a screaming started inside my head I just lay, numbed and dead inside. My battle was lost, a battle that it seemed I didn't need to fight because it hadn't been true. I couldn't say what it was that made me believe him, but somehow I did. I lay silent, unmoving, the concept of time and life lost. I was drowning in my sea of emotions and had no desire to surface for breath.

****

My Sarah was dead. A cold motionless corpse never to be reanimated into the loving soul that I had come to depend on and gifted a part of myself to. The pain was physical, my heart had cracks in it, I could picture rivulets of blackened blood, tar-like, dripping from my broken soul onto the floor, forming a deep puddle that would soon envelop me. The tears had long since subsided and my face felt crusty. I didn't care. I didn't even trust that the sensation was real. I didn't know what reality was. I felt the feeling build up in me, like a tsunami, it built until I couldn't contain it anymore and I let out a gut-wrenching shout, developing into a scream that burned my throat, tearing my vocal cords. I let it carry on until it faded into a crackled whisper and felt all remaining tendrils of energy leave my body.

I heard the door knocking in the distance, miles away. There was no one in this world I wanted to see ever again. I ignored it, anger mounting that anyone would impeach on my privacy and home, my personal grief. The knocking grew louder, someone was really going to town. I expected to hear the wood splintering any second now, but I wasn't at all inclined to go and open it. I was dead. I could hear the commotion, someone was shouting at me,

"Sir, we are going to have to enter by force if you do not open this door in the next thirty seconds!" A man's voice, muffled like he was shouting into the wood itself.

"Sure," I mumbled to myself, "enjoy." I counted to thirty in my head using the Mississippi's and right on cue, I heard a great crashing noise behind my head and the scuffling of multiple people's feet entering the flat at speed. I still didn't turn around to greet my visitors. They probably weren't real. I was probably just lying on my sofa, imagining all of this and my door would be intact the next time I looked at it. My thinking was soon corrected when rough hands yanked me upright off of the sofa and into standing. I came face to face with a burly police officer whose expression was a mixture of anger and disdain. I imagine he took one look at me and thought I was just a drunken fool.

"Sir, why did you not answer the door when we knocked. We had a distress call to this address." I shrugged my shoulders impertinently in response.

"It wasn't me, I don't want you here." I looked up to meet his gaze and flinched when I saw my own face in his. Mottled and grey, blood pooling in all of the orifices. Pushing myself away from him abruptly, I shouted at him to stop. I blinked and his face turned back into what it had been. He was looking across at his fellow police officer and looking confused.

"Sir, are you OK? Do you need assistance?" I watched his gaze slowly move up to my head, the scar not quite fully covered by my hair yet. I reached up to see something when a thought struck me and felt a jab of confusion when I felt the plaster was there. Did I get so deep into my delusions that I even put that on my head and imagined it was Sarah? Surely not, renewed doubt tingled at me again, but not doubt in myself again this time. "Sir?" he repeated. Then he shot a look over to his colleague, who nodded at him wordlessly. "Sir, we are going to take you to the hospital for a check-up. Nothing to worry about, just routine."

"Wait! Just wait a second!" I threw my hands up in front of me to stop him coming towards me for a moment. If there was a plaster there, then it had to mean that Sarah had put it there, right? It felt like false hope, but it was hope nonetheless. My mind was swirling the same thoughts around over and over. If I was going to go crazy, I wanted to go with some hope still coursing through me. I looked to the door and another police woman was standing there in the doorway, kind face offset with a hard posture. Next to her was my neighbour, Mrs Tempera, in her usual attire of a loose-fitting just below the knee floral skirt and a baggy shirt. She was wringing her hands nervously and I assumed it must have been her who called the police. The first officer who had spoken to me took my arm gently like I was a patient and led me towards the door. His whole attitude towards me had changed now.

"We will get your door fixed for you in no time, sir, don't you worry." I didn't even care. I was running through possibilities in my head, my conviction getting stronger with each passing moment.

As we got closer, Mrs Tempera reached out a wrinkled hand to me spoke to me, "Dear, are you OK? I hope you don't mind. I heard a god-awful noise coming from in here and I thought the worst, especially after the other day." I swung my head round to face her full-on.

"The other day? What happened the other day?" I asked, pushing her to say the words I needed to hear.

"You don't remember?" She looked confused and unsure about whether to speak.

"It's alright, Mrs Tempera, I'm just having a bit of a rough time. I know I did a stupid thing the other day and I won't do it again. But was I on my own?" She looked relieved at my reassurance. Then she shook her head.

"No, that pretty little thing of yours knocked on my door and asked for the key. Is she not here?" She craned her head into the flat curiously. My heart pumped harder, hope built into a crescendo, then anger. I had believed him. I believed that son of a bitch Dr Muggor. He nearly won. He nearly broke me, and I nearly let him.

I turned to face the officer holding my arm, "Apologies officer, I don't think I need an escort anywhere." He looked taken aback and looked to his colleagues for a moment.

"I think I must insist." He spoke, putting on an authoritative tone.

"I will insist harder. I shouted, made a lot of noise. This is why my neighbour was worried about me. I have a lot of pain in my head you see," I pointed to my scar as a demonstration, "and when it gets bad, I don't know how else to cope with it. It was wrong of me to be so noisy and disruptive and to not have opened the door, but I couldn't get up." He frowned at me.

"So, why did you shout at me to stop?" I thought for a moment and tried to work out what was best to make him leave so I could work out my plan.

"When you moved me, it made my head hurt more. I was telling you to stop moving me." Judging from the look on his face, he wasn't buying it. To say I was unkempt was a huge understatement and he will have been judging me more on my appearance at this moment than my words.

"Well, if you insist. Should you have any problems, please don't hesitate to call it in. I will have someone contact you about your door." He nodded briskly to me and then at his two colleagues and left. Mrs Tempera hovered in the doorway looking guilty and I reassured her it was fine, she did what any caring neighbour would have done. She smiled gratefully at me and tottered back to her place.

I retook up my position on the sofa and thought about what to do. If it hadn't been for Mrs Tempera, I wouldn't have known for sure that Sarah was here just a couple of days ago, which couldn't have been possible if she had died over a week ago. I bet she was a factor that Dr Muggor wouldn't have taken into consideration, he would have had no reason to. I felt like I didn't have too much time to make a decision, I needed to make it fast. If he had already told me she was dead, then if he hadn't killed her already – a possibility I was studiously ignoring – she was in massive danger and I needed to somehow go on a one-man mission to save her. But with him feeding my brain with countless issues and problems, I was limited. My first port of call had to be to destroy his database. Even if he had a backup somewhere, I needed to get rid of the main one he was using to give myself more time without his interference. Clicking the button on the side of my phone, I checked the time, 11:32 pm. That was as good a time as any. Without a second thought, I set out of my flat, not giving any cares as to whether anyone wandered in through my smashed door whilst I was gone. Bigger fish to fry and all that.

****

I decided to grab a taxi around the corner to save time walking there and conserve what little energy I had. Jumping in the back of a nondescript black cab I gave the address and leaned back. I probably should have brought something with me for protection, but having a lack of weapons in my flat made that impossible unless Dr Muggor was willing to go face to face in a butter knife duel with me. No, what I needed to do had to be undercover and quiet. First, I would smash up his computer and then I would find Sarah, the hope of seeing her face again was driving me on. This wasn't about me, this was about her now. If it wasn't personal before, it was now, he had ensured that.

I realised I never had confirmation that he had her, but I was pretty damn sure. She had been helping me and he would have seen this, I had even told him that she was watching the footage with me. I also realised now that having her help me put her at risk anyway right from the outset, because if he succeeded in breaking me he would still have to silence her. I made the driver stop around the corner one street over so I didn't alert them to my presence if they were still here. The chances of them being in the 'medical clinic' at this hour were slim at best, but I wasn't willing to risk it. Thanking him, I handed him a £20 and climbed out. The streets were lit badly around here, it really was the back end of town. I walked slowly towards the end of the street and turned the corner. There in front of me was the clinic. No lights seemed to be on and there were no cars parked nearby. I also noted with interest that the green plus sign wasn't there, they must have put it up there especially for my visits. I waited for a minute or two to see if there was any movement at all. Nothing. I moved in. I could hear my heart thudding in my chest, loud enough that I was sure if anyone came close enough, they would hear it too. Making a break from the shadows of the last house, I ran across the road and straight to the door of the clinic, eyes darting around to see if anyone was around. Still nothing. Skirting around to the back of the building, I looked for another entrance, there must be more than one for fire hazard reasons.

Coming around the corner, I breathed out a sigh of relief, there was one. I ran hunched over and reached the door. It was very old school and didn't look particularly sturdy, so I was hoping the same would apply to the lock. Checking it anyway, I pulled the side of the door in the vague hope it would save me the trouble to attempting to lock pick it. I had no luck, it was locked. Crouching down, I looked at the mechanism in the slot. It looked like it was just your average door lock but with no handle on this side, meaning it could only be opened from the inside unless you had the key. Pulling my wallet out of my pocket, I looked for a credit card. I had never done this before and frankly felt a little James Bond about it. I found an old bank card and I slid it neatly into the gap and angled the corner above the slot. Pushing down nothing happened, so I tried from the other side. Still nothing, I frowned, they made this look so easy in the movies. Looking again, I could see the triangular-shaped metal bit was facing away from me and that was what I needed to push in.

Reangling the card, I tried again, wiggling it a little and pushed downwards hard. Something clicked and the lock popped out, swinging the door out by a centimetre or two. I held in my desire to whoop for joy. I couldn't wait to tell Sarah about this when I got her back. Keeping my breathing steady, I pulled the door a bit more open and peered into the thin gap to see what was on the other side. I could see something flickering in the room and as my eyes adjusted to the gloom, I jolted in shock and threw myself away from the door and pinned myself against the wall. I tried to calm myself down breathing more erratically now, I chanted internally to get my head together. I hadn't expected to see anyone in there now, I had convinced myself that the building would be empty. But sitting with her back facing me at the desk in the far corner had been Steph with her arms twitching away like she was writing or typing. That was a close call and I was thankful she hadn't heard me opening the door. I wondered where Dr Muggor was and Sarah. I don't really know what I had been expecting, but I hadn't thought he would be likely to keep her here.

The problem was I didn't know any other location she could be and a quick scout of this place could potentially give me a lead. I took a deep breath and poked my head around again, Steph hadn't moved, she was still at the desk wittering away at whatever task she was doing. I needed to create a distraction, something to take her away for at least five minutes. Her head tilted a little and with excitement, I saw she was on a laptop. It looked like the same one Dr Muggor had been using before. Pushing the door to but not fully closing it, I ran around to the front of the building, sticking to the wall and out of sight of any potential cameras and motion activated lights. I slunk up to the door and with little time to change my mind smashed it hard with my fist three times in succession. That should do it. Darting back around to the back door, I could just about hear Steph shuffling around and muttering under her breath about always forgetting keys. She must have thought it was Dr Muggor, good, that may even buy me more time if she sees no one is there and looks outside for him.

I slid into the room silently and ran to the laptop. She was on the database with the viewing portal, full of videos, countless now. Looking at a couple of the thumbnails, I could see they were all ones from fairly recently. I scrolled down quickly to see what the last entries were and for once, luck was on my side. It would appear I had a moment, although not realised it, just outside the clinic. The footage thumbnail was me looking at the front door time-stamped from only three minutes ago. Very lucky for me, she had been looking through other ones and not watching the bottom of the screen. I needed to find a way to corrupt the computer, but I didn't know anything about them. I had a laptop years ago that I 'blue-screened' otherwise known as the 'blue screen of death', but no idea how I had achieved it. I had a computer tech friend who probably could assist me, maybe I could ask him for a virus that wipes everything out of the system. But that didn't help me in the here and now and time was of the essence, pressing on me with its invisible ever intensifying force.

God knows where Sarah was or what she was going through and my stomach did a sickly flip even considering the possibilities. I needed to find something to help me find her, I needed to see if there was any paperwork here with a different address on it. If I found anything, I would go to it, no questions asked, I wasn't seeing straight now, everything was blurred and panicky with a bizarre twist of clarity overriding it all telling me I had to do something. I raided through the various small piles of paper strewn all over the place, my ears straining for any sound of movement outside. I must have been in here for at least a few minutes now and I wondered why I hadn't heard her footsteps coming back through the waiting room. Surely she must have realised that there was no one there and put it down to teenagers playing knock down ginger or something by now.

As though she sensed my thinking, I heard the clip-clop of her coming back towards the room, steady and slow, not in a rush. I hunted for somewhere to hide and came up blank. The room was too open plan with nothing but the chair in the centre of the room and the cabinets and desks pushed up against the walls. I was breathing in pants now, knowing I was seconds from being foiled and I knew the ramifications of being caught would be terrible. I couldn't help Sarah or myself if they caught me now. I kicked myself for realising she was taking longer than expected and not using the opportunity to get out then.

I spotted a fire extinguisher hanging on the wall and felt the hint of a grimace cross my face and a small sense of pleasure fizzed through me at the dark idea that struck me. I grabbed it from its hooks and slid behind the door where she wouldn't see me as she entered. I made it just in the nick of time, the heavy door started to swing inwards as I froze in place. I waited for the perfect moment. Too soon and I may not be effective enough. Too late and she would see me coming and make a move to stop me. The moment presented itself all too soon and without any thought, I silently raised the extinguisher and in one swift downward move cracked it into the side of her appealing little face. She didn't see me and now, she couldn't see anything. Her body crumpled instantaneously out for the count. I was surprised I didn't feel wrong about it, I felt pleasure, power and strength coursing through me. Also, I felt like some level of justice was served, she was after all the one who killed Dr Smyll without emotion. Fighting the urge to crunch it down on her skull again to ensure she never got up, I stepped neatly over her giving her a menacing scowl for good measure.

Going back to my task of finding some clues, I raced through the piles of envelopes and printed out sheets without much luck. All of them seemed to be addressed to here although tellingly, none of them mentioned the words 'medical clinic', not that I really thought it was one anymore. Turning my attention back to the laptop, I clicked on to the desktop to see if there was anything in there. The background was some generic splashes of colour, nothing of note. There were numerous folders scattered across the desktop and a little bit of me was surprised at how messy it was, I had half expected it to be overly organised and neat.

But then looking around the desk in here, I should have known better. One folder was titled billing and I figured that could be my best bet, so I opened it. Opening the last one labelled 'Electricity – Farm' my head started to race, not because I was having any sort of turn but because I felt it could be a break. The fact there was a bill for a farm meant that had to be a potential location for Sarah. The bill was addressed to Dr Muggor and the address was around thirty minutes' drive away. Every now and then I checked to see the unconscious body of Steph was still motionless and unthreatening, not really sure what I would do if she came around and saw me. I think I would gladly jump at the excuse to hit her again, I'm anti-violence generally, but this one sure was an exception.

Figuring my best move to make here was to just take the laptop with me and break it later. I unplugged it, grabbed the phone off the side that I assumed was Steph's and started to leave when something in the back of my mind niggled at me. I paused in the doorway and made a quick decision. I put the laptop on the dental chair and ran around the room pulling out drawers and throwing various books on the floor. I upturned the bin and knocked the stale coffee on its side spilling the contents across the desk. I was content with the level of destruction I had caused and happy that at least on first glance it would be plausible that a bodged robbery had taken place. I grabbed the laptop off the chair and exited, pulling the door closed behind me, but not all the way.

I was just pulling my fingers away from the door when I heard the inner door of the office open and froze. I heard the thud of the door hitting Steph and an exclamation of, "Oh, fuck!" Taking the opportunity, I sprinted across the ground and straight across to the other side of the road, not looking behind me until I reached one of the alcoves of the houses there. As yet Dr Muggor hadn't looked outside to find a culprit, maybe he hadn't seen the back door slightly ajar yet. Hopefully, he would be too preoccupied sorting Steph out for a while, giving me even more time to get to Sarah.

****

I ran through the next part of my plan in my head. I needed to get to a hardware store and get myself something to defend myself should the need arise and I felt like it may do. These people were capable of more than I could possibly fathom, and as my limited experience so far with them had shown, they were capable of a lot. Luckily, I was just on the outskirts of the city, and there was an abundance of hardware stores open all hours near me. I knew there was one just around the corner with a taxi rank practically on its doorstep. I ran most of the way, only slowing my pace when I reached the door with a garish neon light announcing it was open. It hung from a small hook at the top of the door. Panting, I went in and grabbed the first backpack I could find, a torch, a hammer and gloves. I half considered finding a place that sold guns – unlikely at this hour I knew – and going full out crazy to find her like in the movies, but discarded this idea knowing it was impossible and not even remotely feasible. I threw the

150

money at the cashier and told him to chuck the change in a charity pot of his choice and exited again, all within five minutes.

I spotted a taxi idling on the curb and ran straight to it, opening the door and tumbling into the back, breath coming in short spurts. I didn't need to open the laptop to remember the address, it was seared into my mind. I ran it off to the driver who just looked at me and rolled his eyes. He probably assumed I was your average drunken punter. I looked at the time on his dash, half one in the morning. His assumption could be true, could be true to the former me too, by this time on any given night I was usually well on my way to being heavily intoxicated. I realised I hadn't really had any drinks since the accident and was pretty happy with that fact. Focusing on the matter at hand whilst I was transported, I threw everything into the backpack except the laptop. I had time to burn whilst we travelled and whilst I was feeling so with it – most likely because at least for now, I had removed their means of administering their 'treatment' – I wanted to see what other information I could glean.

Putting it back on to the desktop, I browsed through the folders without opening any. What I found interesting was that there were multiple folders with names in them. Some had the letter 'x' next to them. I saw my own name on one of the folders but chose to first have a look at one of the ones marked with an 'x'. Bill Smithers. Inside the folder was an array of word documents and a few videos. I opened the word document titled 'Termination of Treatment'. It opened up into a sheet that resembled a medical form. I scanned through it. At the end, there was a box with the name 'Termination', which was what I was looking for and I read the contents:

'The subject had proven to be highly responsive to all methods of electrical pulse treatment except one. After administering strength 4 QTPN, his hallucinations extended beyond our handling. Rapid deterioration of mental capabilities and non-responsive to commands. Mr Smithers resorted to violence and breaking and entering our property with threats to our lives. Termination was required.'

I wondered briefly if that was what the commotion had been when I was in the office with him that day when they had become flustered. Had they just killed someone whilst I was waiting in there? My blood was running cold. I opened the next one and scrolled down straight to the last box:

'Subject suicidal. Future reference, subjects must be of a strong nature with a stubborn will. She sought outside assistance, terminated threat. Subject committed suicide.'

Two more deaths to mark against his name. With interest, I saw there was one for Jane. I opened it and went to the last box. This one was just titled 'Progress of Patient':

'After years of varying treatments, subject is now responding entirely in line with expectations with minimal input.'

That was it. Nothing more written about it. I looked up through the other boxes and read in titbits that he had treated her with all sorts of methods; injections, tablets, electric shock therapy. I didn't know whether to hate or pity Steph. At one point, he had even considered terminating her, but it looked like she ranked as his best 'subject'. That was all that we all were to him, not people, just subjects to toy with and experiment on.

Scanning through all the other ones marked with 'x', I was saddened to see how many people had fallen victim to him, all of these people were dead. But how did he get away with it? How did he live with himself knowing about all the lives he had destroyed? My blood ran colder still as I saw there was one labelled Sarah, but in a backwards way, a sense of reprieve came seeing there was no 'x' there. I opened the file. There was only one box:

'This is an interesting subject to work with. Strong will power, intelligent, has a lot of fight in her. Challenge will be to break the spirit enough that she becomes pliable to commands and responds correctly. First stage completed, implant in place. Strength one pulses administered for all chemicals, reasonable reactions. All further experiments will be carried out under observation in confinement. The current most effective vision is viewing a loved one being terminated. Will continue to observe and implement new visualisations.'

My heart dropped reading it, my poor Sarah, she was now going through this first hand when I wouldn't wish it on my worst enemy. Intense sadness mixed with raging fury swamped me. He had cut her open and stuck that poisonous piece of machinery in her head. The only consolation I had was knowing that whilst I had the laptop, he shouldn't be able to 'administer' anything else. That said, I wouldn't be surprised if he had another one. It would make sense keeping in mind that Steph had been on one in the office. If she was busy doing some other task Dr Muggor had set her, he would need access too from another platform. I prayed that if there was another computer or laptop, I would find it at

152

this farm. I could picture Sarah in my mind's eye. Sure, I know she isn't a fragile girl, but what she must be seeing was enough to break the strongest of spirits, myself and the list of other names was a testament to that fact.

I looked back at the screen. I didn't know if I wanted to read mine, in fact, I was beyond certain that I didn't want to. The fact he hadn't 'terminated' me yet was good, however, I didn't know if his mind had changed on that in the last few hours. As it stood, he thought I was under the illusion that Sarah was dead. I saw that there were videos in many of the folders, but I had no desire to see someone else's suffering. I could relate to it only too well without having to watch it in high definition. I was sick to my stomach reading it all. Closing the laptop with a heavy sigh, I asked the driver how far away we were.

"About fifteen minutes," He grumbled. OK, plenty of time for me to prepare myself for whatever may await me. I settled back into the chair, all the things I had seen and read swirling around my mind like a sick and twisted merry go round, never stopping.

****

I stepped out of the cab and the cold air cut through me like a knife. I was on a dirt track about one hundred metres long with a small farmhouse planted at the end of it. A little letterbox sticking out of the mud with rusted letters on it indicated to me that I was in the right place. The farmhouse was small, old and looked unlived in. There were shutters across all of the upper windows and the front door was slightly off-kilter in its frame. There were several missing bricks in the walls exposing dark holes where they should have been. It looked lonely and derelict. I scanned the surroundings. There wasn't another house in sight, just groups of trees dotted around the fields. I could see the outline of what could potentially be another house in the distance but in this dim light, it could have been miles away. The terrain was flat all around, I imagined it was not an animal farm in its day, but a harvesting farm for corn and wheat and whatever else was in demand that year. I wondered for a moment if this could be a dead end, it looked so abandoned. I ignored the thought, it was a fantastic cover for Dr Muggor, of course he made it look like this – no-one would suspect a thing.

Except for the surrounding trees, there were no decent hiding places to choose from. The cab pulled away and with it the last light source. I reached to my backpack and pulled out the torch I had bought for just in case of an event like this. I flicked it on and kept the beam low to the ground, checking for any trip hazards. I couldn't even hear the main road from here. Everything was silent, just a slight whistling sound from the wind rustling the leaves. I took it as a good sign that there were no cars parked here, it meant Dr Muggor must still be back at the clinic or he could be on his way here, but he wasn't here yet. I took that positively and worked with it.

Abandoning the attempt at being quiet, I sprinted the rest of the distance to the house, closing it in less than ten seconds. Catching my breath from the excursion, I leaned against the wall of the house. I was right next to a window and I peered into it. It was completely pitch-black inside, just a few shadows were visible when I squinted. I could feel my adrenaline pumping through my veins, this was it. I would finally have one up on Dr Muggor and save Sarah. I knew she was here, I felt it in my gut. Figuring I had to get this done quickly because he could be back any moment, I faced the front door and reared back on my left leg. Propelling myself forward, I shoved my right foot into the centre of the door. It gave way without any resistance and caused me to follow the motion of the smashed door and go tumbling into the house, landing hard on my knee and only just avoiding my head bouncing off the floor. Dust poured up into the air around me and I started to choke. Waving my hands in front of my face I tried to disperse it and got to my feet again, rubbing my tender knee with my hand. I looked around for a light switch then thought against it; if Dr Muggor was on his way back here it would call like a beacon to him and he would be on guard for someone here or even prompt him to call the police.

What I had in mind required a lack of law enforcement. A grim smirk crossed my face. I edged down the hallway, everything was covered in an inch of thick dust, papers were strewn haphazardly across all the surfaces, cups discarded on sides. On my left was what look like a kitchenette. I glanced in there not expecting to find anything, it looked like it hadn't been used in a decade at least. Crockery piled high in a stained sink, pots and pans with a residue that would never come off no matter how long you scrubbed it. The thin curtains hanging on the window had holes in and I imagined the during the day time they were ineffective in their role as shade givers.

I turned away from the kitchen and looked to the door on my right, the room that I had tried to peer in from outside. It was a lounge. In place of sofas, there were a handful of wooden chairs, all in varying states of decay with a thin bits of cloth draped over the bases. The floor was covered in debris, cigarette butts, plastic bottles and yet more paper. A few medical journals seemed to be scattered here and there, but I had no interest in looking closer. My sole purpose here was to find Sarah and get her out as soon as possible. But having only seen these two rooms, my optimism was already waning. This place looked as abandoned on the inside as it had on the outside, maybe I was wrong again, I sighed inwardly completely dejected at all this doubt and fear. I didn't even have a gut instinct any more it seemed. I figured I may as well continue the search anyway, but the little hope I had mustered up before was dwindling.

I pointed the torch to the back of the room and spotted a rickety staircase running up the back wall. It struck me as an odd place for a staircase, and for some reason it made me more alert again. It looked like it was handmade out of old pallets, not by a skilled carpenter though, to say it was a bodged job was an understatement. I wandered further into the room taking care not to step on anything, I didn't want to trip or cause myself any more damage than I already had. Considering how terrible my body felt, I was amazed it was still functioning, but what astounded me the most right now was the clarity in my head. Everything felt clear and unfuzzy, the slight sounds I was making almost sounded melodic to me, not coming at me with strange volumes and twists. My thoughts were coming neatly and unconfused. I thought about the laptop I had taken from the medical clinic, and once again wondered if it was the only laptop they had. I hadn't had any bad turns for a while now and my alertness was reaching highs I hadn't experienced in over a week. Finally, it felt like something was going better. I flinched at the sting of guilt that coursed through me when I realised how selfish that was. But in all fairness, this state of mind was certainly going to be of more use in rescuing Sarah than when I was a blubbering scared mess. I reached the back of the room and assessed the staircase warily, it led up into a hole in the ceiling. This staircase was definitely not an original, I wondered where the other one was, perhaps back down the hallway, I hadn't finished exploring. The steps looked like they'd been used a lot, so I decided to go for it.

Keeping my feet to the outsides of the steps because the centres of them didn't look like they would hold the weight of a bag of sugar, I ascended. I poked my head through the hole and aimed the flashlight around. The view up here was quite a contrast to the one that had met me downstairs. Entering the room completely, I took it all in. A large bed stood proud in the corner, a nightstand piled with books and medical memorabilia. A wardrobe stood at the end of the bed, one door hanging open, I shone the light in there and saw a collection of white overcoats and black trousers lined up neatly on the hangers. Black loafers, four pairs that were all identical, lined the floor.

I turned my attention to the other side of the room next to the window that should be overlooking the front of the house, if I had orientated myself correctly. There was a huge collection of strange looking posters all over the wall, consuming it. I edged closer to have a look. This must be where Dr Muggor actually stayed, leaving the downstairs area as a decoy, I guessed. I wondered how many people from his experiments had tried to find him and if that was the reason he lived like this. As I saw the photos and paperwork on the wall my breath caught and I had to look away. There were sections dedicated to different people, notes pinned up next to sheets with things written on them like 'Less SRTNN', 'Result of More NRDNLN', 'First Termination'. These were shots of people in different states of mind and at the bottom of a handful of them was a post-it with 'Termination' scrawled on it and the photo was the victims unseeing eyes gazing towards the camera modelling for their final picture in their deaths, faces mottled and bruised. None of them looked peaceful in their demise and I couldn't handle it. Despite feeling like I was really holding it together a minute ago I could now feel it slipping away. I felt the beginnings of a panic attack, but I knew this was all me and nothing to do with whatever Dr Muggor was doing to my brain. I stood away from the haunting images and took deep breaths, refusing to look at them anymore. The reason I hadn't looked at the footage in the folders on the laptop was due to the fact that I hadn't wanted to put faces to the names, now I had no choice. They were ingrained in my memory.

I heard a rumbling in the distance and my heart jumped in my chest. Flicking off the torch, I moved to the window and looked out. I saw headlights coming down the track, bumping along through the potholes. Dr Muggor. Shit, shit, shit shit! I realised I hadn't put the door back and started to get flustered. I then had to stop myself emitting a manic laugh at the absurdness of panicking about not returning the door to its original position when it was split and splintered. I crouched down, knowing he couldn't see me in the gap of the shutters I was looking through but paranoid all the same. Any moment now he would see that the door was down and come looking for an intruder. I hit myself in the forehead with the palm of my hand, cursing myself for being so stupid for imagining I was in some action movie and kicking the door in rather than trying to pick the lock. I watched as he came up the dirt track towards the house and to my surprise, he drove straight past it and out of my line of sight.

156

Confused, I looked around for another window to see what was happening. There wasn't one, just a door leaving this room. Moving over to it quickly, I opened it and found myself on a small landing area. On my right was a window looking across the back of the house and on my left was another set of stairs. Looking down them I could see why a new set had been made, the centre section of them was completely collapsed, unusable.

Shaking my head to myself to rid my momentary distraction, I looked through the dirty window to my right. I saw the car had come to a stop and the door was left open on the driver's side. I looked for the driver and spotted him off to the left. With surprise, I saw there was a metal shed tucked away at the back of the farmhouse. I could make out in the glare of the car's headlights Dr Muggor fiddling with a lock on the door. He pulled it open and turned and walked back to the car, oblivious to his captivated audience of one. His body language spoke volumes, he was jolty and agitated. He stomped to the passenger door and hauled the door open; I could see someone's legs in the footwell. He reached in and roughly pulled her out, she was wobbly but conscious. I couldn't see their faces from here out of the reach of the lights but I didn't need to. Steph leaned into Dr Muggor and they walked side by side into the metal shed. I wondered what was in there and if that was where Sarah was being held, because she wasn't anywhere here that I had looked so far. There was actually no sign of her at all. I chewed the skin around the nail bed on my thumb, worry and the need to do something building up again. I waited for five minutes to see if they would re-emerge but the door remained closed.

Then I was hit by another worry. If Dr Muggor had a lab in there of sorts, chances were he would have access to the database and all his equipment. He would be able to access my visions and re-control my chemicals to trigger all my visions and bad turns. I started to panic, swinging my head from side to side seeking inspiration from the peeling walls or wispy carpet. I needed to get in there, save Sarah and destroy whatever he had. I opened the door the other side of the landing and found myself in a dingy bedroom or at least what may have been one before, a broken bed frame sat against the wall and that was it. The mattress was upturned and leaning against the wall too, a dark stain covering most of it. A singular small pole jutted out from the wall with empty hangers telling a sad tale of a life once lived here. I wonder if he kept someone here before. The conditions were pretty awful and it had no homely touches. The window was taped over with black plastic bags to ensure no light would ever enter this room.

I went back into the hallway to check the window and felt the hairs on the back of my neck stand up when I saw the door was opening on the shed. Dr Muggor was walking out, rubbing his head and it looked like he was shouting something, but I couldn't make out his words. It pleased me to see him in such distress, I wanted to times that feeling in him by a thousand, watch him squirm, plead and cry for a mercy that would never be granted. He swung the door closed but didn't lock it and I noted that Steph didn't follow him out. He climbed in his car, slammed the door shut and screeched away. I wondered where he was going.

I quickly turned on my heel and ran through the Dr Muggor's bedroom and took the rickety stairs two at a time, jumping the last four and sending up a heap of dirt when I landed. Moving quickly, I ran through the front door and saw in the distance the lights of the car driving away. Good. I skirted round to the back of the house, now was my chance to see in there. Especially whilst injured from the hit to her head, Steph was of no threat to me. She'd likely be sleeping it off, at least I prayed she was. I didn't want a confrontation just yet. I needed to see Sarah safe before I made any moves that let them know what I was doing. But if push came to shove, I would incapacitate her again to stop her from intervening. I tiptoed to the door and listened for any noises. I couldn't hear anything. I put my eye to the slight crack in the door and tried to see inside. A small green light was the only thing I could see, so throwing caution to the wind, I pulled the door open fast to have the element of surprise on my side. I stared blankly in front of me, all I could see was the silhouettes of garden tools lined up on the wall. There was a light switch on the wall next to the door and I flicked it on, blinking to adjust faster to the harshness of the fluorescent bulb. There was nothing else apart from some old fishing chairs stacked in the corner.

The third wall had some kind of bar running across it, with a painters table in front with nothing atop of it. The floor was wooden, same wood as the stairs, I assumed, but with bits here and there that were off colour. My confusion mounted, where was Steph? I didn't see her get in the car with Dr Muggor. Unless she had already got in by the time I looked out of the window. But what could they have been doing in here, there was nothing in here or maybe whatever was in here they had taken? Maybe she had gone back in the house, but I would have passed her on the way through. Uncertainty rattled in my brain as I tried to work it out.

I scratched my head, the sense that time was slipping away from me was growing stronger with every minute that passed. Sarah needed my help and I had no idea where she was. My rush of adrenaline faded off rapidly with the realisation she wasn't here, I had come to the wrong place. I left the shed and walked away from the house, backpack over my shoulder, dialling the number for the taxi service to pick me up at the end of the dirt track. I felt like whatever monitoring and interception system that Dr Muggor and Steph may have in place wasn't going to be being monitored at this moment with everything they had distracting them right now. I went and sat down underneath one of the lonely trees next to the road and waited. If Dr Muggor came driving back now, I could slip behind the tree trunk and he wouldn't know I was here. Resting my head against the trunk for a brief pause, I inhaled deeply, then unzipped the bag, pulling out the laptop and set to work on figuring out my next play.

****

My instincts were telling me to not head home just yet and that was just fine as I had no intention of heading in that direction yet anyway after some further research. The taxi came pretty quickly and I realised I hadn't even noticed the time passing. I didn't even feel the cold, my body was pumped full of energy and anticipation. I had found my next step and on the way to it, I asked the driver to make one quick stop off that only took around twenty minutes, I told him to keep the meter running. I should have been speedier than that, but I had to wait for the right person. If the driver was at all concerned or confused by my actions, he didn't show it, he had the perfect poker face. I hopped back into the cab and rang off the next address I wanted him to take me to and like the last taxi I took, I told him to pull up around the corner. The information I had left at our first destination should provide me with just enough time to get Sarah if this was the right address.

There was another property that Dr Muggor had bills sent to and this one was in the city. I had just assumed due to the movies and countless stories I'd read over the years that someone was being held hostage they would be held in a far-out place, not in a city. How wrong I'd been. Praying and chanting a mantra to myself that all would be alright, that I would find Sarah and we would be OK, that he hadn't hurt her seemed to quell my nerves a little. I needed to rescue her, stop Dr Muggor from doing any further damage and then what would be, would be. I truly didn't care about the rest of it. I thanked the driver and stepped out onto the pavement. The sky was beginning to lighten, night slowly giving way to morning. The warm orange glow was just coming over the horizon and in a few short hours, people would be rising from their beds to go about their days, oblivious to anything but their own movements and agendas.

I scanned the street for the address I wanted and found it fairly quickly. It was a couple of houses in from the last one on the left. I wandered towards it and looked for Dr Muggor's car. Wherever he had gone, it didn't seem to be here. Well, he could have come here and gone again in the time it had taken for me to get here, but what mattered was that he wasn't here now. I walked straight up to the door and rang the bell just to be sure. If he asked any questions, I would feign innocence. I read in the files that on occasion the 'subjects' had become mentally unstable without input from him, so that could be something I could use to my advantage should the need arise. As I thought would be the case, no one answered the door. I looked around me to make sure no nosy neighbours were observing and I began my hunt for a spare key. It didn't take long. For someone so intelligent, he didn't put too much thought into where he would hide his spare. It was under the second rock I picked up in the flower bed. Schoolboy error. I brushed it off and inserted it neatly into the lock and turned it. The door clicked open and I stepped in, closing the door behind me.

I was inside. My heart was beating an erratic rhythm in my chest, making my eardrums thump in an echo. I looked around me, this was more like what I had expected the home of the great doctor to look like. A red runner ran the length of the hallway, silver gilded mirrors lined the walls and mahogany side tables and cabinets lined the bottom half of the hall. True to the style and habit I had repeatedly noticed of him, a bunch of paperwork lay in disarray on top of the surfaces, but it was all very 'upper class' in its appearance and air. He had the same air of superiority about him, his house reflected that well. Or maybe it didn't, maybe it was just because that was what I had anticipated I would feel in his home. Not that it mattered either way, I didn't need more ammunition emotionally to hate him.

I wandered down the hall, choosing to avoid looking in the mirrors and pondered where the most likely place was that he would keep someone against their will. It wouldn't be in the living room, kitchen or bathroom, so I headed straight for the stairs. Climbing them in twos and quickly reaching the top, I was faced with a choice of four doors. I opened the first one directly in front of the staircase and was faced with a grand bathroom. It positively gleamed in all its

160

glory, resembling something from a magazine spread. A huge two-man bathtub sat dead centre in the room with shelves carved into the marble itself, golden faucets and feet finished the look. I would feel like a king just to wash my face in it. Where the hell did he get the money for this if he didn't technically have a job? The sink was of the same style and there was nothing else in here except plush rugs lining the floor surrounding the bath and a toilet in the corner with a pretty little basket full of magazines and loo rolls placed neatly beside it. I could spend hours here relaxing, I bet with some wine and tasteful music, you could lose yourself to the world. On the other hand, I would be fearful of making a mess or breaking anything, so it was just as well I had my run of the mill average bathroom set up back at home.

I shut the door and proceeded to the next one, this one opened up to a towel closet. I couldn't help myself and touched one, it was softer than anything I had ever felt. Dr Muggor went all out when it came to home comforts it seemed. I tried the next door, expecting it to be a bedroom, I was right. It was medium-sized but luxurious all the same. It barely looked lived in, everything was spick and span in its place and even the bed looked like it had been turned down by a seasoned maid. It was a bed larger than any I had seen, way bigger than a queen size, you could probably fit a football team in it. I scanned around to see if there were any more doors in here but there was nothing but a few large paintings adorning the walls, all of the landscapes, all containing mountains and trees. They reminded me of the artist I used to watch on TV, Bob Ross. I turned to the last door, hoping it was the right one and I would find my Sarah behind it. I turned the knob and nothing happened.

The moment triggered a fresh bout of adrenaline, the locked door was all the evidence I needed to convince me that she was right behind it, waiting for me, "Sarah! Sarah! It's me! I'm here for you! I'll get you out of there, hold on!" I looked around frantically, trying to find where the key could be. Realising I didn't have time for this, I hauled the hammer out of my backpack and started smashing it into the door lock. All it resulted in was painful vibrations being shot up my forearms. I tried a new tactic. I started to hammer into the wood around it, pleasure mounting as the wood splintered away. Very quickly, there was a hole above the knob and I reached through ready to turn the handle. My movement was stopped when something very sharp stabbed into the top of my hand. I pulled it back with a gasp and saw the skin peeled back torn to the bone. I clasped my other hand over the top to stem the bleeding, adrenaline numbing the true extent of the pain and I moved a foot back and lined up the hole in the door so I could see through.

The room beyond was fairly dark and I thought for a moment I must have been careless and cut my hand on the jagged wood. Then sending me flying backwards in surprise, an almighty bang caused the entire door to bend from its frame for a moment and a foundation shaking roar filled the air. Confusion mixed itself with complete terror and I saw a shaggy coat, orange and black pressed up against the hole. What the hell was this? Was I looking at a tiger? A god damned tiger? I shook my head again, grasping my injured hand. Who on earth keeps a damn tiger locked in a house? Well, Sarah surely wasn't in there. Was she? My head started to sway and my tongue picked up the familiar sensation of feeling swollen and tingly. The hallway warped suddenly and the door that was my only protection from the tiger melted before my eyes, like hot wax.

I shimmied backwards down the hall, frantically searching for a way to escape what would undoubtedly transpire next. I saw no way out, I couldn't outrun this beast. The doorway was empty, but I knew he was there somewhere lurking out of sight. I could practically feel the floor shaking with the depth of his growl. He stepped into view, mammoth in size, a tiger in all its fear inducing glory. He sized me up, yellow tipped teeth razor sharp and bared at me in a warning, lips peeled back with his whiskers twitching. His eyes were shining so brightly I could see myself in them, shrinking away in sheer terror. He lowered the front half of his body to the ground, back end raised and wiggling ever so slightly. His tail was waving side to side matching the motion of his magnificent shoulder blades rolling up and down to a rhythm that I couldn't hear, showing me he was preparing to pounce. I threw my hands up in a vain attempt to defend myself against the imminent 350kg hit and as I closed my eyes, I just saw him flying through the air, paws ready to pin me in place and his mouth wide open ready to consume me, then the pink coloured ribs in this throat blocked out everything else in my vision.

****

Consciousness called me and I went to put my hands to my face and realised nothing was happening. I tried again and no matter how hard I pushed, nothing happened. I tried to look down to see if I was restrained and my view remained the same, I was looking at a dark wall in some room that looked like a cellar. I tried to speak, but my voice failed me. What was this? I was trapped in my own body unable to move or speak. I could feel my eyes flickering about in their sockets but again, my view stayed the same. I must be in some full-body restraint, but how and where? With some frustration, I realised the tiger must have been a hallucination, meaning that Dr Muggor had regained access to the system. A voice came out from somewhere close by and I realised it was coming from my mouth, but it wasn't my voice. It was Sarah's. My disorientation ramped up another notch, I seemed to be trapped inside Sarah, watching and listening from the inside with no control over what happened.

"What do you want from me?" her voice was pleading, but with an edge of defiance. Dr Muggor came into view as she spoke, standing above her like we were sitting down. He leered down at her like she was dirt on the bottom of his shoe.

"That isn't for you to worry about, my girl." Ah, so that was something he used for everyone, glad it wasn't just me. "You just have to relax your pretty little self," he reached forward with his hand and although I couldn't feel it, could guess that he was touching her face, I felt repulsed, "and let me do all the work. Soon enough, I will be able to free you from the constraints of your own mind and you will live a life you could never have imagined. You won't have worries, pain, sadness or anger. Admittedly, you won't experience happiness or joy again, but you will live without the darkness that threatens to consume you every moment of every day."

I listened in bewilderment, you could see he truly believed in what he was doing and thought he was doing a good thing. At this point, Sarah chose to look around the room, showing me more of the elusive place Dr Muggor had stashed her. It was a cellar; I could see now. There was a barred door off to the right and a makeshift bed of tatty stained rags bundled in the corner with an old-fashioned shackle bolted to the wall above it. That was probably where he was making her sleep, the sick bastard. A small bucket on the left-hand side of the room must have been where she had to relieve herself. Completely stripped of all dignity. There was nothing else in the room, just one small chair by the door and I imagined whatever Sarah was sitting on now. Was this a vision? A nightmare? I didn't know if I was awake, but I certainly wasn't myself. I didn't know if I was noting the details of the room in vain, this could all just be made up, it certainly felt it. I made one last effort to speak and move and found myself incapable again. I grunted in frustration soundlessly.

Sarah spoke again after a short pause, "And you, Dr Muggor?" Her voice was sickly sweet with just a hint of bitterness. "Do you feel anything? Ever?" he laughed in response. She tried again, "Where is Arnie? What have you done with him?" He laughed again with more strength this time. Then the laughter turned to something akin to anger and he came up close, inches from her face.

"Arnie is well, don't you worry yourself about him anymore. You will be seeing him soon enough. In fact, he is seeing you, right now. Say hello, my girl." My view started to swing around again. Sarah was looking for me, I could hear her breath coming in pants, the mention of me watching her almost sending her over the edge into hysteria. I tried to call out to her to reassure her and remembered I couldn't. I had no substance or being here in where I assumed I was, inside Sarah's head.

"Arnie! Arnie!" I wanted to reach out to her, console her but I couldn't. I could now hear something moving behind me and Sarah strained to see, not quite able to move all the way around. What I had thought would just be a wall behind Sarah was more space and from it, Steph moved into Sarah's line of sight, holding the laptop in her hand like a waitress presenting food. Sarah looked at the screen and on the screen, all there was what she was seeing in a mirrored effect. "I don't understand what you are showing me." She sounded insolent, trying to show strength when she was really struggling. Steph spoke up this time, her voice was monotonous and level. I took some pride in seeing that one side of her face was black and blue with a few broken blood vessels, a large gash above her eyebrow was crudely stitched up.

"This isn't what *you* are seeing, this is what Arnold is seeing." No beating around the bush, just a plain statement, to the point.

"What do you mean? How is this possible? What the hell happened to your face?" she asked.

It was Dr Muggor who spoke next, "Did he not tell you about his dream? It is the same concept of implanting visions and ideas, but what we have now developed is a way for his implant to read on command, whatever you are experiencing. And the same applies to yours. So, he can witness real-time what is happening to you. He is currently in an unconscious state, allowing us to penetrate his mind better. He is a strong one, your 'Arnie'." He said my name with distaste, like dirt on the tip of his tongue. "He has been lucky though; he will be one of our best once we finally break him. This fact is the only reason you do not have to refer to him in the past tense, however this can still be the

164

case. You will not be given such liberties. But," he looked deeper into her eyes at this point and I felt it wasn't her he was looking at but me, "you should be aware that the goodwill and allowances we have given you have reached their culmination. Any further foolish behaviour will result in the termination of both of you."

My non-existent stomach dropped. He now had the power over Sarah too and what I witnessed in the nightmare, the termination via electrocution directly into the brain, was something I would avoid Sarah experiencing at all costs. I had to tread carefully if I even had any steps left. I wondered just where I was exactly. Sarah wasn't speaking anymore, and I felt my concern grow. She was clearly in no good state, I had to do something to stop her meeting this same fate that so many others had and I most likely would. Her head bowed as she looked down to her left arm and watched silently as Dr Muggor injected something into the vein. My view slowly disappeared into slits, fading until it was nothing at all. I felt myself drifting away and pulled on the wave of darkness.

****

Something was cutting into my wrists and ankles and I couldn't see anything when I opened my eyes. I blinked a few times to see if the darkness would dissipate but nothing happened and a fear grew that I had also been blinded now, considering most of what I saw of late was in some sort of dream state it could still work for Dr Muggor. I could hear shuffling around me, footsteps close to where my head lay and I tried to maintain steady breathing to not give away just how terrified I was. I wriggled a little to ease the pressure off of my right hip, digging into something hard. The bone ached like it was about to crack from the pressure. I heard the approaching footsteps stop somewhere near my face. Then something was pulled off my face and I took in my dank surroundings and in spite of what greeted me as my eyes adjusted I was thankful to not have another hurdle to overcome. Dr Muggor was looming above me with a grim expression, in his hand the blindfold that he had just removed from me. He started to tut, emphasising every one with a little click of his tongue.

"So, what do you think, my boy? Have you had enough?" I moved my tongue around my mouth, I was parched. My throat felt scratchy and in need of water, I must have been inhaling dust of off this floor for God knows how long.

"Enough? From the beginning, I had enough. What kind of a stupid question is that?" I hissed in response. He bristled at the venom in my voice, he clearly still expected me to bow down to him and mutter yes sir, no sir. Perhaps I should, but I had nothing to lose; the only purpose I had left in this life was saving Sarah and getting us out of here and as it stood I wasn't doing a very good job.

"Arnold!" he nearly shouted my name, fighting to keep his tone level. "Why can you not see the bigger picture? Look, this may help." He reared his foot back and neatly booted me in the chest, winding my already short of breath body. I thudded backwards and could see Sarah sitting in a small wooden chair, arms and legs tied to it. Her head was lolling around, like her muscles couldn't bear the weight of it any more. I felt my heart heave with the pain of seeing her like this. "You need to think about your actions and your next steps. The repercussions of you not following any and all instructions that I lay out to you will be dire as I'm sure you've been able to fathom." Dully, I nodded my head. The game wasn't up yet, but he didn't need to know about that until the time was right. It was my last chance and I couldn't let anything cause it to fail. I just had to hope that the person I had spoken to before thought outside of the box.

"Where are we?" I asked, straining my head to look up at him. "Where is Steph?" Dr Muggor's lips pursed a little when I asked where she was, interesting.

"It is of no concern to you where she is, but in light of the fact that you cannot do anything here, she is currently trying to repair the laptop that you crushed in your fall, after you so kindly broke into my office and stole it. Tell me, did you truly think you could get away from me and what you voluntarily got yourself into?"

"No, sir. I was acting out, I suppose, in rebellion. Not unlike your average mindless teenager begging for attention. Given my newfound knowledge of what your true aims are and the risks involved I can readily assure you that I am sorry for my actions." Despite the current circumstance, I took an element of pleasure in watching him seethe at my sarcastic words, not sure whether to take me seriously or not. He didn't bite the bait completely.

"Wonderful, right, so I can take this will not be a repeat event. You have reached the end of my tether with your actions. I have never allowed anyone else to have such an amount of leeway when training them, however, you have a mind that will be of great use to me. But again, I will remind you that even that can't be your saving grace if you push me any further." Well, what I deduced from that was that he would have killed me already, but something about my mind was preventing him. Good. His manner of speaking had become even more direct too, no-nonsense. "Your little lady here, however, may not prove as useful to my research and if she steps out of line, she will meet the same ends as those I demonstrated to you previously. Understood?"

My bravado was gone, I nodded mutely at him in response. I began to wonder how much time we had been here, how long I had been unconscious. There was no concept of time in here, no windows. The room and smell in here only strengthened my belief that we were in a cellar of sorts, underground at least. What I wouldn't have given to see rows of wine lining the wall and to be able to pour myself a healthy measure, drinking away the rest of my short life. Whether or not I was actually alive didn't matter. What Dr Muggor was trying to achieve was killing the person you truly were. So, for all intents and purposes, if he succeeded, the Arnold Shack that I am now would be dead. And Sarah too. And how ever many other people he managed to coerce unknowingly into his sick ploy.

I wondered why after this amount of time I hadn't completely gone out of my mind, perhaps I had and just didn't know it yet. But not in the way that he wanted and yet he persisted. Maybe this is what he was talking about, I flashed back onto the documents I read of the other people. With this method of implantation, it took a mere few days, maximum a week for them to lose all contact with their beings and become shadows of themselves. Maybe I was like Jane or Steph as we know her. Maybe this is why he hadn't just terminated me as he liked to describe it. It was a politer way to describe murder, I guess, it was as if it somehow made him feel better about it, not that I was under any false illusions that he suffered from any meaningful feelings. I also found dark amusement at the fact that he thought he was 'training' people. As terrifying as being inside my own mind had recently been, I felt that inside his was a whole other game, a different dimension.

I was still hanging onto a strand of hope that we would get away from this, I had one trick left up my sleeve but I was finding it hard to retain any positivity. Now more than ever, that strand of hope was incredibly bleak, but to have it was better than to not. I just had to hope and pray things panned out the way I had tried to make them, with a slight twist now, as we were now being held captive by him, in a location I didn't know. I couldn't focus too much on my fraying strand of hope for I feared it might snap under the pressure of my scrutiny and then we would have nothing to hold on to. I looked back at Sarah again, longing for her, wanting to touch her and reassure her and rip that damned implant out of her head. In part I wanted her to wake up so I could talk to her, but at the same time I was relieved that she was unconscious and not having to deal with all of this.

"Dr Muggor, please, would there be any way you could take it away from her. She won't say anything, I promise. We will keep quiet. Just don't do this to her." He chortled, holding his hand over his stomach exaggerating just how funny he found the suggestion. I felt my skin prickle and burn in rage, I repressed it, now was not the time and besides, lashing out was futile whilst I was in constraints.

"My boy," he said in his pitchy tone, and I inwardly cringed, "you just don't understand and perhaps you never will. Luckily, you don't need to."

"But you can say she had a mental breakdown, she works in a stressful job, it isn't unheard of," I pleaded.

"That isn't the point. Of course, I could say that and you could too, we could even convince her. But I don't care for the idea, it is of no interest to me to remove the implant, no benefit at all. You are stupid to suggest such a thing, foolish even. You have both come to the point in your lives that this was meant to happen. Fate put you here and you must accept it. Nothing will change it."

Again, I reflected on how utterly insane this man who stood before me was and how unnerving it was to have not seen it before, anything that had felt 'off' in the beginning, I had put down to my own instability and dismissed. I allowed my head to sink more into the dusty ground, my eyes losing focus. I could feel them fogging up, but I didn't want to give him the joy of seeing my broken spirit. There was nothing I could say to him, nothing that would impact him, not even the most powerful being in the universe could reason with a mind so warped. My body was crying out in pain, my mind weeping from sheer exhaustion and pressure. I was using all of my reserves to keep it together at this point. Apparently, that last shred of dignity I was trying to hold on to wasn't OK with Dr Muggor. He used the toe of his shoe to lift my chin to make me look at him again and I watched as he gestured to someone behind me and small hands came underneath my armpits, with Dr Muggor roughly shoving me backwards. I assumed it was Steph behind me. I could hear her panting from the effort of trying to move me into sitting position.

Dr Muggor lost all patience at this point and dropped me in place, "Can't you do anything right? All of this, everything Jane, is your fault. So, I would appreciate it if you would stop that horrific puffing and get on with what I have told you to do." Trouble in paradise again, I thought back to Dr Smyll's house, they were arguing then too about the ineptitude of Steph/Jane. She was now to the side of me and I could just about see her bruised face, she looked unaffected by the put-down from Muggor, just gave a slight nod and moved over to Sarah and pulled her chair around to face me more.

I was now propped up against the wall, the cold stones providing no comfort to my aching body. Steph moved to my side again and picked up the laptop, pressed a couple of keys and looked expectantly at Sarah. I followed her line of sight nervously. Dr Muggor was standing back and observing his little circus. I watched as Sarah's eyelids fluttered and so suddenly, her chest threw itself outwards and her head launched back, all the veins in her neck straining from the effort. She was letting out harsh gasps and slowly her body relaxed and she started swinging her head around, looking at the room and confusion was rippling across her face. Tears filled her eyes when she saw me and she realised what was happening again. The reality was almost as bad as the nightmares she will have been enduring. She tried to speak to me, but a light croak was all she managed. I watched her eyes, the moment that she realised that if I was here with her tied up, I couldn't come and save her. Her iris's dulled and her cheekbones became more pronounced as her expression lost all animation. She was close to giving up already. I needed her strength, she had to be stronger if we were to get out of this.

I sent out another silent prayer, laden with begging tones and promises to be thankful this time. Almost at the exact same moment, a quiet noise could be heard from somewhere above us. It sounded like a rumbling, possibly a car? Dr Muggor shot to attention, he strode into the middle of the room and bashed roughly into Sarah, who shrank away from him, nearly falling sideways in her now teetering chair. Steph took a few fast steps to get to his side and I managed to throw my tied legs out straight in front of me at the perfect time. I couldn't have anticipated how well my sudden idea would go, and definitely couldn't have dreamt it would go so well as it did. I felt her foot catch underneath my ankle and she fell forwards, the movement slowed in my mind. I caught a glimpse of the laptop screen, a large crack running down it, not good, but clearly not broken enough. Her grip didn't stay on the laptop and it fell to the left towards me. She came crashing down in a mini-explosion of dust and grime and let out a cry, the noise coinciding with the cracking noise of the laptop crunching into the ground on its side. I let out a gleeful 'ha!' and it quickly dissipated when I watched Dr Muggor angrily bring his foot back and kick Steph in the side of the head, the same side I had hit her with earlier. He didn't do it full power but it was enough. She cradled her head and lay silently, no response, but conscious. He glared down at her,

"You damned idiot! Shut up! Who could that be? Hunters? You better hope it is hunters." I felt a flush of energy come through me but kept my facial expression completely neutral. Dr Muggor snatched the laptop up and looked at it grunting in anger. The rumbling stopped and we couldn't hear anything more. Sarah's eyes were darting around, terror oozing out of every pore. I didn't know if she was actually with us in the room or suffering a hallucination. Steph had been tapping away before the noises from above. Sarah suddenly flinched and turned her head away with a cry, giving me the answer to my question, she was seeing things. I had no time to bestow sympathy or worry. If this was the moment, I had to be ready. I felt like I should have smashed my feet down on the laptop to try and do further damage but it looked like the screen was black now anyway, plus I didn't have any more time as Dr Muggor picked it up so swiftly.

Steph slowly rose to her feet and hung her head waiting for Dr Muggor to speak. He shoved her towards the gate and told her to check it out without being seen. She nodded silently and padded away and Dr Muggor swung round to direct his unbridled anger at me now, "Tell me, my boy," this time, he spat it at me, "will she find hunters up there?"

I tried to shrug but the movement was minor and I wasn't sure he picked up on it so spoke instead, "I don't know. I don't even know where we are."

"Yes, you do. You have been here before, you just didn't do a good job of looking around. Lucky really or you would have found Sarah before now." I frowned at him, was I at the farmhouse? It must have been because they definitely knew what I was up to by the time I went to his house in the city. How did I miss something that led underground?

My thoughts were stopped rapidly by Sarah letting out a pealing scream, "No! Please don't get away from me!" She was kicking her heels into the ground and pushing the chair backwards, balancing precariously on the hind legs. There was nothing I could do to save her as I watched her topple over backwards and her head cracked neatly off of the wall behind. She stopped moving and her eyes were closed, only the gentle rise and fall of her chest gave me any relief of knowing she was at least partially breathing.

170

"Fuck!" Dr Muggor muttered to neither of us in particular. "She gave too much to her, now they will have heard that." He looked back at me, "You stay here, you move, you die." I didn't have any choice, I was bound. He stalked away and walked up the stairs through the barred door, laptop stashed under one arm. The moment I felt confident he couldn't hear me I tried to shuffle across the room, barely moving a millimetre at a time.

There was about ten seconds delay before a sudden bang echoed down to us and a high-pitched cry cut through the air. I pushed harder to get over to Sarah, trying to ignore what was happening above us. A loud crashing noise came next and something came tumbling down the steps, clanging as it went. It stopped at the bottom and I looked at it, it was a pair of shears. The realisation hit me like a brick to the chest, we were at the farmhouse, in the shed, somehow underneath it. I didn't see any entrance though, but I guess it would make sense that he wouldn't have had directions on the walls for just anyone to follow. I stopped where I was, waiting to see if anyone would follow the garden tool down the steps. I could hear shouting, there were multiple voices up there. I restarted my attempts to move when I saw feet approaching, coming down the stairs. My heart dropped in defeat, black shoes and trousers, Dr Muggor. He paused on his descent, then I heard a voice call out, which didn't belong to Dr Muggor and I wondered if I was having a vision again.

"Hello? This is Officer Smith of the local county police force. If there is anyone down there please put your hands behind your heads and get on your knees. Any resistance will be met with forcible arrest." His feet started to move down the steps again and I noticed his voice sounded a bit shaky, A belief that this was reality and not another vision started to form in my mind. "I have with me two more colleagues and back up is on its way." He reached the bottom and blinked a few times taking in the room. More footsteps came from behind him and the woman whose name I never took entered the cellar too. She looked around in disgust, taking in Sarah laying on the floor strapped to a chair unconscious and me lying in the dirt too, looking at them waiting for them to come and help me. I felt all of my energy drain out of me, all fight gone. Help was here and so the last part of me that was holding on and being strong finally caved.

I managed to speak, "Get her first, please. She fell over in the chair and hit her head really hard." The woman officer went straight to her assistance, picking

171

the ropes apart that held her legs in place first. Officer Smith came to me and crouched down and started fiddling with my wrist restraints.

"Good call, Arnold. We went to the first address you gave us and saw that there was some glass of sorts on the landing area upstairs," I assumed that was from the laptop, "and it looked like there had been a struggle there. So, we looked up Mr Muggor's known addresses and this one came up listed as his fathers. We thought it was best to check after what you said to us. Have to say I'm glad we did. Are you alright?" He looked genuinely concerned about my well-being, I couldn't even imagine what I looked like. I wondered what the struggle had been in the house. Maybe it was the same as before, a memory blank. Or just the mess I had left from my imaginary tiger fight. All I knew with certainty at this point was that I fell unconscious and then ended up here with Dr Muggor.

"Did you get them? Dr Muggor and Steph? They heard you moving around and came to see." His eyes dimmed a little and his head bowed, he took a deep breath before he spoke.

"Yes and no. We reprimanded the woman, Steph as you called her. She is now in custody in the back of the cruiser. Mr Muggor managed to get away, he attacked my other colleague and knocked him into us. He was out of the door before we could catch him and we couldn't see where he went. I have called it in, so you don't need to worry. He can't have gotten too far and the whole area will be crawling with officers shortly."

Don't worry? Don't worry? He had the laptop! My panic rose again. If he got that working again, he had full power over us and now that all this had happened, there was no way he was going to let us live. All it would take was the press of a button and we would become nothing but a statistic, a mushy, bloodied and electrocuted statistic. I stared at the officer, not knowing how to convey the sheer panic coursing through me. Sarah was sitting up again, rubbing the back of her head and looking woozy. I lowered my tone.

"You have to understand, if he got away with the laptop, and he gets it repaired, he can do unimaginable things to us. I know it wasn't easy for you to get together your colleagues to come and help us, I understand it all sounds completely crazy. But believe me, what he is capable of is beyond what anyone can imagine." Officer Smith frowned slightly at me, clearly wondering if I was ranting on because I had just been through a traumatic event. I tried again, "Look at us, look at where we are. Did you look up Muggor's files? See his history? He is a very dangerous man with the ability to cause really big problems. I need you to help us. Look at my scar, look at Sarah, over there. You will see she has a small incision in the side of her head near her ear. In there is a small implant the same as mine. It can control our minds and hormones, leading to us losing our sanity." My hopes faded when I saw the look on Officer Smith's face. I wasn't explaining very well obviously. He looked at me wide-eyed like he was facing a madman. He had finished untying me and put his hand gently on my knee.

"Sir, I am going to take you to the station, we will run through everything there, OK?" I nodded dully. We were not away from it yet, it seemed.

I got up, knees not quite sure if they could take my weight yet and I felt a steadying hand come under my elbow. I thanked him and moved over to Sarah, stroking my hand across her forehead. She looked at me hazily, her face ashen and lips slightly parted. She took a moment to take me in, then she reached out a hand to me and started to cry softly. I tried to pull her up to me, but I didn't have the strength. Both of the officers helped her up and Sarah fell gratefully into my arms, crying into my shoulder. I felt someone tugging at my arm and felt a pang of annoyance that anyone would interrupt this moment. I didn't care what it was, we needed to comfort each other right now, we were both scared and fragile and it felt like the only people in the whole world who knew what we were going through was us. No one could ever understand. Or maybe they just didn't care to because it didn't fit in with their ideals of the world.

The tugging came again when neither of us responded and the culprit spoke up, "Sir, we need to get you both out of here. You have been through a traumatic event and we need to first take you to the hospital for a check-up, then in for questioning." There was no point in fighting it. Maybe there would be a way we could convince them of everything that had happened, then they would find someone with the ability to remove these implants. The sooner we did that, the better. I submitted to his pushing and we wearily went up the stairs.

Coming out on top, I looked around out of curiosity. We had come out in the shed as I thought we would. The entrance into the underground room was actually via a trapdoor, currently open. It looked like it took up much of the floor space and I couldn't see, even now, anything to indicate how to open it except a small lever like the ones you get on car seats. It was small enough that you would miss it unless you actually looked for it. The opening was actually where the table had been and I could just see the legs folded up behind the door. Clever really, not that it was much of a surprise considering everything else Dr Muggor had shown himself to be capable of. Imagination and creativity were things that he clearly had an abundance of. As exhausted as I was and as much as I wanted to see the back of this place, I wanted to see how the trapdoor worked. It annoyed me that I had missed it.

As if sensing my trail of thought, Officer Smith spoke to me again, "We have to leave everything as we found it. When the team arrive shortly, they will need to take photos and note everything down. So, please don't touch anything. Let's go." He waved his hand at the door of the shed and put his hand on my back to direct me out. Sarah was hanging on to my arm with the other officer keeping guard the other side of her in case she fell. We were led to one of the police cars stood idling on the track at the back of the house, there were three of them. I wondered which one Steph was in when I saw the middle car had the other officer sitting in the driver's seat. So, it would be that one then. She would be handcuffed and unable to escape. I wanted to open the door and hurt her. But I was stuck between two minds. I hated her, with all my soul, for everything she had done and been a part of. But the other part of me felt like she wasn't really her; she was what Dr Muggor made and abused, a first edition of what he was trying to make us into.

I felt a nudge and realised I'd stopped in my tracks, just staring at the police car. I shook my head to myself and Sarah now took control, taking my hand and leading me to the next cruiser, having regained a bit of her strength. They opened the door for us and we slid into the back seats. All of the adrenaline that had been running through us had run its course and I felt numb with tiredness. My head felt too heavy for my neck and I let it drop back onto the headrest. Sarah was in the same boat and did the same. We sat holding hands waiting for our driver to get in the car. The door swung closed with a thud and Officer Smith climbed into the front. He looked back at us.

"Are you both alright?" We nodded in unison even though we were completely not and it was bordering on comical that of all things Officer Smith could have asked at the moment, it was that, a question with a glaringly obvious answer. "Well, I need to get you both to the hospital, where we will make sure that you," he nodded at Sarah, "don't have a concussion. Then we will get your statements. Officer Duthie will stay here and wait for the others to arrive." He nodded out of his window at her and she patted her holster reassuringly. Reassurance for us or herself, I had no idea. I nodded at her as well, not sure if she could see me through the tinted windows, but I wanted her to know I was grateful that someone had come to fight our corner when it all seemed so far-fetched and unbelievable.

****

We pulled away and Sarah and I got lost in our own thoughts. The bumpy track bounced us around and I found it soothing. Sarah tried to put her head against my chest but found it too uncomfortable with the pain in her head to keep being bumped up and down against my chest, which suited me fine at this time as I was in a lot of pain too, especially after taking a boot to the chest from Dr Muggor.

I thought about my visit to the police station earlier in the day, now overly grateful for the decision. I had been in two minds about it. But now if I hadn't have gone and found the officers that came to my apartment, we would still be tied up in a cellar, under the direct control of a madman and his sidekick with our fates unsure. They were still unsure now but marginally better. I hadn't really divulged too much when I went in and found Officer Smith. I just told him that my girlfriend had been kidnapped by someone parading as a doctor, who wanted to do experimental treatments. I then had to explain how I knew who it would be, but I kept it short and sweet. I told him that if he could help me get her back, I would tell him everything from the beginning, but that our lives had been threatened if we went to anyone about what was happening and so they couldn't let on that I had been to see them and let me go. I had also sweetened it by telling them that I could lead them to information regarding his involvement in the deaths of multiple other people. It seemed to work. They agreed to let me go if I promised not to interfere and try to save her myself, I had agreed, noncommittally, of course. Luckily that seemed to be enough, they probably took one look at the state of me and figured I was harmless anyway. Plus death was a powerful threat. I told them Dr Muggor's name and gave his house address in the city where I thought Sarah was. It was luckier that they didn't give up at that point and went on to find more addresses related to him. Now we had to work to finish all of this.

I was haunted by the thought that Dr Muggor managed to get away from the three officers who arrived, I didn't know where he was or what he could be doing. The rumbling of the road and low humming of the car was sending me into a drowsy haze. I decided that for now at least, we were safe and allowed myself to drift off until we arrived at the hospital.

****

I felt a gentle pushing on my hand and opened my eyes slowly. I forgot where we were for a moment and felt disorientated. I had been dreaming about something very mundane but blissfully so. I had been going about my daily business in my apartment doing a little bit of work, watching some TV, making some food. All the stuff that I would never take for granted again. Sarah had been there too; she was lounging around in a fluffy pink dressing gown just keeping me company. I didn't want to come back to reality, I wanted to stay in that dream world a bit longer. Maybe that was what Dr Muggor was trying to achieve? Once we had lost our minds, we would surely be in that continuous state of not worrying, just going about our business with no pressure. Then I thought of Steph and revised that. He wanted robots, people to do his bidding in a blink of an eye. No, the two scenarios were very much different from each other. Officer Smith was looking at me, patiently waiting for me to regain consciousness. I blinked at him and he looked over to Sarah. A split second passed when a wave of panic washed over his face and made my stomach lurch in fear and whip my head round to look at her, "Shit! We shouldn't have let her go to sleep! You never let someone with possible concussion go to sleep!"

He jumped out of the car and started waving his hands to the nurses hanging around outside having their cigarette breaks. They quickly discarded their smokes and came briskly over. A male nurse pulled the door open on Sarah's side and asked what happened. Before I spoke, Officer Smith offered the explanation, "We have two victims here of kidnapping. I called ahead to the desk. The female may be suffering from concussion and the male needs a check over too." The nurse nodded quickly, bopping away. He called for someone to get a gurney to transport Sarah and a wheelchair to assist me. I tried to tell them I was OK to walk and they said it was not an option due to protocol. He was pursing his lips at Sarah, clearly not pleased to find a patient with possible concussion asleep in the back of a police car.

As a team, they carefully pulled her out and laid her down, then rushed in through the doors leaving me behind with another nurse. She was what I would describe as fluffy and welcoming, not fat per se, but not small. She beckoned me and I sat in the wheelchair she presented to me. It was comfortable and I sank into it gratefully. She wheeled me in, ignoring my pleas to stay close to Sarah and have someone tell me how she was doing and give me any and all updates as soon as possible. She took me straight into a room and told me to climb into the bed. I did as I was told, no point in pissing off the help. She called in another nurse, who promptly stuck an IV in my arm and attached me to the machines.

"Seriously, I am OK. It isn't me you need to worry about! Can you take me to Sarah?" The nurse who had inserted the IV looked at me sympathetically.

"Not just yet sir, we have to give you a quick check first. You have been through quite the ordeal yourself and it wouldn't help anyone if we just let you go wandering off to see her. She is in good hands; you can trust us to look after her. Soon enough, you can go and see her." It didn't really help me, but I nodded in response and agreed to let them do all their checks. They were muttering something about severe dehydration and possible post-traumatic stress disorder. They checked all my vitals and their facial expressions didn't instil much confidence in me. It didn't take them too long to run through their checks, and determine nothing was broken which was surprising really considering the hits I had taken recently. They then smiled politely at me and told me to get some rest whilst I could, then departed leaving me to my own devices. In this moment, I felt incredibly lonely and tried to calm my racing mind by watching the monitors beeping to themselves and soon got lost in my head.

****

I was still completely on edge, conscious of the fact that until Dr Muggor was caught and put behind bars, we were not free or out of danger. If he fixed his laptop, we would be at his mercy once more and that mercy would not be kind to us. It wouldn't have taken him long to figure out that I had managed to lead the police to him, it wasn't exactly a place that stood out in the middle of nowhere. Plus, he had asked me directly if it was hunters, his tone suggesting that if it was anyone other than hunters he knew it would be because of something I did. They would have had no reason to go and search his property except for me. No, if he got his system up and running again, it would be the end of our lives. He would not think twice about hitting that key and killing us. Also, now he was on the radar, he had nothing to lose in doing so. In fact, it would be clearing up loose ends. I wondered what they were doing to Steph and if she would speak. I doubted it, she was utterly devoted to Dr Muggor, willingly or not. I was so lost in my thoughts that I didn't realise that a doctor had come in and was standing next to me, waiting for my attention. I gave it to him.

"Mr Shack? I'm Dr Mann. I'm happy to tell you that other than a few small things, you are absolutely fine. We are currently giving you a dosage of vitamins and fluids as you were quite low on both. If you feel up to the task, Officer Smith and Officer Sabe would like to speak to you soon. Just let me know when you are ready." I assumed Officer Sabe was the third man, the one who had Steph in the back of the police car.

"I'm ready, but can you tell me how Sarah is?" I asked, and something flashed across Dr Mann's face.

"She is not quite out of the woods yet. She took quite the bump to her head. Luckily, she doesn't have a concussion but she has been through a lot and needs some time to recover. When she came around, she suffered from a small seizure, so we need to give her a CAT scan, we are waiting to take her down. I have a few questions for you both, but I will wait for the police to speak to you first."

"Is she awake? What kind of seizure? What happened?" The doctor started to wave his hands at me to get me to slow down my barrage of questions.

"She is fine for now, we just need to keep her under observation, that is all. We are looking after her. I will take you to her as soon as you've had your interview." I wasn't going to get any further by pushing him, so I said thank you and he left with the two police officers entering the room right after. They must have been waiting outside. Officer Sabe introduced himself officially and then allowed Officer Smith to take control. I assumed that as he was here now, he must have already taken Steph to the police station.

"So, Arnold, I'd like to run through everything. Don't leave anything out. You are not the one in trouble here, nor is Sarah. I need to know everything in order to take the necessary actions."

"Did you find him yet?" Both men looked at me, pausing for a moment before Officer Sabe spoke,

"No, but we are searching for him now. Both properties we have listed under his name are under observation. We have also taken the liberty of posting officers outside of a third property. I believe you may know it, on the outskirts of town."

"Yes! Yes, I know it. That was where they would make me meet them." They both nodded and jotted something down in their mini notepads.

"And Steph? You know her real name is Jane now, yes?" They nodded at me again, impatiently this time. Officer Smith retook the lead.

"We know how to do our jobs, sir. Now if you could please run through everything for us." So, I did. I went right from the crossing of the bridge with the thugs and small boy, meeting Dr Muggor in the hospital – which raised both of their eyebrows, I didn't need to mention the security flaw there – the implant, which I now felt sure he had actually done before I had come around and he introduced himself, Dr Smyll, Steph, aka Jane, the hallucinations and nightmares, the laptop and control with other victims, all the way up to the kidnapping, breaking and entering, to the here and now. Every now and then, I noted that one of the officers head's would tilt sideways quizzically, not quite sure how believable the story was. I fought the urge to reassure them it was true. I didn't need to. Once they caught Muggor and his laptop, they would see it all for themselves, even just seeing his wall of victims in his farmhouse should be enough evidence to put him away forever. Once I was done recounting everything, I was spent. Both officers looked much the same, notepads full of information. They were just wrapping up when another officer came storming into the room, panting and winded.

"Officer Smith, Officer Sabe, I need to speak to you outside, now." My heart rate spiked. What happened? They exchanged a look, glanced at me and with small nods left the room. They were outside mumbling for around five minutes, I couldn't tell what they were saying because they had their backs to me. I watched as they brought their hands up to their heads and bowed them in unison. It didn't look good. The third officer departed and Officer Smith and Sabe spoke a few low words again, and Officer Sabe left too. Officer Smith came back into the room, an unreadable look on his face.

"Mr Shack, I am required elsewhere for the moment, but I will have another officer posted on your door for the meantime. I will return shortly." His voice kept breaking as he spoke and I wondered what they had spoken about.

"Are you OK, Officer? Is it Sarah?" He shook his head, sadness now present on his face.

"You will hear it soon enough, we have an officer down, Officer Duthie, the officer who was left at the farmhouse." As he spoke, the sadness transformed into anger, radiating from his very pores. My heart dropped and I felt sick.

"Can I ask what happened?"

"As you and your partner are both at risk, I can inform you that Mr Muggor is in possession of a firearm. But as I said already, we have officers posted here now to offer you both protection." His voice broke a little again and he made the motion of a cross. He excused himself and left the room without any further conversation. My feeling of sickness increased, this was all my fault, now someone else was dead at the hands of Dr Muggor. I sat in silence trying to absorb this latest blow. I didn't know how much time had elapsed but soon enough I was pulled from my reverie by the sounds of Officer Smith returning to his post and relieving his colleague.

One of the nurses came back in, with the professional smile in place that never belied any bad feelings or news. She told me that if I wanted, I could go and see Sarah. I gave her my thanks and moved unsteadily over to the wheelchair next to the bed trying to process the latest news. The nurse wheeled me down the hallway and into another room. Sarah was sitting upright in the bed and looking worse for wear. She looked over at me tiredly expecting to see someone else and her face lit up when she saw it was me. Just that expression alone made me feel a bit brighter, like not everything in the world was broken. She tried to swing herself out of the bed and the nurse standing by pushed her back and warned her not to move. I got to her and stood, I leant into her and gave her a strong embrace, pushing my energy into hers until I felt them combine and grant us both a bit more strength and calm. I assumed she didn't know about Officer Duthie yet and I didn't want to tell her and make her panic more. I stood back and clasped her hand in mine, ignoring the wooziness that was washing through my head. She looked trustingly up at me.

"Arnie, they said I have to go and have a scan on my head because of the fit. I don't want to go on my own, I'm scared."

"I know Sarah, but I can't come with you into the room. I will ask to come down and wait for you outside but this is for the best. They need to make sure everything is alright and they will see the implant too, which can only help us. They will see that everything we have told them is true and find a way to remove them."

"I know, but they haven't found Dr Muggor yet, have they? What if he does something?" I could hear the pitch of her voice rising as she thought about the possibilities.

"No, they haven't, but Steph dropped the laptop when we were still there and smashed the screen again. I don't think it is working. But we have to work fast,

OK? You will be OK. I am right here, always." I kissed the top of her hand and the nurse standing to the side stepped forward and cleared his throat.

"We are going to take you down now, Miss Balet. You can come down too, but you will have to sit outside. I assume that the officers will also accompany you." He nodded to Officer Smith and his colleague standing with their hands clasped in front of them by the door. They nodded neatly and moved out of the way. I told them I could walk and this time they didn't argue with me. They wheeled Sarah out of the room in the bed and we all went down in the elevator, none of us speaking. Sarah was lost in thought, rolling her thumb between her fingers looking at something in the distance that none of us could see. Now her hair had been pulled back, I could see a small shaved square behind her ear where Dr Muggor had put in the implant. I felt anger rise up again and I battened it down, it wouldn't change anything here.

We arrived at the room and I sat down on one of the squeaky green chairs lining the wall and thought about having a cigarette. That would be a treat right now. The officers didn't sit, they stood and kept glancing around. Guards ever more up now that I had told them Dr Muggor had been known to enter the hospital unknown and he had downed one of their beloved colleagues in cold blood.

****

We had sat patiently waiting for them to do the scan on Sarah for around ten minutes and I tried not to focus on the palpable grief of Officer Smith, he must have been closer to Officer Duthie than the others here, I could see the mourning tearing through him. I felt for him, it must be awful for him knowing someone he cared about was killed in the line of duty such a short time ago in a place that he had left her to stand guard. I think they call it survivor's guilt and I was surprised they hadn't taken him off duty now although I was grateful for the familiar face.

A loud commotion came from the room they had taken Sarah into and my stomach turned when I saw three doctors hurtling down the corridor towards us. They rushed into the room and I stood, ready to run in there. Officer Smith sensed my intention and put a hand roughly on my chest and grunted at me, "Stay." He looked to his colleague, "Check it out." The other officer nodded briskly and went to the door, but he was pushed back by doctors shouting at him to stay out of the room. My bruised chest was throbbing from where Officer Smith had just restrained me. I felt my knees giving way and I was overcome by fear and panic at what was happening in there. I could hear shouting and beeping coming from the door which was now sitting ajar. Officer Smith's hand remained on my chest to stop me from going near them. We stood for another agonising five minutes whilst all the possibilities ran through my head. I imagined them coming out and telling me she had died or them coming out and telling me not to be silly they'd actually taken Sarah to another room and this was another patient. I knew the latter wasn't really possible but I toyed with the idea to keep myself calmer. When the doctors started filtering out, they were removing gloves, hats and all coated in a thin film of sweat. I stopped one in his tracks, pulling on his arm, Officer Smith didn't stop me this time, he understood my need.

"Is she OK?" I blurted it out, it came out like a squeak, I wasn't sure I wanted to hear the answer. He looked at me sympathetically.

"For now, they will move her shortly. You need to take a seat and relax, sir." With that, he walked away. Relax? Was he having a laugh? I held back an actual laugh that bubbled up in response, I had to remind myself that he obviously didn't mean relax as in kick back with a pint. But he said she was OK, so that was something. A few minutes later, Sarah was wheeled out, this time she wasn't conscious, she had breathing tubes up her nose and I could just see the pads on her chest where they must have used defibrillators. I wanted to cry, shout, scream, hit a wall, run a mile. Instead, I looked at her sadly and followed their journey back up to the room, the nurse pushing her was looking glum and stressed. They put her bed back where it was before and the nurse reattached everything, giving a final check before turning to me and the officers.

"If anything happens, please let us know by pressing the red button. We will be monitoring the machines anyway, but if there is anything we need to know, that is the quickest way to get our attention." We nodded our agreement and understanding and she left the room. Once she left, I felt my emotions come through even stronger. I fought back my tears and I felt a hand on my shoulder. I looked and Officer Smith was looking at me, sharing in the grief and pain with me. He told me they would wait in the hall to give me some privacy and left. I stood next to Sarah, not sure what to do with myself. I stared at the tubes coming out of her nose and felt my fight leave me, the tears flowed down my cheeks and I bowed my head in silent prayer. My moment was rudely interrupted by the arrival of the doctor.

"I'm going to have to ask you to return to your room for monitoring, Mr Shack. Miss Balet needs to rest."

"Can I ask what happened to her? I have a right to know."

"We are waiting for her family to arrive; we will discuss this matter with them."

"I am family, she is my partner. Please, tell me." My overriding fear was that somehow Dr Muggor had played a part in it.

"Fine, she had a reaction in the MRI machine, we managed to get a small part of the scan completed, but she suffered another seizure. We have spoken to the police and understand that you also have this electronic implant in your head and we believe that the machine somehow reacted with it. She needs her rest, she had a very close call in there, we managed to pull her out before it was too late."

"Did it electrocute her?" I asked.

"I don't know, the reaction was similar to that of being electrocuted, yes."

Was this Dr Muggor? It can't have been, it must have been the machine. If he had access to his laptop again, I was pretty certain I would not be breathing right now. He ushered me out of the room and I felt this whole scene was incredibly insensitive. Didn't he know that at a time like this we needed to stick together? He seemed to be one of those doctors where it was nothing but a job.

I walked down to my room again, Officer Smith on my tail with the other officer left standing outside Sarah's room. I settled myself in the bed but couldn't bring myself to rest. My mind was whirring. I needed to know where Dr Muggor was and what was happening. I asked Officer Smith again and he just told me when there was more information, he would be sure to relay it to me. I sat back and rehashed everything in my mind until it felt like I was inducing a mental breakdown. I had to do something. A nurse came back in to check my fluids and asked how I was doing.

"Not great. Do you have anything to help me? I can't rest. My body hurts. I need to be doing something." She tutted in response, nodding. She didn't say a word and simply inserted a needle into my IV. I started to ask what it was and felt the room start to spin. I opened my mouth again, but I was washed away in a wave of very welcomed darkness.

****

I came to slowly, greeted by a very quiet room. An amber glow was coming from the hallway, it must be night time and they dimmed the lights. I could just see Officer Smith leaning against the wall next to the door. I wondered why they hadn't done a shift swap yet. I cleared my throat and he jumped, then looked round to see me. I raised my hand feebly, still half asleep from whatever the nurse had given me. He gave me a tired smile and nod in return. I made a mental note to myself to let the police department know how good of an officer he was. He moved forward from the wall and started to come into the room.

"How are you feel–" His question was cut off by a gloved hand coming across his face and muting him. A glint came off of something metal in the other hand that was coming around and before Officer Smith could react, it sunk deep into his neck. I watched in horror as his eyes rolled back and his legs gave way. The assailant aided his fall to make sure there was no noise. I don't know if it was the adrenaline, but everything slowed down and as he approached me, hood pulled over his face, I pressed the alarm button repeatedly, frantically hoping that a crew of people would come to our aid. For some reason my voice was failing me and I couldn't shout out. The man pulled down his hood and I came face to face with the man whose location I had been wondering about for a while. His hair was in disarray, teeth bared in a snarl with crazed eyes. This was no sane man; he had now completely lost it.

I looked around for an escape and found none. I yanked the tube from my arm and jumped out of the bed on the other side. My only option was a window behind me and it was shuttered closed, I didn't have enough time to open it and escape. Muggor approached me tantalisingly slowly. My pulse was beating a steady rhythm in the pit of my stomach and I was sure my heart would break through my ribcage any second now. I waited until he was at the end of the bed and took the only shot, I could see. I took one big step back then launched myself over the rail of the bed, tucking myself into a ball when I hit the ground the other side to lessen the impact. I sent a silent apology over to Officer Smith as I bounced up onto my feet again the other side and sprinted out of the door, narrowly avoiding smashing into the wall in front. I pushed myself off sideways and ran towards Sarah's room, looking for the other officer. He was nowhere to be seen. Shit. Where was Sarah? Had she been moved? I reached the door and looked inside very quickly. She was in there, still much the same as before, the steady rise and fall of her chest showing me she was sleeping and alive. I looked behind me to see if Dr Muggor was close and didn't see him. I hoped this burst of adrenaline didn't fade off yet, I needed it.

What didn't make me feel better was the fact I couldn't see anyone at all. Of all times for a hospital corridor to be empty, it had to be now, just our luck. I didn't have time to worry about where he was. I ran into the room and started pressing the red button marked 'Urgent'. It let out a high-pitched beep. I needed to get her out of here, but she needed the machines right now. I didn't know if she was breathing on her own. I hesitated too long, I heard someone approaching outside, no attempt to quieten their footsteps. I wanted to think it could be a doctor or nurse, but my intuition told me otherwise. I heard him before I saw him. I was frozen in place, only made worse by the fact that as he came into the doorway in all his manic glory, he started to laugh. Deep rumbling laughs, the complete opposite of his normal high pitch of speaking. He got about a metre away from me and stopped laughing. His face took on a serious menacing look and he glared at me, staring deeply into my eyes.

"My boy, you definitely crossed the line. And now you must pay. All of this is your doing. All these lives lost and disrupted, all on your shoulders. I am doing the right thing in eliminating you. You understand, of course." I racked my brains, I had to stall him.

"How is this all of my doing? If you hadn't have started all of this, none of this would have happened. You killed people, you hurt people, you put crazy little devices into people's brains!" He laughed again.

"Yes, I suppose you may think like that. But all of this links back to you."

"And you!" I retorted.

"Be that as it may, I don't have long to chit-chat. I disconnected the alarms in the nurse's office, but they will probably be wanting to do their rounds shortly." There was nothing I could say to him. Anything I said would be futile. I tried anyway.

"What about Jane?" That got a reaction, his face jolted. I pushed, "You will lose her if you do this. Don't you want to save her?"

He responded first with a small grimace, "My boy, she is no longer with us. Thanks to you, the laptop is broken and my other equipment is under the control of pigs. She will have taken a lot of work to fix again. She knew the drill whilst I was still able to direct her, I gave her very specific orders, which she will have carried out by now."

I felt intense sadness wash through me although I wasn't too sure who for. I sensed Sarah stirring next to me and I prayed she didn't bring any attention to herself. Dr Muggor didn't notice yet, still thinking about the loss of his most successful victim I imagine. He started moving forward again and I shied away from him. He chuckled at me.

"Don't worry just yet, you still have some time. I need to open this window, once I dispose of you two, I need a route out. They will hear the gun and I can't very well walk down the hallway after that. That would be rather stupid, don't you think?" I wondered if that was rhetorical.

"Well, why would you use a gun then?" I was still working through. if I could get Sarah out, I could've run, but I couldn't leave her behind.

"Because frankly, I don't like blood too much. I don't mind seeing it, but I don't want it on me, it's…well…icky." I let out a surprised laugh in response. I wasn't amused, just taken aback. He was just tying the blinds in at the bottom and I saw an opening. I launched forwards in a rugby tackle position and smashed him into the wall, my head impacting as well. My vision wavered but I held on. I felt him grunt and start to rain down punches on my back. I didn't let go. I felt the punches lessen and realised he was reaching for something in his pocket. I pushed my feet off the ground and shoved my shoulder hard into his ribs, hoping to wind him and delay him. It worked, just. He cracked his knuckles down on my head and I lost my grip for less than a second, just enough for him to slide his hand into his pocket and pull out a small pistol.

Panic threatened to overtake and I felt myself against my own wishes accept what was about to happen. I threw a hand up to try and push his arm away, but he brought one leg out from underneath me and over my arm in a quick swoop, pinning me in place. I knew that in just a second a shot would ring out and it would be the last thing I heard. I clenched my eyes shut and heard it, it burst through my eardrums and made white lights flash up in front of my eyelids. The ringing continued and I wondered why I could still hear it. Was this death? I felt something hot and wet drenching the back of my head and felt confused. Then I was yanked from behind and fell onto my back. Looking up I saw the other police officer, the one who had been absent from duty at the door holding his gun in shaky hands. I looked down my body to Dr Muggor sitting against the wall, clutching his chest, blood pooling out over his fingers and onto his stomach. He was gasping for breath, eyes rolling in their sockets.

"Don't move!" the officer shouted. I think that wasn't a necessary command, it didn't look like Dr Muggor would be running anywhere soon. I could hear people running in the hallway towards us and suddenly the room was milling with people. I was helped up by doctors and nurses and the officer kept his gun trained on Dr Muggor. Everyone else turned their attentions to me and Sarah and I was caught up in the confusion. Someone asked the officer something and he looked to the side for just a second. I saw it all play out and began to run forward opening my mouth to shout a warning, but I was too slow.

Dr Muggor lifted the gun he still had and shot straight at the officer. I watched as the officer was taken off of his feet and fell into two nurses behind him and Dr Muggor got swiftly to his feet and rolled headfirst over the windowpane and out. I ran to the window and looked down to see him clambering out of the bush below the window and clutching one hand to his chest. He shot one look at me and ran across the parking lot and round the corner out of view. I shouted for someone to get after him, but there was too much of a commotion in here and no one took notice as there were no police officers who could do anything right now; people were trying to help the officer lying on the floor in a pool of his own blood, from what I could see the bullet hit him in the shoulder. Sarah was awake and looking around, completely bewildered and scared. I went to her side and crouched down, holding her hand. I muttered it would all be OK over and over again to her for both of us, blocking out the sounds of everything else in the room.

****

A week later, we were sitting talking quietly in Sarah's new hospital room. It had turned out that the officer, who had been guarding her room, had chosen a very bad time to go to the toilet. His gunshot wound was luckily what they called a through and through, meaning it didn't hit anything important, except his skin, of course. He would be fully recovered in around two or three months. Officer Smith came around a couple of hours later, Dr Muggor had injected him with some sort of anaesthetic. Apparently, he was very fortunate; had it have been even a centimetre to the right, it would have killed him in seconds. A funeral had already been held for Officer Duthie and the entire station and people she knew turned out to pay their respects. Steph had hanged herself whilst in her cell, using the torn fabric of her jeans to create a noose. Dr Smyll also had a funeral, this time one with less judgement from all of those who thought she had fallen victim to drugs. We had been cleared of any wrongdoing in relation to that whole saga, considering the circumstances. I had, however, been given a warning for being a 'cowboy' and trying to save us by myself, but again, they said they understood why I took the actions I did even if they didn't condone them.

They had also found Dr Muggor. He had managed to make it just two streets over before he succumbed to blood loss from the gunshot wound. He was found lying face first, drenched in his poisonous blood. His laptop had been located on the hospital premises and repaired. The officers leading the case couldn't believe that everything we had told them was true, even when they were faced with it. All of his other victims, the documented ones at least, now had some kind of closure. The families had been contacted and for the most part had been relieved that the ends that they had met where not what they had initially thought and had found difficult to believe. In fact, some of them didn't know where their loved one was and it gave them closure to know that whilst not alive, they were not suffering anymore. The police would initiate a search for the missing bodies in the coming days.

I had also been told I still had my job waiting for me and I politely told them I would not be coming back. The hospital had some top cranial surgeon flown over from America a few days ago and they very carefully performed two small operations on me and Sarah, keeping us under local anaesthetic to watch for any bad reactions. So, apart from the general pains of everything we had gone through and the copious mental scarring that would take more than a little time to heal, we were now on a better path facing brighter days again. Sarah seemed to be improving every day, outside of a few dark patches here and there, much the same as what I was experiencing, we were moving on.

I caught Sarah wiggling her fingers and smiling absentmindedly to herself. I took her hand and smiled back at her, the small band glinting off the overhead lights. It was the promise I had made to myself and now I had to follow through with it. I had asked one of the nurses to accompany me to the jewellers once her shift was finished, even offered to pay for her time but she turned the money down, telling me she loved a happy ending. So, I bought a small unobtrusive ring and presented it to Sarah, who loved it. Now we could plan our future again.

I had learned to appreciate life and what we have in it and to not wish it away or have regrets. We were just waiting for the go-ahead to leave and a lot of people had turned up to wish us well and somehow it reminded me of what it felt like to have a family, and I realised it was something that I missed. News had spread fast of the ordeal we had been through; the local paper even wrote a story about us and gave us a handsome sum of money for the privilege. The doctor finally joined the group of people in the room, all talking amongst themselves and said with pleasure and an exaggerated bow, "You are officially discharged, Miss Balet." She grinned up at him and swung her legs over the side of the bed. She was dressed and ready to go, so we gave hugs to all the well-wishers and wandered down the hall hand-in-hand.

Once we reached the exit, I took one last look back at the building and thought out loud, "I hope I never have to set foot in that place ever again!" Sarah nestled her head into my shoulder and laughed lightly. Then she tugged on my hand to start moving again. We dismissed the taxi idling at the curb and carried on walking. Enjoying the sensation of being outside, the sunshine on our skin, the wind giving soft caresses through our hair. With small smiles we walked home to rebuild our lives and move on from everything that had happened to us.